NASHVILLE NIGHTS

JULIE CAPULET

He's *crazy* for her …

Vaughn Tucker is the hot as hell drummer of the Tucker Brothers band, whose four albums have all hit number one. Vaughn is drop-dead gorgeous … and completely out of control.

Gigi Hayes's life is a million miles from packed stadiums and high-profile tour schedules. She's a small town girl who spends all her time working in the library and studying to become a qualified social worker. For … reasons.

When Vaughn meets Gigi, for the first time in his life, he's the one who's star-struck. But Gigi is saving herself for true love. And even though she's drawn to the beautiful, trouble-written-all-over-him superstar, she's not deluded enough to believe he's capable of such a thing.

Vaughn has already fallen hard. And Gigi's refusals only make him crazier. She's an angel and he may as well be the devil himself.

But when heaven meets hell, all bets are off …

Nashville Nights is a steamy standalone rockstar romance starring an

*out-of-control drummer and the one woman who's everything he
never knew he needed.*

Music City Lovers

Julie Capulet LLC

NASHVILLE NIGHTS
Music City Lovers Series
Copyright © 2021, 2025 by Julie Capulet

All rights reserved. This copy is intended for the original purchaser of this book only. No part of this work may be reproduced, distributed or scanned in any electronic or printed form without prior written permission from the author.

NASHVILLE NIGHTS is a work of fiction. While reference may be made to actual historical events or existing locations, the names, characters, places and incidents portrayed in this book are fictitious. Any resemblance to actual persons, living or dead, events, business establishments or locales is entirely coincidental.

Nashville NIGHTS

1

VAUGHN

I WAKE up to the sound of birds chirping.

Where the …?

My head is pounding hellishly.

A vivid image of my mother's face fringes at the edge of my awareness. Her dark hair and her green eyes. *I love you, Vaughn.* It's the very last thing she ever said to me.

My eyes are suddenly wide open.

Her image fades but it's jarring. The heaviness of the loss of her is as raw as it ever was. It never seems to soften or fade out.

I look around.

I'm in a barn, sleeping in a goddamn pile of hay.

Which is surprisingly comfortable.

I crashed out after an all-nighter with my brothers, I remember now. We wrote three complete songs.

And drank a lot of whiskey.

Too much whiskey, if my hangover is any judge.

The place is huge, with dusty beams and an old-timey, rustic vibe. Morning sunlight streams through thin gaps in the wood, painting the whole place in stripes of … beauty, maybe. The kind that makes you feel deeply, fully inspired, I realize as I lie here. Absorbing it.

You're a beautiful soul, Vaughn. Don't be reckless. Don't throw it all away.

Shit.

Having my mother speak to me knowingly from beyond the grave is not something I had on my bingo card this morning.

But I'm feeling it. Too deeply, as always. It's a pain I do my best to numb whenever the need arises. I slide my flask out of my back pocket and check its contents. Hair of the dog and all that. But it's empty.

I look almost eerily like my father did but people used to say my mother and I had the same personality. She was fun and enchanting to be around but there was a pronounced vulnerability to her character that was all about her kindness. She cared too much.

I don't see those similarities in myself at all. Unfortunately, my habits mirror all my father's worst tendencies. No matter how much I wish I wasn't, I basically *am* my father. And it's this realization that makes me want to self-medicate like nothing else does.

Whatever. I don't feel like analyzing my personality flaws this early in the morning. Or ever, more accurately.

I'm covered in straw and I'm dusty as fuck but the slant of the sunlight feels different today. Soft and colorful. Almost magical.

I must be really hungover.

I climb out of the hay and try to brush some of it off my clothes but to hell with it.

When I step outside into the daylight, the world is basically on fire with blazing sun, blue sky and green, rolling landscape as far as the eye can see. I have to shield my eyes for a few seconds from the glaring brightness of it all.

There's a pond in the distance.

Now there's an offer I can't refuse.

I take a few seconds to adjust to the sunlight and to make sure my equilibrium is more or less intact, then I walk down toward the pond, half-amazed at how scenic this place is. I've spent too much time in the city lately, on tour buses and in hotel rooms. It's good to get away from all that.

I'm running commando so I strip down and wade into the water, which is clear and clean-looking, and dive under.

Damn, it feels good.

I swim for a while and wash off the dirt and the sweat.

It's been a crazy few months on tour. I've overindulged in every way it's possible to overindulge. I've played my heart out and squeezed every last drop out of each day and—even more—each night.

It's just how I happen to live my life. Fast. Hard. Might as well make the most of the more-money-than-I-could-spend-in-this-lifetime, the whiskey on tap, the God-given gifts I happen to appreciate the hell out of. I have blue eyes and black hair. I'm 6'3" and built as fuck—in every regard. Women give me whatever I want whenever I want it. I thank my lucky stars for all of the above by enjoying the ride every chance I get. Why wouldn't I?

I'm famous, not just because I was recently listed among the top five drummers in the world but also because I tend to make headlines for a variety of reasons.

I prefer to let my fire burn bright.

I'm borderline out of control, maybe, but who isn't?

Anyone who tells me they're *in* control is full of shit, I figure. Even if such a thing was possible, it wouldn't be something I would aspire to. I have zero interest in living my life by a set of arbitrary rules that might be considered "acceptable."

To who?

No one *I* happen to know or care much about the opinion of, is what I've come to realize.

Even so, I can admit I feel sort of wrecked. Not just physically, from all the insane excesses. Those are easy enough to bounce back from. I'm 24 and brimming with virile energy and blazing lust. It burns hot and borderline feral, all the time, so if I don't *use* it I feel like I might spontaneously fucking combust.

It's the existential exhaustion that hits harder. Sometimes it dawns on me that it would actually be nice to care about what other people think of me.

But all those impulses died on one particular stormy night, years ago now. Its effect still has the ability to exhaust me from time to time. Lately the memories have felt like more of a black cloud than usual. Having my mother revisit me in a surprisingly realistic hallucination out of the blue makes me realize how jaded I am. Maybe I'm closer to the edge than I thought.

The cool water feels nothing less than miraculous, like I'm somehow in the process of being reborn.

After a while, I walk up the sandy beach and grab my clothes but I don't bother putting them on. I'll dry off in the sun. There's no one around. I happen to be a person who's intensely comfortable in my own skin, with good reason. I don't know if I'm arrogant or just secure enough to know from experience that I happen to look like a guy who can show a girl the time of her life on around ten different levels. And then deliver on each and every one of those promises in spades. At least for one night.

That's just the way it is.

I notice, up a slope, there's a cottage situated in a small grove of trees. Travis mentioned that there were two or three of them, along with the main house and the barn. Part of the property he bought only days ago. He wants me to move into one of the cabins for a while.

I know my family worries about me. I take things

further than either of my brothers or my sister. Travis and Kade mostly stick to whiskey and Roxie doesn't drink at all.

But, hell, we all have our demons and we all handle them with different medicinal remedies. I tell them there's nothing to worry about.

I walk up the slope to check out the cabin.

It's got a small front porch with two wooden chairs and a nice view over the pond and the hills. I'm mostly dry so I pull on my jeans but leave them half-zipped. I toss my shirt onto one of the chairs and check the door. It's unlocked.

Whoever Travis bought the property from left everything behind, like they were planning to come back to it but never did. The house is furnished and so is this cabin. It's rustic and dusty but fully equipped as a guest house with all the modern conveniences. There's a small kitchen, a table next to the window, leather couches and a fireplace. There's one bedroom with a king-sized bed and a small but luxe bathroom.

Perfect.

There are even paintings on the walls. One is a geometric design, in black and white. It doesn't really go with the rustic furnishings or the wood of the interior, but I like it. It shakes things up.

After our next tour, which is only twelve shows, I might settle down right here and Jack Kerouac my way through a couple of weeks to see if I can create some music that digs so deep it goes down in infamy for the rest of time.

Or something.

All three of us write music and we all have different styles. Travis's is more country, Kade's leans toward bluegrass-meets-edgy-folk and mine is more rock 'n roll.

Yeah, that's what I'll do. Write. Let the angst and the regret and the feverish love of life pour out of me without distractions.

I find it interesting that the urge to write feels remarkably like lust. It's a spiritual lust but it spills over into a physical lust that's fiery and more voracious than any other kind.

Right now, I'm feeling it. I want to write something down and then fuck my way leisurely through a steamy afternoon with some willing nymph. Of which there are always plenty. Except that I'm out in the middle of the countryside and around fifty miles from civilization.

So I'll start with the writing, which can only be good if I'm feeling as feverish as I do right now.

Here I am, standing in the doorway of my new digs, leaning my shoulder against the doorjamb, jeans only partly zipped, appreciating the view as I contemplate the state of my own raging lust, when into that view walks … down by the pond … a girl.

Shit.

For a second I wonder if she's paparazzi. The last thing I need is for fans to start camping out in the woods. Or photos of me half naked all over the internet.

It wouldn't be the first time. Roxie sued some girl over a leaked photo that was taken of me about a year ago. It was eventually removed, but women still mention it to me from time to time. I don't remember it being taken but apparently it was memorable.

But I can't see a phone in her hand. Or a camera.

She's carrying a book.

And she hasn't seen me yet.

But then, as she walks along the track toward me, she feels my gaze. She looks up at me. And she stops walking.

She's a distance away and I can't clearly see all the finer details of her face. It's enough, though. She's cute. In fact … hell. She's dressed in a faded pair of jeans and a white button-down shirt, tied at the waist. Her hair, which is pulled up off-handedly, is a light, vibrant shade of red. It's what you'd call strawberry blond. The term could have been invented just for her. She's wearing a pair of black-framed glasses. I find myself wishing she wasn't. They're hiding her face. But even from this distance I can see a warm blush coloring her cheeks as she stares up at me.

I imagine what I might look like to her. I glance down out of curiosity. I'm mostly decent. At least I'm partly dressed, even if I am half-cocked. Which can't be helped. That's just how I live my life and there's not a damn thing I can do about it.

She's shocked by my presence. She wasn't expecting anyone to be here.

Who is she?

Where's she going?

I want to know.

"Hey," I yell out, raising my hand in a sort of greeting.

She doesn't wave back. Or answer me. She walks backwards for a few steps before turning in the direction she came from.

I almost laugh. "Wait."

She doesn't.

I zip myself mostly up and I start walking down the hill.

I don't want to scare her but, fuck, she can't just wander into my view like that in all her strawberry glory and expect me not to at least want to find out who she is. I'm too amped up to stand there while she walks away.

She follows a trail on the far side of the pond. She glances back to make sure I'm not following her. When she discovers I *am* following her—and in fact gaining on her in ground-eating strides she'll have to take off in a full run to possibly escape—she stops and turns to face me, her thick book hugged in front of her chest like a shield.

As I walk closer I can see that, behind her glasses, her large golden eyes are wide.

I exhale a laugh. "Shit. Don't be scared of me."

Then again, when you look how this girl looks, all

pure and sun-touched and gently studious, maybe she *should* be scared. I'm tatted up to the nines, built as fuck and wild with lust and life. I probably weigh twice what she weighs. I'm suntanned and barefoot and shirtless.

She checks me out slowly, lingering on the tats on my arms and my chest. My stomach. The way the top button of my jeans still isn't fastened. To my face. My hair.

I can't tell if she recognizes me. She's not fangirling or swooning. There's a thread of curiosity, like something about me seems vaguely familiar but she can't quite place it. I don't want to break that bubble. I don't want her to freeze or to run.

"I'm sorry," she says, and I realize I got the wrong impression. She's not scared. She's feisty. Ready to fight.

Which makes me smile. The last thing I want to do is *fight* with this gorgeous little stranger who, now that I get a better look, is not just cute but seriously stunning in an I-wake-up-in-the-morning-looking-like-this kind of way. She's as natural as the sun-bright hayseeds waving in the wind and her hair is the exact same color. She has long, gold-tipped eyelashes that blink at me from behind her glasses, mesmerizingly smooth skin and the kind of plump, bee-stung lips that crank my half-cocked problem several notches higher. I feel hot and hungry to eat her mouth and can only hope like hell I don't bust out of my barely-fastened jeans.

I could sling her over my shoulder and carry her home with me. She couldn't stop me.

"I'm trespassing." Her voice is soft. Calming. It's the kind of voice that could soothe your nightmares or talk you off a ledge. "I didn't know anyone was here."

"You can trespass any time you want."

Her gaze wanders again over the many tattoos across my chest and lands on the smallest, a single word inked over my heart. I'm surprised when she asks it. "Who's Savannah?"

I don't answer right away. I wasn't expecting it, the weight of the name spoken in this girl's gentle voice, handled so carefully.

"My mother," I finally say, and my voice sounds more husky than usual.

She watches my eyes for a few seconds and through her glasses I can see that her tiger-yellow irises have a kindness and depth to them that makes me want to … do something. To dive in. To lose myself in the comfort of her.

"I have to go," she says. "It was nice … running into you. Bye now."

Bye now. "Wait. What's your name?"

She half-smiles and starts walking away, not even giving me that.

I walk along with her. I hold one of my wrists behind my back as I walk. Hiding my fist, which is clenched for no particular reason. So I don't seem as threatening to her as I feel.

Her clothes aren't particularly tight-fitting but do little

to hide the fact that she's got the kind of body that could —and just might—make a grown man cry. Curvy and lush. Her shirt is tied at the front, revealing a thin strip around her waist that shows off the smooth skin of her stomach. Her jeans are fitted around her hips but slightly looser around her waist, leaving a small gap at the front between her waistband and her skin. That little space, for some crazy reason, is … insanely tantalizing.

I want to touch her there, and slide my fingers inside, gliding over her soft pussy, getting her wet, playing her clit, slipping inside.

Fucking hell.

"I'll be away for a few weeks but then I'm moving into the cabin," I tell her. "Give me your number."

I never ask girls for their numbers. Or follow them. *Or* call after them. I don't need to.

We get to a fence. She climbs over it, ignoring my question. "This is me. I hope you have a nice trip."

She's dismissing me?

She's dismissing me. As she should. She's clearly wholesome and good. Clean and pure with golden aspirations and kind-hearted intentions.

The unfamiliarity of this situation amuses me for a couple of seconds. Every woman I've ever met has gone to lengths even I'm sometimes shocked by, to get my attention, to get into my bed, to taste, feel and own every inch of me they can get their hands on.

As for this one, for her, I'm a big black hole of experiences she doesn't yet know she needs.

"Tell me your name or I'm climbing over this fence and banging on your door until you tell me." She gives me a look that's slightly exasperated or maybe even annoyed and this, for some reason, makes my chest sort of ache, with … I don't know. It feels almost like happiness.

"What's yours?" she asks me.

Her mouth, holy hell. It's making me feel depraved. *I want to kiss her. Taste her lips. More than that. I want to spill myself all over her and inside her. I want to lick her and eat her and fuck her until she's crying because I'm so deep and I feel so damn good.*

"Vaughn." I almost say my last name, but hold it, in case she still isn't sure.

It's enough. A little crinkle appears between her eyebrows and those flags of pink warm her face again. Like it just clicked. She recognizes me. "I have to go."

I don't want her to leave me yet. I climb the fence and, because there's a huge tree next to it, I sling myself up onto a thick, low branch.

"You'll fall," she says. "You don't even have shoes on." The sound of her bell-toned Tennessee twang is just about the sweetest thing I've heard in a long time. I'm not sure why. Her feisty, gently-scolding delivery is getting me hot. Even hotter than I already was. My cock is now fully hard and borderline painful and my jeans still aren't fully done up.

I want to lay her down in the summer grass and kiss those

pillowy lips. Peel off her clothes. Run my tongue around her nipples until they're taut and ripe for me. Until she's moaning. I want to find out if she's strawberry blond everywhere. And rub my hard, bursting cock against her pink pussy until she's all slippery and ready for me …

Fuck.

Calm down, you maniac.

This hotness feels tangled. With a weirdly wild joy and a craving. For her to fix those golden eyes onto me with all their kind depth and sassy gorgeousness.

For her to care.

I want her to scold me again.

I want to do things that shock her and make her *feel* me. My lust and my pain.

I'm sitting on this tree branch six or so feet off the ground and from here I can see the back door of her house. It's red. "I just want to know what your name is. Since we're neighbors now."

Her eyes are studying me softly and I'd pay a million dollars to hear what she's thinking right now. "Gigi," she finally says.

Gigi. I love that. "It's nice to meet you, Gigi."

"Nice to meet you too, Vaughn. Now will you please get down?"

"You can walk through that land anytime you want. Swim. Walk the trails. Spend time in my cabin, if you need some time alone to read your book. Anything you want. We'll be gone for a few weeks."

She barely tilts her head, like she's surprised by my offer. "Thanks."

I jump down, landing on the soft grass. She watches me do this, taking in the dirt on my jeans from the bark and my bare, inked, suntanned chest. She's staring at me like she's wary I might be borderline crazy.

She's right.

My phone rings in my back pocket.

She takes this as her cue. "Bye, Vaughn," she says.

"Maybe I'll see you when I get back."

I take my phone out of my pocket, but I'm watching her as she walks away. As I do this, a wave of loneliness hits me right in the middle of my chest that clashes with the bright light of the sunny day. Maybe my flashback is having its way with me again.

Fuck.

I need a drink.

I look at the phone still ringing in my hand. It's Travis. "Hey."

"You up? We're leaving soon."

"Yeah. I'll be there in twenty." I hang up on him. He's distracting me.

I'm still watching Gigi as she walks up the steps of her house, glancing back to see me standing right where she left me.

My new tiger-eyed neighbor.

Chances are I'll forget about her by the time I get back from our tour.

Maybe.

Not a chance in hell.

What I find myself thinking is … I want to make her blush again. And show her how good my kind of trouble feels.

I want to hear the feisty little stranger with the sun-bright hair and the flags of warmth on her face moan my name as she comes hard around me.

Watch out, strawberry girl.

What I want, I always get.

2

Gigi

Two hours earlier ...

I WAKE up earlier than usual, despite all my attempts to sleep in. Which I can never do. The sun is bright, even at 6:18 a.m. I grab some clothes and my phone and quietly make my way out of the bedroom so I don't wake Ruby. She was out late last night working again, at the new job she got as a cleaner for the house next door.

Something's changed in her recently, though. Even though she hasn't told me the details of whatever it is, I'm getting the feeling there's more to the story of her new job than what she's given me so far. We've both been busy but she's also hiding something. I know her too well.

You don't clean for fourteen hours a day, I don't care how dirty that house is. And she looks all starry-eyed in a way that's new.

I'll get it out of her. We tell each other everything, we always have. I'll talk to her later about it, in case she needs help with anything. The past few weeks have been an emotional time for her. She just graduated and is saving up to move to Nashville after the summer. It's a big deal to have dreams as wild as Ruby's are, to feel the whole world opening up in front of you because you're finally free to start following your own path.

She wants to write songs and sing to big crowds and become a superstar. I can see all of that happening for her, even though the competition is so fierce. She's got the talent and she definitely has the drive. Not to mention the looks and plenty of glittering X-factor.

Ruby wants to make her voice heard. To entertain and inspire. She will, too, I know it.

As for me, I have a different kind of dream.

I want to help people.

Which sounds sort of cheesy or tame or even lame, possibly, but I know it isn't. When you think about it, helping people is the wildest aspiration there is.

I want to save a life that otherwise wouldn't have been saved. That's it. That's my dream.

I often think about something called the Butterfly Effect. How the flicker of a butterfly wing in one direction or another can lead to an entirely different sequence of events that changes the course of history and everything in it. If a tiny wing can do that, what can an entire *life* do? If you save a life, what could the continuation of a beautiful soul that might have otherwise been extinguished from the world lead to?

What none of my sisters know is that it wasn't an out-of-the-blue heart attack that killed our father. It was an addiction to pain killers that caused it. I found him. I was the only one home and I called the ambulance. My mother knew, although I don't think she ever knew the extent of it, and I never told her the darker details because I don't think it would have helped her. It would just have made the pain even more brutal than it already was. He told me, as I held his hand in the ambulance. He started taking the prescription after he'd injured his shoulder in some farming accident. He was addicted and he'd tried to stop but he couldn't. He was buying them illegally and he knew the ingredients weren't pure. They were dangerous. In the end he was injecting himself with whatever he could get his hands on. He already had heart problems and the drugs made them worse. Much worse. He'd been warned. But he couldn't stop himself.

And I couldn't save him.

He told me something else, too. That I should use the gift I'd been given. The empathy that went deeper than most people's, he said. He wished he'd told me but he didn't want to burden me with the depth of his problem. He said it felt like quicksand and he didn't want to drag me down with him.

By the time we got to the hospital, he was already

dead. They had to pull his cold hand from mine because I didn't want to let him go.

My father was kind and beautiful, with an edge. He was cool and fun and handsome. Ninety-nine percent of him was outrageously good, and steady. But there was a spark there too, behind all that. That one percent of him had a taste for danger. An urge to touch the fire.

Ever since he died, I can feel that spark in myself sometimes too. A fever for something I can't even name. When I feel the glow of that spark, I try to curb it in directions that'll help me get what I want in life. I study harder. I take long walks to burn off the energy. I help my sisters and Momma work through whatever issues they're having—and there are always plenty of those. I've taken on the role of a sort of counselor for everyone in my family and I'm fine with that. If I can help them in any way at all, I will.

The thing is, if I'd known earlier that my daddy was in trouble, I'm sure I could have helped him. He *wanted* to be helped. He told me that as he was dying.

I think everyone, deep down, wants to be helped.

And I could have done that. My understanding and my love could have changed his mind about taking the wrong path, the path that killed him. I *know* that, somewhere deep inside my heart.

I've got a way of seeing things and convincing people of their own worth that makes an impact. It's sort of my thing. My gift, my father called it. Other people have musical talent or can play football or design buildings or whatever. I can change people's minds when it comes to their own psyche. I can help them see the things that are good and unique and amazing about themselves that sometimes they can't see.

It's partly why Ruby is so confident and so ready to take the world by storm. She *is* talented. She also *knows* she's talented and worthy and ready for her life, partly because I taught her to see that in herself.

I go into the bathroom. I get dressed and splash my face with cold water. I put my hair up and brush my teeth. Here I go getting all philosophical. I wasn't expecting to *feel* things so deeply this morning. Maybe having Ruby home, all hopeful and excited, has kicked up some of my protective instincts. I just want her to be okay. She's a free spirit and I don't want her getting into trouble or taking things too fast.

I just hope she's not heading down the same road as our two older sisters, getting hooked on men who then proceed to take over every aspect of their lives, down to the music they listen to and the clothes they wear. Both Rose and Scarlett are hard-wired that way. They aspire to being taken care of by men. They fall for any good-looking guy who happens to flick them a half-interested glance and then cry when the boys don't call.

It's a trap I plan on avoiding.

My phone rings. I take it outside and sit on the bench

under the tree so I don't wake up the others. "Hey, Scarlett."

"Hi, honey."

"You okay?"

She's sniffling and she sounds exhausted. "The baby just won't stop crying, no matter what I do. Her colic is getting worse. I didn't sleep at all last night."

"What did the doctor say?"

"She said Clemmie will grow out of it but it sometimes it gets worse before it gets better."

"You should come home for a while, then we could all help you with her. You could sleep."

"Johnny doesn't want me to leave. And he's already talking about having another baby. Can you believe that? I can barely handle one, how am I going to handle *two*? I'm too tired to even think about that, let alone do anything about it. Which of course he complains about."

"Wow."

"Yeah. Tell me about it."

"I'm sure it'll get easier."

"Oh, God, the baby's awake again. I have to go. Can I call you later?"

"Of course you can. Anytime you want. You'll be okay. Make sure you sleep when the baby sleeps."

"I will. Love you, Gi. I miss you."

"Miss you too."

She ends the call.

Scarlett's happy enough with her new marriage and

her beautiful baby girl. But when things get hard, like when money's tight—which it always is—or her husband is too controlling (something she loved about him to begin with but lately … not so much) or the baby cries so much (all the time), she calls me. I'm the one she vents to. There's no point now worrying about whether she rushed into family life when maybe she should have taken more time to think things through. She *wanted* that baby and that husband to take care of her. She went for that outcome like an arrow for the bullseye. All I can do now is tell her how lucky she is. To help her appreciate the good stuff and provide a shoulder to cry on when she feels overwhelmed.

As for me, I don't plan on getting involved with anyone until I've graduated, found a job, saved some money and done some traveling. For myself.

Do what you love, my daddy used to say. *Shine your light, Gi. You're such a bright one.*

I don't want the distraction of a relationship.

Besides, all the guys I meet are only after one thing and it's a thing I don't want to do with someone I don't completely love. Which sounds corny and old-fashioned, but it's true. I don't want to have sex until I'm in love. All the guys who call me up or come into the library where I work are … well, not even close. I don't even *like* most of them so the thought of falling in love with one of them feels like it might be a fantasy that's located in some far corner of another galaxy at this point.

Something that happens to other people, but not to me.

Anyway, I'm too busy working my way through my degree in social work at the community college to worry about it.

Maybe after I graduate I'll go on to become one of those therapists you see on TV, in a big office with city views. In New York or somewhere exotic. Once I get qualified I'm thinking of taking a job somewhere else for a while. I've hardly seen the world beyond the fifty mile radius of my own house. I've never been on a plane. I've only been to the city a handful of times. It would be cool to check out a few different states. Or countries, even. It's hard to imagine how that would feel when you've never been anywhere.

I go into the kitchen and pour myself some orange juice. I make some toast. Then I sit at the table and open my *Critical Self-Reflection in Social Work* textbook and start reading the fourth chapter.

I'm taking some notes when my phone rings again.

Dylan flashes up on the screen.

He's a guy in my Ethics class, even though he's studying to become a banker. When he told me that, I joked about bankers not having any ethics. He only shrugged and said the class was required.

He even *looks* like a banker, like he's already got one foot in middle age. He has light brown hair and eyes such a pale color gray they look see-through, as though you're staring right through him.

"Hi, Dylan."

"Hey, Gigi. I hope you don't mind me calling so early." I glance at the clock. 8:42. "You mentioned you're an early riser."

"It's fine."

"Listen, I was wondering if I could borrow your Self-Reflection textbook for the next assignment. Have you read chapter four yet?"

"I'm just reading it now."

"Can I borrow it when you're finished? We could meet here and discuss the assignment." After our first class of the semester, we discovered we're neighbors. He lives on the other side of the field from my house, across the expanse of property now owned by Ruby's new boss.

Dylan hasn't bothered buying any of the textbooks. This is the third one he's asked to borrow. And he seems to be relying on me to help him with his assignments.

Even though I fully realize he might be using me to ease his way through this course, I always find it hard to turn people down if they ask me for help. Maybe he can't afford to buy the books or something. I'm trying to make a point of getting more staunch when it comes to "self-care and the power of saying no," as it's outlined in one of my other textbooks. But it's the ambiguity that stops me. Maybe he really needs the help. "Okay. Sure."

"How about now? Do you want to bring it over?"

"Give me an hour or so to finish taking notes. Then I'll walk over."

"Great. Thanks, Gigi. See you soon."

I end the call and take down the notes I'll need to write my assignment. Momma and Rose come in and start making breakfast. I stand up from the table and close the book, sliding my phone into my back pocket.

"I'm going to walk over to Dylan's."

Momma pours herself a cup of coffee. "Is he the boy from your class? The banker?"

"He's not a banker yet."

"The *aspiring* banker." Rose is grinning. "How romantic. He's called you every day for the past three days, Gi. He's obviously got the hots for you big time."

I can always trust Rose to fixate on whether or not I'm planning to have sex with someone. "It's not like that, Rose."

"Of course it's like that, Gi. Why do you think he keeps calling you?"

"Are you dating him?" asks Momma.

"No, Momma. I'm not *dating* him. I'm letting him borrow my book. I'll see you both later."

My lack of a love life is a huge joke to Rose, as always. But her teasing has a caring edge. "One of these days you're going to meet a man who can melt through that thick icy forcefield, Gi. I can't wait until some super-hot alpha bad boy waltzes into town and sweeps my oh-so-studious, hyper-responsible sister off her feet, unleashing her ravenous and totally suppressed wild side. *That* will be something to watch."

"Would you stop?" Then, because I can't resist, "As if I'd ever fall for a bad boy. What even *is* that?"

"Definitely not the banker," she laughs. "I stalked him online after the second time he called you. Despite the fact that you insist on wearing those bookworm glasses and those tomboy outfits, my gorgeous sister is still a million miles out of *that* guy's league."

"Whatever." I'm tired of the topic, even though I think she might have just given me a rare compliment. She smiles at me as I close the screen door and I make a face at her.

Carrying the book under my arm, I walk across our backyard and climb over the fence.

It feels strange to know that someone's now living at the property, after so many years of the place being empty. I even heard music last night. In fact, I probably shouldn't be trespassing. But if I keep to the track on the far side of the pond, I'm not even within sight of the house, so I figure they won't even notice.

The pond looks inviting. And, as I get closer, sort of muddy at the beach end. Like someone recently went for a swim. The rocks by the shore are still wet.

Maybe this was a bad idea.

I keep walking but I get the prickling, heated sensation that someone's watching me. I look up to the abandoned cabin that overlooks the pond to see … oh.

I stop in my tracks.

Oh my God.

A guy is standing there.

He's big. Wet. Muscular. Shirtless. Tattooed.

A bad boy. Definitely.

Wow.

He's young but probably a few years older than me. He's very tan, with longish, thick, sort of glamorously-wild black hair.

His shoulder leans against one of the wooden beams of his porch and he has one hand slung into the pocket of his jeans.

He's … not even fully zipped up … and he's *filling out those jeans like nobody's business—holy shit!* My face feel hot. I try not to stare. I can feel my heart beating fast.

He looks dangerous. Reckless and untamed, in a lazy, ultra-confident way. In a way that makes my stomach do a funny little flip.

I'd have to be made of stone not to notice that he's … handsome. More than handsome. Sort of … absolutely gorgeous. In fact, I don't think I've ever seen *anyone* as gorgeous as this guy is. Or as freaking … *hot.* It hits you like a freight train. You can't *not* notice how beautiful and how outstandingly built he is.

I can see that his eyes are blue even from this distance.

I can also see that he's got Trouble with a capital T written all over him. You can tell he'd kill you with the kind of pleasure you'd never recover from. I don't know why I say that, but the promise sort of radiates off of him.

You can also tell that he'd demolish your heart and your life in the process.

How do I know that?

Because I've seen two of my sisters get similarly demolished—or close enough—by men who were far less *alpha* than this guy clearly is. Even from here, it's easy to guess that he's a man who could have any woman he wanted, and probably—no, definitely—has *had* every woman he's wanted.

Not my type at all.

Not that I have a type.

He's not the type I'd *want* to be my type, when I get one.

I don't want to be demolished. Or have the kind of pleasure I'll never recover from.

Do I?

No. Absolutely not.

"Hey," he calls out.

I take a few steps backwards, hoping maybe he hasn't noticed me.

But of course he's noticed me. He's staring right at me. He's talking to me.

And my heartbeat is thrumming in unusual places.

I turn and start walking back home.

"Wait," he yells.

I almost start running, but I randomly think about

something my father told me once, that if a dog starts chasing you, you shouldn't ever run. You should turn and face them and stare them down until they walk away.

Not that that applies to this situation but my instincts are on overdrive. I can hear him following me and I probably couldn't outrun him even if I tried.

So I hug my book against me like it could offer me protection even though I refuse to be terrified and I turn to face him.

As I watch him walk closer to me ... *wow, he's good-looking.*

His eyes are an incredibly vivid shade of blue. His eyelashes are thick and dark and long enough to give him an almost romantic appeal, like he belongs in a fashion photoshoot staging Roman gods and their harems or something. Or in a band-of-brothers cowboy movie and he's the one that everyone would die for and all the women fall in love with. He inspires crazy visions. Because he's completely over the top.

His black hair is still damp from his swim, framing his head in a halo of haphazard, perfectly-mussed waves. His eyes are slightly bloodshot and there are faint shadows under his eyes as though he hasn't had enough sleep lately. These details don't detract, though, not at all. They make his irises look even more striking and give him a hint of sincerity, like under all his rough sexiness, he feels things. Deeply.

He's not angry. Something's funny to him.

Me.

That I would walk away from him.

Maybe that's never happened to him before. It wouldn't surprise me.

"Shit," he says. "Don't be scared of me."

I'm not scared of him. I get the vibe that he's as wild as they come but that his heart is good. I have a knack for reading people's psyches and his feels … complicated. But not threatening.

And now that he's closer, there's something almost familiar about him.

Have I met him somewhere?

But that's impossible.

I would have remembered.

"I'm sorry," I tell him. He smiles lightly at this and I lose my train of thought for a few seconds. His blue eyes. His white teeth and the shape of his mouth. "I'm trespassing. I didn't know anyone was here."

"You can trespass any time you want."

His chest is sculpted and … ideal. Seriously. He's like a roughed-up, inked-up, living work of art. Lean but sort of gracefully muscular. I notice a name tattooed over his heart.

Savannah.

His girlfriend, maybe. But I've already figured out he probably has more than one of those. And I don't know why I ask him. I get the feeling I already know what he's going to say. "Who's Savannah?"

My question hits a place in him that hurts, I can see this before he answers. When you spend as much time counseling your sisters, friends and random people that recognize you as a sympathetic listener, you start to develop a knack, and you can usually read their pain in the hesitations. "My mother," he says.

There's something difficult about his relationship with her, maybe, or her memory.

And if I stand here too long analyzing this god-like bad boy, I'm going to want to find out more.

Which isn't going to happen.

He's a stranger. And he's too beautiful to get to know. I don't *want* to get to know him.

Why?

Because he's the kind of guy—and I've never met one before, but it's obvious—that would hurt you just by being around you. I *already* feel hurt. He's too much. His unruly, masculine magnificence is too much. Most of all, his threads of vulnerability and pain are too much—and the more time I spend in his company, the more pronounced they become. The entire cocktail would force you to care about him and then every time he made a mistake or behaved in a way that was as loose and reckless as every-thing about him promises to be, it would break your damn heart.

"I have to go," I say. "It was nice running into you. Bye now."

"Wait. What's your name?"

It's best to not even go there. That would make us friends. Or acquaintances. Which I've already decided to try to avoid. So I start walking away.

He walks with me.

I glance over at him and my eyes feel glued to some of the details of him, as much as I wish they weren't.

He's a good six or seven inches taller than me. His hair lifts gently in the breeze and the softness of it clashes with his ink, his bronze skin, his low-slung, still-unfastened jeans, the pronounced V-line at his lean hips, and all the hard lines of him—one in particular I make a point of not staring at but it's kind of impossible not to notice that it's as wildly and dangerously outrageous as the rest of him. "I'll be away for a few weeks but then I'm moving into the cabin. Give me your number."

As if.

We're at the fence. So I climb over it and do my best to breeze past his demand. "This is me." He mentioned he was leaving. "I hope you have a nice trip."

"Tell me your name or I'm climbing over this fence and banging on your door until you tell me."

I glare at him, as much as I can without becoming sort of dazzled again by his face. His eyebrows are thick and dark. His mouth is … made for sin. *He'd be dirty as all hell.* His lips are beautifully shaped and there's a hint of his beard. He probably hasn't shaved for a few days. *I bet there's nothing he wouldn't do. There's probably nothing he hasn't already done.*

I don't want to be rude. And I don't want him banging on my door. Rose would have a field day. "What's yours?"

"Vaughn," he says.

Wait a minute.

Holy hell.

That's why he's familiar. *Is it?* No, it couldn't be.

But I think it might be.

It is. It's Vaughn Tucker.

The famous drummer.

The *very* famous drummer who plays with his brothers in the Tucker Brothers Band. Whose songs play on the radio all the time. I have a bunch of them on my playlists. I love their music.

Vaughn Tucker, the famous drummer who's always making headlines for all the trouble he gets into and all the women he sleeps with.

I wonder how many hearts he's broken. Hundreds, I'd wager. Probably more like thousands. "I have to go."

He climbs over the fence and up onto a low branch of the old oak tree. He sits there like he doesn't have a care in the world. I wish he wouldn't do that.

"You'll fall. You don't even have shoes on." I really don't want him to hurt himself.

"I just want to know what your name is. Since we're neighbors now."

I can't think of any way to get out of it at this point. So I tell him. "Gigi."

He smiles and catches my eyes and my stomach does that little flip again. Slowly and sexily, which is clearly his M.O., he says, "It's nice to meet you, Gigi."

"Nice to meet you too, Vaughn." He's making me nervous up there in the tree. I wish he'd be careful. "Now will you please get down?"

"You can walk through that land anytime you want. Swim. Walk the trails. Spend time in my cabin, if you need some time alone to read your book. Anything you want. We'll be gone for a few weeks."

I think I read something about a tour coming up. That must be why he'll be away. I've always wondered what that cottage looks like inside. It's so cute from the outside. Sort of a picture-perfect little log cabin. "Thanks."

He jumps down onto the grass effortlessly, dirty, sweaty, clearly not worried about heights or any of the rest of it.

He's close to me now and I can feel him, like his heat and his raw energy might give me an electric shock if I get too close to him. I take a step back.

I'm almost relieved when his phone rings. I use his distraction to make my escape. "Bye, Vaughn." I start walking up to the house.

"Maybe I'll see you when I get back," he says.

I don't bother answering him. *Or maybe not.*

You're hot, you're beautiful—and you're a playboy of the highest order. The last thing on earth I want to do is fall in love with you, only to have my heart squashed like a slug on a country road.

And yes, I do realize the spin of my own thoughts.

You just said fall in love. You've never said that before.

It means nothing. Just because he's the kind of man you could fall in love with very definitely doesn't mean he's the kind of man you'd *want* to fall in love with.

I don't.

I won't. Obviously.

At least a hundred million other women are *already* in love with him, no doubt crying by their phones waiting for him to call them. I'd rather run a mile from him than join their ranks.

I glance back at him and he's still standing there, watching me as he talks on the phone. Looking off-hand-edly drop-dead gorgeous and sort of … sad.

Damn him. As if the gorgeous part wasn't bad enough.

Maybe he needs someone to talk to. Maybe he needs help.

I'm sure he'll get plenty of that where he's going.

What I'm thinking as I go inside and shut the door behind me is, *I hope I never see him again.*

Somehow I get the feeling I won't be that lucky.

3

VAUGHN

"WE'RE MEETING THE FAMILY?" I almost laugh. "Shit."

Travis gives me a glare that's half pissed off and half totally whipped. It's a new look for him.

And I'm in a shitty mood.

I feel restless.

I want to see her again. I want to exasperate her again and make her blush. It wasn't enough time.

"She's moving in with me, going on the road with us for a month and she's only eighteen," Travis says.

My brother thinks he's in love. I almost feel sorry for the poor sucker.

I pat him on the back. "Sure thing, bro. Why not. Let's go and meet them." I glance at Kade behind Travis's back and Kade shakes his head as he packs up his vintage Fender P-Bass.

We're entertained enough by Travis's new obsession that we've agreed to stop by Ruby's house on our way back to Nashville. My brothers and I camped out at Travis's new country house last night and got drunk on whiskey and stayed up most of the night working on a couple of new songs we're putting together. Ruby lives nearby and went home for the night before things got rowdy.

I'll admit the girl can sing. We gave four or five others a fair shot at auditioning to be our opening act for the 12-show tour we've got coming up. She outshone them by a country mile, we all agreed on that. It's her look as much as her voice, which she can effortlessly shift between a smoky rasp and a pitch-perfect clarity that makes you stop what you're doing and listen to the glide of it. She was fast-tracked by the muses, is how Kade put it, being born with a talent like that. Especially since she has no formal training and is straight out of some strict boarding school she just graduated from.

Which made me laugh.

Figures my brother would fall for innocence incarnate. To the point of ridiculousness.

She didn't even know who Travis was.

The girl has clearly been hermetically sealed up in her convent for the past four years, no doubt with her chastity belt firmly locked.

Travis is in the process of enlightening her, obviously, but the whole thing is beyond a joke.

And I'm not really in the mood to play nice for the mother and sisters of some naïve crush of Travis's before we sweep her off to the big city. Then again it might be mildly entertaining to watch their reaction to the sight of us.

Travis is probably the most wholesome-looking of the three of us, as these things go. He wears more denim than leather, the length of his hair is closer to respectable and he only has a couple of tattoos. Kade is more brooding and inked and his hair hangs almost to his shoulders, which countryside mothers tend to glower at.

As for me, no mother in her right mind should let me anywhere near her daughters.

The brightness of the sunlight shifts my hangover up a gear.

And the flashback I had this morning along with the girl and her face and her question aren't helping.

Who's Savannah?

My regrets come flooding back to me and I reach for the quarter-full bottle of whiskey sitting on Travis's piano. I take a long swig, then I fill up my hip flask. I can already tell it's going to be one of those days where I need to medicate. To drown my demons and keep them firmly locked in their back-corner-of-my-subconscious cage.

Once we're packed up we go out the kitchen door and out to Travis's car.

"Behave, okay?" he grumbles as we climb into his Shelby. "I fucking mean it. Just act normal for once."

"I always do," I reply, offended, which for some reason makes Kade laugh.

We drive down Travis's winding road. This part of Tennessee is absurdly picturesque with its blue skies and the hazy humidity rolling off the lush hills, softening the scene whimsically. Hanging out in this neck of the woods could almost turn a person romantic if they let it.

I like it, I realize. I'm looking forward to my hiatus in the cabin.

I find myself wishing I could skip the goddamn tour, and go there now.

Because she's nearby.

Because I need a break.

Travis pulls his Shelby out onto the main road, taking the first left into Ruby's driveway. It's a modest house with a neat little front garden and potted plants on the front porch. It's so orderly and so damn *homely*, it almost gives me a pang of … something. Some long-ago memory gets briefly triggered. Which is never a good thing. I take another drink from my flask to dull it.

The flowers in the garden have taken on a neon-bright glow and the daylight has a buzzy edge.

I notice then that the front door is red.

Like … the back door.

It's her house.

Gigi is Ruby's *sister?*

Fuck.

"Be polite," Travis says, as we get out of the car and

start walking toward the house. I'm suddenly a lot more receptive to this whole idea.

He looks so uptight I can't help grinning at him as he eyeballs me pleadingly, clutching his bunch of flowers.

"Could you be any more cliché?" I can't remember the last time any of us had to go out of our way to try to impress someone.

And I think about what I might look like to a small town mother and her three wholesome daughters.

A heathen, very possibly, but there's nothing to be done about that. I'm a fucking rock star, after all. This is how I'm *supposed* to look. They call me the wild child of my band, and it's true enough, although it's not entirely by choice.

I'm wearing black jeans with a chain that links my wallet to my belt loop. For legit reasons: so I don't lose the damn thing while I'm passed out or get pickpocketed by a groupie. They're always trying to get their hands on me, my money and my number.

The sleeves of my black denim shirt are rolled up, showing off the tats that cover my forearms. I've got a few new ones on my hands and my neck. My black hair is wild and hasn't been combed this decade.

But I'm the life of the party, so there's that. And I get to see her again. So I'm now fully prepared to toe the line and charm the pants—or at least the socks—off Ruby's mother and sisters.

One in particular.

Before Travis can knock, the door swings open. Ruby invites us in.

I take in the scene, which is so neat and cutesy and … *feminine,* we might as well be three feral bulls who just wandered into a china shop.

I haven't been inside a kitchen like this in a long time. Where things are all in their place and the table is one that people actually sit around while they eat. A percolating coffee machine and a toaster sit side by side on the counter, clean and shiny. Magnets on the fridge hold symmetrical photos of Ruby and her sisters in place. There's a window seat with floral cushions and carefully tied back curtains I'd bet money Mrs. Hayes sewed with her own hands. The windows are clean and the warm late-morning light spills in unfiltered.

The quaint, orderly domesticity is jarring somehow.

It's … nice.

We stand there sort of awkwardly inside the doorway for a few seconds, bunched together. It reminds me of when we were kids for some reason, traveling in our pack like we still tend to do. Kade is the oldest by a year. Kade is 26, Travis is 25, I'm 24 and Roxie is 22. Our parents were apparently extremely busy over those five years. So we're close and we always have been.

Kade is less outgoing than Travis but always acted as our protector when we were younger. He has a presence people tend to take seriously. He's aloof and full of the kind of depth that's star-dusted and hard to read, if you don't know him. People respect him just because of the aura he gives off. Like he knows things you wish *you* knew. Which is actually true. His creative spark is one of the most pronounced things about him.

All three of us are tall, built and roughed-up the way you get after a solid three months of touring, partying, working out every chance we get and playing our guts out to fully packed stadiums. The lifestyle tends to leave you half-wrecked and half-enlightened and it's a state of mind people notice. Our stage presence tumbles over into real life.

Like now.

They're all shell-shocked for a few seconds.

"It's nice to meet you, Mrs. Hayes." Travis steps forward and hands Ruby's mother the bunch of roses.

Ruby's mother comes toward us, wiping her hands on an actual apron. "That's so sweet," she says, taking the flowers. "I'll put them in some water."

"Momma," Ruby says, "this is Travis and his brothers, Vaughn and Kade." To us, she says, "This is Rose and Gigi, my sisters."

I glance at Rose, who's red-headed and pink-cheeked. Her amber eyes glow with the kind of awe we've become very used to.

And then there's Gigi.

Even though it's a colorful room and each of the

sisters have different shades of red hair, all the light seems to somehow land on Gigi.

Her tiger eyes are wide, but not starstruck. She's no longer wearing her glasses and I'm glad. I can see her face without barriers. Her strawberry hair is loose now and hangs almost to her waist.

She a fucking goddess.

She's standing near the fridge, her hip resting against the counter. There's a sprinkling of freckles across her nose, giving her a hint of tomboyishness which is over-ridden by a raw, feminine beauty that only compounds itself the longer you watch her. Her face is delicate, with those large, golden eyes, a small, perfect nose and those full pink lips that give her innocence a sultry sexiness. It's the kind of face you see on fashion magazine covers, even though it doesn't look like she's wearing any make-up. There's an off-hand glamor to her she's completely unaware of. Her white shirt is still tied at the waist, revealing that thin strip of the pale, smooth skin of her stomach.

That fine strip of skin is so pure-looking, so untouched and soft, my cock hardens and I get this carnal rush of hunger—again—to *lick* her there. To bite her. To hold her down and run my tongue over her sensitive flesh until she squirms and squeals.

If her mother wasn't here I'd already be on my knees.

Gigi catches me staring hotly and the rush of pink flushes her cheeks, just like it did earlier.

She's curvier than either of her sisters, in a way that splices through whatever whiskey-enhanced haze might have been fringing at the edges of my awareness. Her arms are folded across her full breasts—*wow*—in way that's almost insolent.

I blink a couple of times. Outside she had to compete with the sun. Inside this room, the magnitude of her overall look is blazing and outrageous. The soft colors of her. The pink fullness of her mouth and the gold-red hue of her hair. The astounding *smoothness* of her skin. She doesn't look real.

She's watching me stare at her. I didn't realize I'd said the word *wow* out loud. And her understated sauciness makes me smile.

Bring it on, sweetheart. I can do saucy.

I can do a lot more than saucy.

I can't wait until those bee-stung lips are wrapped around my big, spilling cock and slick with my cum.

"Hi, Gigi," I say, glad that the others are talking. Gigi and I are on our own wavelength.

"Hi, Vaughn."

"Imagine bumping into you twice in one morning."

"Imagine."

I don't really want to piss off our opening act—and my rabid brother—by making a move on her sister before we've even started the tour. But I'm not sure if I can resist this girl.

Those soft lips and that creamy skin.

Those bouncy breasts.

As soon as I can get her alone, I'm going to feast on her ripe nipples. I'm going to slide my cock between those two perfect mounds and come all over her skin, covering her in my hot seed from head to toe.

My cock hardens even more.

Gigi's gentle smile is more polite than happy, but Rose gushes in a sort of hushed squeal, "I can't believe the Tucker Brothers are in our *kitchen*."

None of us know how to respond to this so we don't.

"Would you like something to eat?" Mrs. Hayes asks, maybe for a distraction.

"Yes please, Mrs. Hayes," I say politely. I can't remember the last time I ate something that wasn't pizza or burgers or something else out of a box. I'm starving.

As Mrs. Hayes starts getting the food ready, I straddle one of the delicate chairs, carefully—hoping I don't break the damn thing—and allow myself a better view of the hometown goddess in my midst. I'm still staring and this is clearly making her squirm.

Which is getting me even harder. Even though I'm making an effort *not* to get hard. But it's impossible.

It's not the time or the place for a fucking hard-on, you maniac.

I'd start with that pouting little mouth. I bet her nipples are the same shade of pink as her cheeks. I bet she's never had anyone suck on them until they're red and sore. Or made her come that way. I find myself wondering if she's ever had her pussy eaten real good until she's moaning and crying and coming hard.

I'd bet a million dollars she hasn't.

I want to do it.

She'll taste as sweet as she looks, there's no doubt in my mind about that.

I want to do it right now.

It would piss off Travis to no end. He's suddenly morphed into someone who cares about what other people think. Or at least two of the people in this room.

But *come on.*

Her soft femininity is blowing my goddamn mind.

Those *curves.* That heavenly smoothness of her exposed little stripe of tantalizing skin that's just begging to be dirtied and debauched.

By me.

It's mine. I'm going to rub myself all over her naked body. Mark her. Claim her.

My gaze arrives back at Gigi's face. She's watching me check her out.

I narrow my eyes a fraction and grin at her wolfishly, to tease her, and she almost imperceptibly squares her shoulders.

Not in a million years, that little shrug says.

She's right. She should keep a very comfortable distance.

But something about that little shrug provokes the

beast in me—which happens to occupy most of the real estate in my psyche, for better or worse. Who are we kidding, it's always worse.

She's dismissing me. Again.

As she should.

Smart girl.

Challenge accepted, whispers the little devil on my shoulder. Both little devils. If there was ever an angel on one of my shoulders, he converted to the dark side years ago and never regretted the choice.

I'll toe this particular line long enough to placate my brother.

Maybe.

If I can hold out that long.

She's so fucking gorgeous.

For now, at least, I can appreciate the view and play with her unease.

She holds my gaze.

She's shy but she doesn't lack courage. She's going to be a fun one to tease. To rile. To test where her thresholds lie. I'd bet good money she's a virgin.

The thought makes my cock throb hotly.

Calm down, you asshole.

I could be her first, I find myself thinking.

I want to be her first.

Can I wait until after the tour?

Her first kiss.

Surely she's been kissed.

Her first *real* kiss.

Her first mind-blowing orgasm.

Her first—

"Gi?" Gigi's concentration veers to the conversation and mine begrudgingly follows. Ruby and Travis have been talking about our tour schedule. "Can you take time off to come to one of the shows?" Ruby asks her.

Gigi glances lightly at me before she answers. "I'm not sure. I'll have to see."

There's something wildly enthralling about the fact that she's not only *not* fangirling all over me, like they always do, but she's already made up her mind about me. After taking in whatever details of me she's decided sum me up, she's written me off as trouble.

I'm the reason she won't commit to coming to one of our shows, that's easy enough to read.

I'm freaking her out with my muscles and my tats. The chains and the double denim. The dark-horse attention and the playful danger.

"Do you all live in the warehouse in Nashville?" Rose is asking.

"We all have other houses," Travis says, "but we stay there when we're rehearsing and recording."

"That's so cool," Rose says.

Gigi glances down at her phone that's sitting on the counter next to her. The screen has lit up. It's distracting her from what's going on here.

Us.

Me.

I can't help myself. "Who's texting you?"

She gives me a look, and I can't help grinning at her. Of course it's none of my business. But getting under her skin is the most fun I've had in a while.

And she's too polite to be rude to me. "It's just someone in one of the classes I'm taking."

"What are you studying?"

"Social work."

"Social work," I repeat.

"Yes."

I slide my flask out of my back pocket and take a sip.

She watches me do this.

"You want some?"

"No."

"What exactly does a social worker do?" I ask her.

"I'm majoring in addiction rehabilitation. So it's counseling and … you know. Rehab."

Shit. I almost laugh. "Maybe you can cure *me*," I say softly.

"I don't work with actual patients yet. Not until next month." She pauses before she says it: "Besides, you look like you're too far gone."

This makes me smile. Gigi Hayes is sassy. I'm going to make her pay for that. With my tongue. At my very first opportunity. "You're right."

She almost smiles back, but not quite. There's a thread of concern behind her expression. That *care,* again. It's sincere and freakishly compelling. Like a hook that gets into the meat of my angst and pulls on it while at the same time calming it.

Only a few hours ago I was thinking about how I don't care what other people think of me. For some reason, this little strawberry glamor girl has a hold on me, already. I have this strange desire for more of her sensitivity. There's something wildly soothing about it. "Give me your number."

It's then that Mrs. Hayes sets a huge plate of food in front of me.

"Thank you, Mrs. Hayes." My manners are still in there, good to know. It's not that often I have an opportunity to employ them.

It's the first time I've had home cooking since—

For a long time. Let's just leave it at that.

I tuck into it like I haven't eaten in weeks. My brothers do the same thing.

Home made fried chicken, potato salad, coleslaw and warm cornbread with melting butter.

"Mrs. Hayes," I tell her. "This is the best food I've had in years." I almost say the best *fucking* food but catch myself in time, even though the qualifier would make the statement that much more accurate. It *is* the best fucking food I've had in years.

Mrs. Hayes smiles. "That's nice of you to say, Vaughn. You boys should come over anytime you're here. Sounds like you could do with more home cooking." She pours us each a cup of fresh-brewed coffee with real cream.

"Yes, ma'am." I plan to take her up on that offer.

I'll be living next door, after all, soon enough.

And Gigi and I are going to be working up an appetite, if I get my way.

Which, luckily for me, I always do.

The only problem is, I don't know if I can wait that long.

I DIDN'T GET another chance to ask her for her number with all the drama of the girls crying because Ruby was leaving home.

We're in the car and Travis cranks up the music and we head out.

It's for the best, of course.

Kade and I are crammed into the back seat of Travis's Shelby. I take out my flask, fish around in my pocket for a couple of Adderall and a Xanax I have in there and pop all three. I wash them down with whiskey, chugging half of it.

Kade is watching me. "What are you doing, brother?"

"Getting fucked up."

He takes the flask and helps himself to a sip. "What for?" Reading me, maybe, or trying to, pocketing my flask. I could fight him for it and maybe I will. Later. For now, I lean my head back and let my eyes close, feeling the numbness ease through my system mercifully.

Because I'd ruin her life. Because she doesn't deserve me.

Just like my father didn't deserve my mother. She paid the ultimate price because of it.

And because of me.

4

AFTER THEY LEAVE, taking Ruby with them, I help Momma clean up the kitchen. Her eyes are all red.

"Momma, you know this is the best possible thing that could be happening to Ruby. She's eighteen and she's ready. This is exactly what she wanted." Ruby gave me a tearful but exuberant hug as she left and told me she'd call me and tell me the whole story as soon as she got to Nashville. She knows I'm here for her whenever she needs me. But what I'm telling Momma is true. Ruby *is* ready. There's no reason for her to wait.

"I know," Momma says. "But it's so fast. And they're so … "

She doesn't finish but I know what she means. Those Tucker brothers are big and rough. They're pumped-up masculinity on overdrive. All three of them are a walking advertisement for sex, drugs and rock 'n roll. There's no doubt in anyone's mind that Ruby is going to or possibly already *has* gotten down and dirty with Travis Tucker—and that she'll have the time of her damn life while doing it. They're the kind of men that, as a mother, I would imagine you spend every waking moment trying to keep your daughters away from. As a sister, I couldn't be happier for her.

"They're so freaking *hot*, is what they are," Rose says, wiping her eyes. "And *filthy* rich." Rose is also crying, because she wishes it was her. And because her ex (as of ten minutes ago), Jackson Cole, was the former opening act for the band, a gig now assigned to Ruby. "Ruby is *so* lucky."

She's also crying because of Travis's assurance to my mother as they left. *I'll protect her with my life*, he said. We all just stared at him. It's the kind of thing Rose has waited her whole life to hear. It's basically her dream to have a man say something like that about her.

In a fit of despair, Rose disappears to her room to cry it out.

"Jackson was cheating on you, Rose," I call after her. Kade confirmed it just now, to warn her, but Rose already had suspicions. To me, it was always obvious. "He's not worth crying over."

As for me, I make a point of forgetting about Vaughn Tucker.

My early morning walk by the pond with him was crazy enough. With his brawny bare chest and all his sexy-as-sin vibes. Having him in my kitchen was even worse. His energy filled up the room and infused everything with his scent. Of leather (of course), man-lust and hot summer sun. The kind that'll burn you.

I go into my room and sit on my window seat.

I'll give myself five minutes, I decide.

I google him.

There are hundreds of articles and photos. Some of Vaughn and his brothers when they were younger. Their rise to fame. Interviews about their music and their inspiration. Some of him sitting behind his huge drum set, his muscular arms inked and flexed, his hair wet with sweat.

The dirty thoughts playing behind his devil-blue eyes as he watched me.

There's a photo of the Tucker brothers on an awards stage, accepting a Grammy for album of the year. For their second record, the article notes. Vaughn is smiling and holding up the golden statue.

The wideness of his shoulders and the dark sun-bronzed skin of his corded neck. The little hollow at the base, where his pulse played.

There's a photo of the three of them standing on a country road for some photo shoot, looking sort of hipster and romantic. His eyes gleam blue.

His hair, so black and silky-thick.

There's a link to a recent interview of the three of them, from less than a week ago.

The curl of his wicked mouth.

I click the link to the video. The interviewer asks Vaughn if he's dating anyone. Vaughn exhales a smoke ring. "Dating is probably overstating it," he laughs. "But I'm considering calling back these two girls I—*bleeeep*—last night. Damn, those girls could do the most amazing things with their—" The clip is cut where the profanity was edited out. The interview continues.

But I've seen enough.

I return to the image results. There are dozens—hundreds—of photos of Vaughn with his arm slung around different women. I recognize a famous super-model. A European shipping magnate's daughter on her yacht. A reality TV star. A glamorous country music singer, who's feeding him grapes while sitting on his lap at some super-swanky party.

Page after page of articles and interviews are more of the same.

"Vaughn Tucker is sexual dynamite!" according to one Dallas socialite. "Vaughn, call me back, you sexy beast. You've ruined me for anyone else and I'll never forgive you! If you read this, call me when you're in town, honey. Please."

From a fan who won a backstage pass to one of the band's shows in Atlanta: "He invited me and my friend to party with him and let's just say it was the best night of our entire lives. He's the eighth wonder of the freaking world! He's crazy as f*** but the hype doesn't even come close to doing him justice. It was the best O of my life! But his people won't answer our calls. It's so devastating. We just both totally fell in love with him."

Of course you did.

There's an interview with pretty red-headed triplets from Phoenix who are all wearing identical cowgirl outfits in their photo. "He invited us back to his penthouse hotel suite and if anyone ever thought one man couldn't satisfy three women, well, let's just say they've never met Vaughn Tucker. All *three* of us couldn't keep up with him. He's half lunatic and half sex god. But he was gone by morning."

If I ever had the thought that maybe Vaughn Tucker was in need of help, that maybe the joke I made about him being too far gone was closer to the truth than he wanted to admit, it seems like these articles confirm otherwise. He's having fun. He's living his best life, which, for him—a hot, rich, talented, clearly-virile-as-all-hell beefcake in the prime of his life—involves sleeping his way around the world, partying hard and having a blast while doing it.

My phone rings and I jump a little.

It's Dylan again. There are also texts from another guy, Troy, who keeps coming into the library during my shifts and asking me out. I have no idea how he got my number. "Hey, Dylan."

"Hi, Gigi. Everything okay?"

I texted him earlier to let him know I wasn't going to

make it to his place with the textbook after all. I took a few minutes after I got back home to take photos of the pages Dylan would need, along with my notes, and I sent them to him. "Sorry I couldn't bring the book. Something came up."

"Thanks for sending the photos."

"No problem."

"Hey, I was wondering if you wanted a ride to class this afternoon." Our class goes from four to six. "And then … do you want have dinner with me after?"

I sigh, but make an effort to do it silently. He asked me to a movie last week and I made up an excuse.

As usual, I don't really want to get involved with someone I don't see myself ever falling for. And Dylan … isn't that person.

Then who is, Gi?

Vaughn Tucker?

Are you seriously deluded?

It's ridiculous to imagine that the bad boy drummer who just left my house is "falling in love" material. He's a recipe for heartbreak on steroids. I'm holding in my hand an endless scroll of reasons why.

And if Vaughn Tucker is the only person I've met so far that I can see myself falling in love with, then maybe it's time for me to reassess what the hell I'm doing.

Maybe my parameters are skewed. They say that can happen to girls who lose their fathers. You can get lost.

Your radars for finding healthy relationships need readjusting.

"Sure," I hear myself saying. After all, at least Dylan might be capable of being faithful. At least he's not an out-of-control hedonist who sleeps with at least two different women every night and never calls them again. Dylan's probably steady and predictable and normal. Maybe that's *better* than a wild love affair that devastates you in the moment and then continues to devastate you for the rest of time because you'll never find anything as intense.

Maybe I'd *rather* be content than blown away.

Wouldn't I?

Yes.

I would.

And I'd rather be secure than on some uncontrollable rollercoaster ride of total bliss and absolute destruction.

"Great," says Dylan, surprised. "You know, this is the seventh time I've asked you out."

"Is it?"

"I was beginning to think you'd never say yes."

"Yeah, well, I … " I feel a weird wave of sadness as I say it, because I understand fully what I'm doing: I'm lowering my expectations. I'm no longer counting on true love to ride into my life on a white horse and offer pure, undiluted happiness. Because I've just touched fire and it hurts too much. A piece of my heart is *already* in love with Vaughn Tucker—*damn him*—like a small, devil-blue ember the exact same color as his eyes is now lodged there, burning me. And I hate him for that. Because he's gone now, back to his life of women and whiskey and the adoration of millions. They're all in love with him, because he's extraordinary. He's what everyone wants but no one can really have. It would be like trying to hold a shooting star in your hand. "I changed my mind."

5

VAUGHN

Regret is an interesting emotion. The way it sits there quietly under every other emotion, biding its time, like a swift river under a smooth, glinting sheet of ice. You can skate along enjoying the sun but eventually it'll melt a hole and send you crashing through.

By the time we get to Nashville, I'm feeling better.

No, not better.

Removed.

Numb.

Lucid but at the same time untouchable.

I climb out of the Shelby and go into our warehouse, which is swarming with people. They're packing up for our tour, getting the bus and all the vehicles that carry our equipment and crew ready.

People swarm around me.

I feel separate. I can't tell if it's my high or *the* high.

The realization that I met someone today whose whispering memory is having an impact on me even now. I don't know if that's ever happened to me before.

It hasn't.

I meet a lot of beautiful women. Most of them are easy to please and nothing more than a good time that lasts a day or two then quickly fades away. Which works for me just fine.

I'm not sure what's different here. Except that my head feels full of the memory of her. The colors and softness and the shape of her mouth.

What's she doing now?

Is she thinking about me?

I shove the inane thoughts out of my head. I've got enough to think about, with the tour starting and the new songs we wrote last night that need to be played out so I can lock into place the beats and the rhythms.

Roxie's here and she walks over to me. "Are you packed?" She studies my eyes for a few seconds and reaches up to push a strand of my hair out of my eyes. My sister is slim and tiny. At only around 5'4", she has to stand on her tiptoes to reach me. "You look so tired."

"And you look so gorgeous." She looks so much like our mother once did. "We were up late last night."

She's assessing my pupils. My sister has the same dark hair as I do and the same blue eyes. She looks like a prom queen but has the personality of a five-star general. She doesn't take shit from anyone and her concern for me has an edge to it. *Don't be like him.*

Not the reminder I'm looking for.

Roxie is easily the most intelligent person I know and also the most stubborn, by a country mile. "Are you on something right now?"

I blink at her innocently. "I'm high on life, honey."

My sister is our manager, and a damn good one, even though she's young. We had another manager for the first couple years but there were always problems, which Roxie kept on fixing, so we got rid of Angelo and got Roxie to do the job full-time. "You know you're going to force my hand one of these days, Vaughn."

I hold her hand and kiss the back of it. "To do what?"

She pulls away, but her eyes have a shine to them, like she's genuinely worried about me. "You said you'd get clean after the last tour."

"I meant this tour."

She glares at me, her eyes glittering with equal parts sorrow and annoyance.

"I'm fine, Rox. Chill, darlin'."

"Chill, my ass." But she's smart enough to know that nagging me will never work. "How's Travis's new house?"

"It's good. How was your date last night?"

Guys fall into the trap all the time of underestimating Roxie or assuming she's as sweet and innocent as she looks. But they soon learn. "Disastrous. He spent the whole dinner telling me about his new tractor and how much horsepower it has. Then he talked about how many kids he wants to have by the time he's thirty and also that he wants to get started as soon as possible because he's already twenty-six."

I laugh. "Shit."

"Yeah."

Three groupies scream my name and come running over to me. They gather around me and start fawning over me. "Vaughn, we want to ride on the bus with you." Our tour bus is huge and has a lounge, a full kitchen and four bedrooms. Mine is usually … full. We drive to our shows for the North American tours because Kade hates flying.

I look down at one of the girls. She's familiar, although I can't remember her name.

I'm staring down at her sort of intently. One, she's blurred at the edges. Two, it's just such a stark difference. Between this girl and *the* girl. I'm not just talking about looks but also the intent *behind* the looks. Not that this girl isn't kind, she probably is, who would know. Her eyes are brown, full of awe and enthusiasm and a yearning to be a part of something. She wants me, not for me, but for her. Which I can hardly blame her for. She doesn't want to love, she wants to *be* loved.

Strangely, in this moment, it feels like an important distinction.

I'm not proud to admit this, but … how could I have settled for *this*? When I could have *that*? The small-town goddess with the golden eyes and the little furrow of sensitivity between her strawberry-blond eyebrows.

I guess the obvious answer to that question is … I didn't know about the tiger-eyed girl before this morning.

But now I do.

I *miss* that little furrow of concern. The gentle empathy that felt like a cool haven I wanted to dive into.

Listen to yourself, you fucking lunatic. What the hell?

"No," I hear myself saying. "I'm busy."

Roxie does a sort of double-take, like something I said was out of character.

"Can we at least get backstage passes to the first show?" asks one of the groupies.

"Why don't you talk to Roxie about that." I wink at my sister as I walk away.

Why the hell did I just say no to three cute-enough girls jumping into my bed?

You know why.

Maybe I *am* losing it. Starting with the flashback of my mother this morning, I haven't felt quite myself.

And now I'm getting some weird fixation on the kindness of a random stranger?

The little country bumpkin with hair the color of ripe, sun-touched wheat and the smooth-as-silk skin. She's taken up residence in my head. And I'm not even sure I *want* her there.

I *don't* want her there.

I get to my apartment, which is cleaner than I left it.

I'll never get used to having staff, who do shit like picking up after me.

I can, however, get used to the shopping list they make sure I have. I grab the bottle of Johnny Walker Red, crack it open and drink a long sip to take the edge off. Then I slide it into my duffel bag, along with some clothes, all the pharmaceuticals in my drawer, my leather jacket and a few other things I'll need for the three-week trip.

By the time I get onto the bus, the others are already there. Roxie's at the table with people from our sound and logistics crews, Travis and Ruby are sitting on the leather couch by the flat screen TV, which is playing a video of one of our recent shows, and Kade and his girlfriend are in his room.

Ruby is sitting there in the sun and I can't help noticing that her hair is a shade blonder than Gigi's. It doesn't have that same strawberry tint.

I want to see her again.

Why am I craving her so badly?

If we weren't leaving on tour I'd be on my Ducati right now, doing a hundred and fifty.

I feel so fucking restless.

The bus starts up and we pull out. Soon enough we're on the highway heading west.

It's risky and I know this as I do it. Travis might react. Travis probably *will* react. But I'm feeling loose enough not to care. So when Travis goes into the galley kitchen I sit down next to Ruby. She's writing in a notebook. Lyrics, I can see. A few chords. "Hey."

"Hi, Vaughn." More scribbling.

"Can you, uh, give me Gigi's number?"

She stops writing and glances up at me. Her eyes are amber-colored but don't have that tiger thing going on.

Only one person I've ever met has that. Topaz with little flecks of fire.

Bad timing, as it turns out.

Travis was already heading back this way and he hands Ruby a Coke. His eyes are all stormy and his voice has an edge to it when he asks, "What do you want Gigi's number for, Vaughn?"

I mean, what's wrong with that? "There's something I want to talk to her about. We met this morning, before we visited the house. I ran into her by the pond."

"Forget about it."

I get that he doesn't want Ruby touched by any of this. But in actual fact it's none of his goddamn business who I call. He doesn't own Ruby's entire family. This has nothing to do with Ruby. "I don't want to forget about it."

He grabs the front of my shirt with his fist. "I said forget about it, Vaughn."

"Why should I?"

"You know why."

I stand up to face him. "No. I don't know why." Even though I do.

"Because it wouldn't end well."

Maybe it could. *Could it?* "You don't know that."

Travis says to Ruby, "Darlin', why don't you go and sit over there next to Roxie for a minute."

She collects her pad and paper. She stands and touches Travis's shirt. "Travis." Like she can see that we're about to clash and she doesn't want us to. "Vaughn."

Still holding the front of my shirt in his fist, Travis tilts his chin over to Roxie. "Over there," he says again.

Ruby obeys, slowly. As soon as she's a safe distance away, Travis answers my question in a low, pissed-off growl. "You want to know why it wouldn't end well, Vaughn? Because you're a fucking disaster. You use women. You're out of control and there's no way in hell you're going anywhere near Ruby's sister."

"That's not up to you."

He takes a swing at me but I see it coming and I get a good right hook in before he can pin me down onto the couch and get a few punches in. We're evenly matched. I push him off me and get him in a headlock on the floor, which he wrestles out of, probably because I'm woozy from the day's excesses. My balance is off.

He pins me down and punches me again but I manage to land another one at the same time.

Roxie's pleading with us. Kade and some of the other guys pull us apart, but not until after my lip is bleeding and we'll both have decent shiners by morning.

My brothers and I fight all the time. Usually it's over

something stupid like the time I dented Kade's car and he went ballistic or the other day when I told Jackson Cole where Travis's new house was, which Travis didn't react well to even though I'd sworn Jackson to secrecy.

This feels more raw.

For what it's worth I don't *use* women. I give women what they *want*. Every single time. I tell them I'm only in it for one or two nights. That's the deal. I'm as up front with them as it's possible to be. I make no promises and I offer no commitments.

They're there because they want to be there.

As for the out of control part, I *choose* to be out of control. Control is overrated.

Roxie hands me a towel for my bleeding lip. I'm thinking about lunging at Travis again, but Kade reads this and slings his arm around my shoulders. He leads me into my room, which is past his room, where his girlfriend watches me, wide-eyed. "Hey, Carmen," I grin.

"Hi, Vaughn."

Kade's been working out a lot lately. He's strong as fuck today. And insistent. He pushes me onto my bed. "What's up with you, man? You need to cool down. We've got a long drive ahead of us and you're going to sleep off whatever this is."

"That never works."

He gives me a look before slamming the door.

I lay back onto my bed.

Alone.

Travis is right, probably.

And Gigi was right to brush me off.

I'm trouble, like they all keep saying.

You're a beautiful soul, Vaughn. Don't be reckless. Don't throw it all away.

Fuck.

Not again.

It occurs to me then that maybe I don't need Ruby's help.

I sit up and pull my phone out of my pocket. What was the name of the town Travis bought his new property in? I can't remember, but I know the general vicinity of it. I go into Google maps and zoom in on the area, searching the satellite view. It takes a few minutes but I finally pinpoint it. The roof of his house. The driveway. The cabin.

And the house next door.

I zoom in closer until I can read the address.

Her last name is Hayes. They grew up in that house so maybe they still have a landline. Some people still use them, possibly.

I search the online white pages.

And there it is. CJ and RM Hayes.

I dial the number.

It rings six or seven times and then a girly, out-of-breath voice answers. "Hello?"

"Gigi?"

"No, it's Rose."

"Rose. Hey. It's Vaughn."

A pause. "Vaughn?"

"Yeah."

"Vaughn *Tucker?*"

"Yeah. Listen, I was wondering if I could talk to Gigi. Is she home?"

"Gigi?" There's a note of disappointment in the silence but the excitement's still there. "Yes, she's home." My heartbeat thuds in my chest at this news. "Have you left for your tour yet?"

"Just now. We're driving straight through."

"Ruby wants us to come to one of the shows, she said. Maybe to Seattle."

Yes. "You should. You could come backstage and we'll show you around."

"Oh my God. That would be *so* amazing."

"Would you mind getting Gigi for me?"

"Okay." She giggles breathlessly. "I'll see you soon, maybe. Hopefully." *Why can't I have this effect on her sister?* "Hang on a minute and I'll get Gi."

"Thanks."

I wait a while.

Will she refuse? Is Rose trying to talk her into it? What's she thinking?

Why do I care so much?

Finally, I hear her voice. "Hello?" The sound sort of spills into me, like a strange, liquid joy. Like she's holding an invisible string that yanks on pieces of my wrecked, jaded soul. It's fucked up how beautiful one word can be.

"Gigi, it's Vaughn. I, um,"—hell, my palms are sweating. I wipe one of them on my jeans and swap hands. "How are you?"

"Fine." She's clearly not as thrilled as Rose was to hear from me.

"I wanted to talk to you about something."

A slightly exasperated silence. "What did you want to talk to me about?"

Jesus. I'm getting hard from the light annoyance in her voice. *I want to hold her down and enrage her. With bliss. I want to show her how good I can make her feel.* "Have you checked out the cabin yet?" My voice comes out sounding deep and husky.

"What? No."

"It would be a good place to study. It's quiet. And it's nice inside."

"I … I probably wouldn't go there by myself."

"Why not?"

"Because … well, it would feel like I was breaking and entering."

"You wouldn't be, though, because I invited you."

"Maybe I'll go take a look when I get a chance." It doesn't sound like she means it. She's humoring me, maybe.

I want to see her again. "You should." This gives me a lightning bolt of an idea. I try to sound relaxed about it.

"Listen, Gi, I hope you don't mind, but I need to ask you a favor." I'm using her nickname. To get a rise out of her. To get closer to her in any way I can.

"Um … sure."

I've already figured out that she's caring. That she'll go out of her way to help people. "There's a painting in the cabin. Travis thinks it might be worth something, but we don't have a picture of it. I was hoping you could take a photo and send it to me."

"Oh. Okay. Yeah, I can do that."

"You wouldn't mind?"

"No, not at all."

"Do you have a pen? I'll give you my number."

"Hang on … okay, here's one. Go ahead."

I give her my number and she repeats it to make sure she's got it right. "The painting is black and white. It's sort of geometric and modern-looking. You can't miss it."

"Okay. I'm sure I can find it."

Someone's calling out to Gigi in the background.

It's Rose. *Gi, Dylan's here.*

Dylan? "Vaughn, can you hold on a minute?" To Rose, Gigi says, "Tell him I'll be there in a second." *Who the fuck is Dylan?* Then she comes back to me. "I have to go. I have a class and my ride is here."

I don't want to let her go yet. "Gigi—"

"I'll try to go over to the cabin tomorrow morning. Is that all right?"

"That's fine."

"Okay. Great. Bye then, Vaughn."

"Wait. Don't hang up yet."

A small exhale that's not quite as annoyed as the earlier ones. She almost sounds amused. "Is there something else you need, Vaughn?"

As a matter of fact, yes there is. "Who's Dylan?"

A long silence. Then, feistily, "As I said, he's my ride."

"You mean … in a metaphorical sense?"

At this she laughs lightly, and even though I feel like I could bend a crowbar in half at the thought of her *ride*, the sound of her twinkling laughter gets me as hard as a pillar of steel.

"I don't know what that even means," she says. "Not that it's any of your business who Dylan is. But if you must know, he's in my class and he's giving me a ride and then we might get something to eat after that. It works out because my mother needs the car to do some shopping later on. And we only have one, which we have to share because my dad's old pick-up truck is in the shop. Anything else you need to know?"

"What time does your class end?"

"Why?"

"What time?"

"Six."

"I'll pick you up."

A stunned pause. "What do you mean? No, Vaughn." I'm definitely riling her. And confusing her. "I thought you were on tour."

They accuse me of being out of control and I figure now is definitely not the time to quit. "We are, but I'm getting off."

"Getting off what?"

"The tour bus. I'm going to come and pick you up at six. I want to see you tonight. I can fly out to California tomorrow." Something occurs to me. "You could come with me."

A little huff, which causes my cock to throb hotly. I can feel wetness and I reach down to unzip because it's painful. I'm slippery with pre-cum. "You're crazy, you know that?"

"So they keep telling me."

A car horn honks in the background.

"Seriously? He's *honking* at you, Gi? Sounds like a real knight in shining armor."

"Knights in shining armor don't exist."

"Of course they do."

More soft laughter. "Sure. I suppose now you're going to tell me *you're* a knight in shining armor?" *Saucy girl. I can't wait to fuck her mouth.*

"I never have been before. But I think I might be about to start."

Another excruciatingly cute laugh. *I can't wait to hear the sounds she makes when I'm deep inside her. When she's squeezing my bursting cock with her tight pussy as she comes.*

"I really have to go now." Something about her sweet

sassiness is bringing me to my goddamn knees. "Have fun on tour and I'll send you the—"

"I'll be there at six, so be ready for me."

"*Vaughn.* I mean it. Stop playing games with me. I don't want you to come here, okay? I wouldn't go with you anyway. I'm hanging up now. Goodbye. Enjoy your tour."

She ends the call.

Shit, the little minx hung up on me. Definitely a first. Why am I getting the distinct feeling Gigi Hayes is going to drag me through a whole bunch of firsts that I'm not entirely sure I even want?

I sit there for a few seconds, working through my plan. Bruno, one of our producers, decided to drive his own car along with our bus and the equipment trucks. I check my phone for his number and it's there.

I make the call and he agrees.

Then I wipe the blood from my split lip with my sleeve and change my shirt. I stuff my raging hard-on into my jeans and check to make sure I'm borderline presentable.

I almost reach for the bottle of whiskey but decide not to.

I get to see her. I don't need it.

Then I go out into the lounge area of the bus. Travis is watching me warily but I go up to him and hold out my hand. "Truce?"

He eyes me for a few seconds. Then he shakes my

hand. We never stay mad at each other for long. He surveys the damage he did to me. "Your shiner's starting to come up real good."

"So's yours."

"I only did it because they always fall in love with you, man. And you don't *do* love. She'll get hurt and then Ruby will get hurt. I don't want that to happen. She has enough to deal with right now, with it being her first tour and her new album will be coming out and she's performing live for the first time. It's a lot. I'm just thinking of them."

"Sure. I get it." I don't bother saying, *Maybe I* can *do love. I've never tried.*

I sit down at the table next to Roxie, because I don't have the bus driver's number on hand and we don't have access to the driver's cab from the main part of the bus. "Hey, Rox."

"I can't believe you two. Can I get you some ice?"

"I want you to stop the bus. I'm getting off."

"Vaughn, come on. What the—"

"I'll meet you in L.A. tomorrow. There's something I need to do tonight. I'm not arguing with you about it, either, okay? Just stop the bus. Bruno is going to give me a lift."

She stares at me for a few seconds. "Is this about—"

"No. All you have to do is tell the driver to stop so I can get off."

"Vaughn—"

"I'm getting off one way or the other, with your help

or without it. Please. Don't make this harder than it has to be."

She knows me well enough to know I'm not joking. "Are you sure about this?"

"Yes. I'll see you tomorrow."

"Vaughn." As though making one last attempt to plead with me.

But she can see it won't make a difference. "Just do it, Rox."

"You're a madman, you know that?" But she pulls out her phone. "You better be on time tomorrow. The show starts at seven."

"I'll be there."

Within ten minutes, I've already made a couple of phone calls and I'm heading east.

6

———————

Gigi

I RUN out the door and slide into the passenger seat of Dylan's ancient Chevelle. "Hi, Dylan. Sorry for keeping you waiting."

The car is idling and the radio's on but Dylan doesn't pull out right away. He's staring over at me. He's wearing khaki pants and a yellow button-down shirt that reminds me again that he's an "aspiring banker," as Rose puts it. He's already wearing the outfit.

"You look really nice today," he says.

When Rose heard I was going out to dinner, she insisted I borrow one of her sundresses—even though I told her it was absolutely *not* a date. I drew the line at a makeover but she talked me into wearing mascara and pink lip gloss. *When are you going to cash in that V-card you insist on clinging to, Gi?* she asked me. Again. *If not the aspiring banker, then why not one of the guys who keeps calling you? How about the one that's practically stalking you at the library?*

Definitely not.

She knows about the vow I made to myself. What's so wrong about wanting to actually love the person you *cash in your V-card* to? To me, it doesn't seem like too much to ask.

Anyway, as it turns out, this dress fits me a lot differently than it fits Rose, and now I'm regretting wearing it. I'm a few inches taller than she is and it only comes down to the middle of my thighs. And it's more fitted than I realized. "Thanks." I try to tug the hem a little lower.

I wish Dylan wouldn't stare at me like he is right now.

And I can't help noticing what song is playing on the radio. The only song on the latest Tucker Brothers album sung by the drummer, what do you know. Travis sings most of the songs but Vaughn and Kade write and occasionally sing too. I know this because I've been listening to their music since they first came onto the scene, around four years ago. They got a lot of press and publicity because their sound was fresh and because they had the look. Authentic country-rock Southern boys, with thrift store double denim in those days and truckloads of superstar potential. They were dripping with talent and it didn't hurt that all three were—and are—drop-dead gorgeous. I remember picking up a Rolling Stone magazine after they first hit the big time and got their first cover. It almost hurt to look at them, they were just so soulful and young and beautiful.

Their fame spread like wildfire, of course.

I didn't follow them online that much back then because I was still at boarding school and we weren't allowed to use social media or surf the internet much at all. But when I could, I always added their new songs to my playlists. Their music has weaved itself into the fabric of my life and my experiences, like good music tends to do.

I didn't bother mentioning any of this to Vaughn this morning. He didn't look like he needed the ego boost.

I've only heard this particular song once before, but as I listen to him sing the chorus … it's good. Like, *really* good. Original and catchy.

He's got an amazing voice. Deep and husky and full of feeling.

The sound of that smoky roughness makes the tiny hairs on my arms lift.

And it's not the reminder I need right now. "Should we go?"

My question breaks whatever trance Dylan is still stuck in and he puts the car into drive. We roll slowly down the driveway. He's a cautious driver, checking both ways several times before he pulls out, but soon enough we're on our way.

"Thanks for sending your notes to me today," he says.

"They were really helpful. I have to admit, though, I was disappointed when you never showed up for our meeting."

I glance over at him, taken off-guard by his tone, but his eyes are on the road. It wasn't really a meeting. He almost sounds mad about it. "Something unexpected came up."

Very up, *in fact.*

If only you could have seen the way his unfastened jeans hugged the hard, defined ridge of his—

Don't even go there, girl.

But the memory makes my face feel warm. If someone had told me that a world-famous superstar who looks like the poster boy for The Ideal Man If You Happen To Like Playboys Who Are Wild, Insane, Built Like a Greek God and Hung Like A Porn Star would be moving into the cabin next door to my house, I would have told them they might consider professional help.

It's not like me to even think about things like *porn stars*. My two older sisters love to discuss how "well-hung" men are. Rating the hotness levels of every guy they see is one of their favorite pastimes. They tease me because I'm less experienced than they are. But I already know how they'd rate Vaughn Tucker. Off the charts.

I still feel flustered from his call. I pull my phone out of my bag and make a reminder to send him the photo of his painting tomorrow.

Message Vaughn Tucker re the painting in his cabin has a surreal edge to it.

Which reminds me of the last thing he said to me before I ended the call.

I'll be there at six, so be ready for me.

It must have been his idea of a joke. He's probably halfway to California by now.

We arrive at the college and Dylan pulls into a parking space. He kills the engine and we sit there for a few seconds. As I slide my phone back into my bag, he leans toward me. Almost like he's thinking of …

I reach for the door handle, trying to be blasé about it.

"Gigi?" he says, all intense.

"Yeah?"

"I really like you."

"I like you too, Dylan," I reply lightly. I'm fumbling for the unlock button on the door and realize it's an old school one. A little knob you pull, up by the window. Like the one on Daddy's old pick-up truck.

"I mean I *like* you. A lot."

The problem is, even though Dylan is the kind of guy maybe I *should* go for, with his career track in place and the steadiness of his lifestyle, there's not even an inkling of a spark here. Not even an ember. *Not like Vaughn Tucker's ember, that's for damn sure.* My golden rule of not getting involved with someone I can't see myself falling in love with is lighting up like a neon sign in a bar window.

Maybe it's the near-controlling smugness of his tone.

Or the yellow shirt that makes him look pale and sort of ill. Or the glaring *beta*-ness of him (another word my sisters love. They're always trolling for alphas). What's the tier below beta, is what I'm wondering. "That's really flattering but I'm not—"

"You don't have to commit to anything right now, Gigi. We can take our time."

Could I ever feel something for this nice-enough but totally bland middle-manager-in-training, who's pushy and at the same time weirdly and easily triggered, like his feelings get hurt over things they shouldn't? *Not in a trillion years.* "Maybe we could just be friends. And see how things go."

He chews on his lip with a pissed-off scowl on his face. "Sure. Okay. I get it. You need convincing. I can do that."

It won't make any difference, I feel like saying. But of course I don't. This is my personality flaw. I hate hurting people. "Great," I say, trying to keep it upbeat. "We better go."

Relieved to be out of his car, it's clear that agreeing to go to dinner with him was a bad idea. I'll try to think up an excuse during class.

As we walk in, Professor Tate looks up from something she's writing on the white board. "You're ten minutes late." She points to the clock hanging on the wall. "This is your one get-out-of-jail-free card, Ms. Hayes. Mr. Smith."

"Sorry about that, Professor," Dylan says. "Gigi was running late and I was her ride."

Really? Then again, I guess it's justified. It *was* my fault. "It won't happen again, Professor," I tell her.

She picks up a stack of papers and starts handing them out. "There were some excellent essays about last week's topic." Professor Tate places my paper on my desk. "Gigi, yours was particularly well done."

"Thank you."

She places Dylan's paper on his desk, next to mine. "Dylan, you seemed to have remarkably similar views to Gigi's," she adds, eyeing him, then me. "Which is becoming a trend. I have no way of knowing which one of you is the brainchild behind the inspiration, but let's make sure your viewpoints don't align quite *so* exactly on the next assignment."

Dylan looks up at her innocently, admitting nothing.

He must have copied the notes I sent him word for word. And now the professor is practically accusing one of us of copying.

Of course I'm not going to tell her. I don't want to get Dylan into trouble.

Don't be a pushover. There's a difference between helping someone and getting walked all over.

Next time he asks me for my notes, I'll just refuse. Problem solved.

Sure you will. Or you'll cave, like you always do because you'd rather suffer than let someone else down.

I put it out of my mind, focusing on the lecture.

My father used to say I was a person who absorbed the angst of other people and gave calmness in return, like a plant that inhales carbon dioxide and exhales oxygen. He said I was like that with emotions. When we were children he would watch us. Once he took me out for ice cream all by myself and asked me if easing the emotions of other people ever hurt me. I remember it clearly. We had the same favorite flavor: cookies and cream. We sat there on a bench in the park eating our ice cream and I felt so lucky that day to have him all to myself. It was a rare thing. I told him no, the feelings didn't hurt. The feelings were good ones, I said, because they made other people feel better about whatever their problems were. I liked being able to do that.

I haven't thought about that memory in a long time.

"The psycho-dynamic model of substance abuse links problems to events that have happened in our lives," the professor is saying, "that dictate how we cope—or don't cope. Someone might drink too much, for example, to deal with the pain of a past experience. Once we know what that experience is, then we can use it to form the basis of our counseling approach. We'll discuss this in much more detail next week. Make sure you read chapters seven through ten by Monday's class."

As we file out of the classroom, I take my phone out of my bag to check my messages. There are four from Troy, a guy who keeps coming into the library, even though he never checks any books out. I never reply to him because … well, my rule.

There's a loud noise coming from outside the building. It almost sounds like a plane is flying too low. The trees are waving as though caught in a strong wind.

"What jerk is landing a helicopter on the front lawn?" Dylan says as we make our way out the front doors.

I watch along with the small crowd that's gathering as a giant helicopter lands on the grass lawn in front of the building. "I don't know," I answer vaguely.

But I do know.

It's a high-tech one. Modern and expensive-looking. As the propellors begin to slow, the door of the helicopter opens.

Out jumps Vaughn Tucker.

Shit.

"OH MY GOD," two girls from my class squeal. "Is that … VAUGHN TUCKER?"

Yes. Yes, it is.

His hard, sinewy body is lean and toned. A dark gray loose-necked t-shirt shows off his muscles and his wide, sculpted shoulders. Tattoos cover his burly arms and curl in tribal-like designs over his collarbone and the tops of his shoulders. His longish jet-black hair is artfully wind-blown. Bronze skin the color of cinnamon gives him an exotic look and the leather bands and gold chains around his neck add an artistic, pirate-king vibe. His eyes catch the sunlight, as blue as the summer sky.

For all the bad boy rebelliousness that makes headlines and trends on social media daily, he doesn't clash with the obvious luxury of his state-of-the-art ride. He *looks* like a rock star. He's practically dripping with X-factor.

He holds his hand up to shade his eyes and he surveys the crowd. After a few seconds, he sees me.

I can't believe this.

My heartbeat lurches into a staccato beat as he starts walking toward us.

The two girls are squealing in low hysterics as though they're about to hyper-ventilate.

As he draws closer, one thing is confirmed beyond a shadow of a doubt: Dylan will never be a consideration. Vaughn Tucker makes him—and everyone else in this growing crowd and possibly on this entire continent—look washed-out and insufferably bland. Like Vaughn is a technicolored superhero and all the rest of us are mono-chrome mortals who could never in a million years compete with so much … *glory.*

I've never in my life seen such a physically beautiful human being.

The girls are actually crying.

He's close to me now, all six foot, three or four inches of him, and I can smell his scent. Of green grass, a hint of whiskey and smoldering, virile masculinity.

The look in his eyes as he stares right at me is playful but also laser-bright and feverishly intense. His squally energy is like something out of a comic book. You can practically see the zinging ions radiating off of him.

"I love you so much, Vaughn," one of the girls breathes ecstatically.

His royal-blue gaze disengages from mine as he stares down at the girl. She's sobbing like he's the Beatles first arriving in America or something.

Vaughn grins down at her, clearly making the girl's day or probably even lifetime.

Then he turns to me. It's a few seconds before he speaks. Softly, like we've bumped into each other randomly and not in the lingering whirlwind of his chartered helicopter: "Hey, Gi." That huskiness, just like in the song he sang, hits me right below my navel, causing a spreading, wildly intimate warmth.

Whoa.

I don't want to feel anything for this gorgeous hellraiser. He's *too* perfect. And too imperfect. The scores of women, from supermodels to groupies to heiresses to his one night stand with the triplets from Phoenix—all scrolling through my mind with dizzying clarity—prove it: he's a disaster waiting to happen to me.

If he *is* here for me—*and how is this possibly happening?*—it's not a good thing. He'll force me to fall in love with his easy smile and his electric eyes full of fun, lust and, worst of all, sincerity. Then he'll leave me in the dust to shower all his masculine gifts over the next powerless-to-resist victim. Ruining me, probably, because how could anyone else ever live up to … *this?*

He only gives one night.

I've got my rule and that's his rule.

That's what all the women in the interviews said. They accepted it because he was honest with them, even though they all wished for more. They accepted it because he's *Vaughn Tucker.*

They *all* chose one night over nothing at all.

Not me, though. I don't want to fall in love with him, and a one-night stand would be enough to do that to me, I already know this. I'd regret it, because I can't think of a worse curse than unrequited love. He'd be a beast in the sack (as my sisters would say), he'd feel too good, and I really don't want to spend the rest of my life pining for him and retracing all that over and over in my mind, wishing I was special enough for him to want for more than one night. Which he wouldn't. Because he never does. For me, it would be better to avoid tasting the Gorgeous Bad Boy Kool-Aid at all.

Why am I even talking about falling in love with someone I've spent a total of an hour with anyway? It's ridiculous.

So my response doesn't sound entirely welcoming. "What are you doing here?"

He smiles, blinking lazily as his gaze dances over my bare legs, my short shirt, my fitted dress. To my face. I have to consciously activate my forcefield, as my family loves to call it. The protective layer that guards my heart and keeps me free. As resolved as I've been my whole life to keep my distance from men who were never quite right, *this* guy could shatter me without even trying. And he knows it. Because he could shatter any one of us. Me, the socialite from Dallas, and any of the girls in this adoring crowd. "I'm proving that knights in shining armor *do* exist. Phase one. I'm taking you out in Nashville tonight."

"Nashville?" It's miles from here. Then again, he does have a helicopter.

Never mind that my question shouldn't be about *where* he's taking me. It should be about my refusal to go with him.

"Gigi and I have plans tonight." Dylan is standing next to me, arms folded defiantly. I'd almost forgotten about him.

Dylan is close to my height and in Vaughn's shadow he suddenly looks somehow unformed. Like he was an afterthought, whereas whatever creator made Vaughn Tucker took infinite care and riotous gusto in his masterpiece.

Vaughn takes in Dylan. The neatly combed hair. The boat shoes even though we live in Tennessee. The outfit that screams nerd-who-aspires-to-Abercrombie-level-sexiness-but-will-never-even-get-close.

"I gave her a ride," Dylan says. "And we're going out to dinner tonight." Almost possessively.

That Dylan thinks he has any kind of ownership over me is insane. I'm about to tell him dinner is off when Vaughn says, "Not anymore," amused and cutting. After a heated glare, Vaughn's gaze returns to me. The shade of his irises has darkened, more sapphire now than azure, and the glimmer takes on a more furious light. "*This* is my competition? You make it too easy, Gi."

This almost makes me smile. He's *so* cocky. Of course he is. The simple biology of this equation couldn't be more obvious. Vaughn is evolution's A-list, an ideal masculine specimen. The little strands of my DNA are practically leaning in, *craving* him because he's just so freaking magnificent.

Even so, I'm about to tell him that this isn't a competition. And how did it even happen that I'm being practically fought over by a random acquaintance from my class and one of the hottest rock stars on the planet?

Before I can protest either way, Vaughn steps forward and scoops me into his arms.

"*Vaughn.* What is this? Put me down."

The cluster of girls gasps rapturously at his manhandling of me, like they've never seen anything so dreamy.

"Hey," Dylan mutters, but no one's listening.

Vaughn starts carrying me across the lawn.

"*Vaughn.* I mean it. What are you doing? I'm not coming with you."

"This is what knights in shining armor *do*, darlin'. They show a girl a good time like no one else can."

"But not by kidnapping them," I point out.

"It's not kidnapping when you take someone out for some dinner and dancing then safely deliver them home again."

God. He's so strong and aggressive—which isn't something I ever thought would be this crazily persuasive. He's *touching* me. The feel of his warm, solid-as-steel arms and his broad chest as he carries me without any effort at all is infusing me with a strangely forceful hunger.

But I can't just go with this. I'll get annihilated.

I know my sisters would already be strapping in for the ride. I can practically hear what they'd be thinking. *Do it, sweetie. You'll be the envy of millions.*

Maybe I'm too sensitive. Or not sensitive enough. Because I don't want to be just another notch on his use 'em and lose 'em scorecard. I can't. I won't. "Please, Vaughn. Put me down."

His frown is just as gorgeous as his smile. There's something hotly adorable about his mischief. As shocked I am by what he's doing, I'm not scared of him. He's a big, burly, inked-up lunatic, but he's easy to be with. His playfulness and his determination are connective. He should be on his way to Los Angeles but instead he's here, chasing after me. And I have no idea why.

He carefully sets me down on my feet.

Then he falls to his knees in front of me. He's so big and muscular—*and hot*—that, on his knees like this, all genuine and romantic, he's sort of … irresistible.

Damn him.

He's wearing faded jeans and clearly doesn't care about grass stains. Or the fact that the crowd is now taking pictures of us.

"Vaughn—"

"Let me put it this way, sweetheart. I'll humor you and obey you—to a point. I *am* taking you to Nashville with me. But I'd rather take you willingly. So let me convince you in a way that only a knight in shining armor could."

He's staring up at me not pleadingly but sort of … zealously.

Maybe he really is crazy.

I notice then there's a cut on his lip and a bruise around one of his eyes. "What happened to your face?" Unthinkingly, I touch the backs of my fingers gently to his purpling cheekbone.

"My brother and I had a small misunderstanding."

"Travis?"

"Yeah."

"You *fought* with him?"

"It was only a few punches."

"Why would you fight with him?"

"Oh, he just misunderstood a few of my intentions. We worked through it." Like it's no big deal. "Then I stopped the bus and jumped off."

I realize my fingers are now brushing a strand of his hair from his eyes, to see his bruise more clearly. His hair is thick and unruly, as soft as coarse silk. With effort, I pull my hand away. "Why would you do that?"

"So I could see you again."

I'm having trouble processing why he would *jump off his tour bus* to come see *me*. "It couldn't wait until after your tour?"

"No." He stands up, towering over me. His man-scent and the sheer size of him stuns me for a few seconds.

"Please, Vaughn. It's best if you go back to your bus and your ... " *Your stable of women. Your on-call groupies. Your glamorous harem.* " ... life. You don't even know me."

"That's why I'm here. It wasn't enough time."

I need to stop this whole thing in its tracks before I become *incapable* of turning him down. Or resisting him. I can see why they all fall for him. It's not fair that he's *this* hot, tall, wide-shouldered, built—*holy mother, the fit of those jeans*—sun-tanned, blue-eyed and inked like only a hell-raising bad boy could be. The cocktail of Vaughn Tucker is sort of mind-blowing. But I plump up my resolve and try to stay strong. "Look. It's a nice offer. Thank you. But I don't want to be one of your ... conquests, okay? I can't handle that. And I don't want to."

"I don't have conquests."

I give him an exasperated look. *What about the triplets? The best friends with their backstage passes? The girl that fed you grapes?*

"You googled me," he says, as though reading the images flickering through my mind.

"I didn't need to google you, Vaughn. You're all over the internet." *Tousled, usually, from your most recent romp with a swimsuit model.*

"They weren't conquests." He doesn't elaborate. "And we need to eat. I refuse to let you go hungry tonight, Gi. And I'm hardly going to let you make the mistake of being bored to tears at the diner by the twit in sensible shoes."

I glance back to where Dylan's still standing, watching us. "Yeah. I was trying to figure out how to get out of that one."

Vaughn gestures toward the helicopter with a flick of his head. "I have a getaway plan."

I know exactly what will happen. He'll charm me with his killer smile and his honesty. He'll break through my forcefield with his blue-eyed lust bullets.

Before I can figure out what to do or how to cling to my last stand, my phone rings in my hand. I'm still holding it. *Momma*, the screen reads. She hardly ever calls me. She usually just texts. "Momma? Is everything okay?"

"Gi, do you know anything about this car that was just delivered? Whose is it? It's brand new, by the looks of it. Fancy, too. I told them it wasn't ours but the delivery man insisted this was the right address. Maybe it was supposed to get delivered next door."

I look up into a pair of spangling sapphire eyes, rimmed with dense, dark lashes longer than any man's have any right to be. "You said you were having car trouble," he says softly.

"You bought me a *car*?"

"I bought your mother a car," he corrects me. "Because she cooked the best meal I've eaten this decade." Carefully, he takes the phone from my hand. "Mrs. Hayes? It's Vaughn here … good, thanks. Listen, I wanted to tell you again how much I enjoyed that meal. And the pie was … what? Yeah, it's for you. It's nothing. Really. You just enjoy it … of course I'm sure … no, I absolutely insist. And in return, I'm going to hit you up for another one of those pies when I get back." He listens, then laughs. "All right, then. You're welcome, Mrs. Hayes."

He hands my phone back to me, grinning gently but you can tell he's irritatingly pleased with himself.

I don't grin back. "Momma?"

"Lord above, isn't that just the sweetest thing you've ever heard in your *life*?"

"Yes. It sure is." Glaring. "I have to go now, Momma. I'll see you later."

After several more lyrical gushes about how outstandingly wonderful Vaughn Tucker is from my besotted mother, we end the call.

I really can't believe this. "You did not just buy my mother a car."

"Sure did, darlin'." He's totally unrepentant. "I have more money than I know what to do with. Sometimes it's nice to share the love. It sounds like she needed one. And I appreciated the pie."

"It was a *pie*, Vaughn. If you did that because you …" I don't know how to accuse him of such a thing. He wouldn't *buy my mother a car* so I'd go out to dinner with him. Would he?

"Are you ready? The champagne's on ice and we've only got the helicopter for ninety minutes, since it was so last minute. Then we're going to Speakeasy. I'll take you home in the limo."

I've heard of Speakeasy. It's a club and one of the best restaurants in Nashville, but it's invitation only. It's a place celebrities go to. It's located on the top floor of a building in the central city and it's guarded by an army of security, so the stars don't get mobbed. And Vaughn Tucker is exactly the kind of clientele Speakeasy caters to. He's probably a VIP or something.

"It's one of the few places I can go to," he says.

"They probably wouldn't let me in. I won't be twenty-one for another few weeks." And I'm not a celebrity, I don't need to point out.

"I can get you in." He runs his hand through his hair, causing a perfect jaunty curl to stick up. "So, what's it going to be, Gi? In my arms or slung over my shoulder? The choice is yours."

I've only been to Nashville a handful of times in my life. I've never eaten at a fancy restaurant. I've never even tasted champagne.

That grin again. The one that could—and has—slayed a thousand women. "Come on, when's the last time you went for a ride in a helicopter?"

"I've never ridden in a helicopter."

"No?"

"Not even in an airplane."

"Then it's time for you to live a little, Gigi Hayes. Come on, baby. Get your halo dirty."

Ha ha. *Baby.* I'm sure he says that to all the girls. I narrow my eyes at him, wondering how far he'll go. Pretty damn far, is my guess. He copies my movement. Then he makes a face and I feel myself relenting.

"Ditch the dweeb. I guarantee I'm a lot more fun."

I know he's right. I also know that, if I do say yes to Vaughn Tucker, I'll have more heartbreak, turbulence and ecstasy than I know what to do with. I'm not sure I'm ready for that kind of roller coaster, or if I ever will be.

He's half lunatic and half sex god … but he was gone by morning.

I take a deep breath, fully aware that I'm setting myself up for a fall. But maybe he's right. Maybe I *do* need to live a little. "Fine, then. But I'll walk."

He slowly shakes his head. "Knights in shining armor *always* carry their guests onto their chariots." I bite my lip and he watches me do this, his irises a smoldering indigo. "It would be a personal insult if you wouldn't grant me that privilege."

Before I can protest any further, he lifts me into his

arms and starts carrying me toward the helicopter, which is already starting up.

I glance back to see Dylan standing there with a what-the-hell expression. "I'll have to take a rain check," I call out to him.

"You'll never want one after tonight," Vaughn says, carrying me into the helicopter, where one of the flight crew seals the door closed firmly behind us.

7

———

VAUGHN

I SET Gigi onto one of the plush seats and pull the seatbelt around her to fasten it. She's wide-eyed but not intimidated. There's fascination there but not mindless, star-struck adoration.

I fucking *love* this.

The blind adoration gets so tedious. Women tend to love the idea of me, the look of me, the energy of my music. The fame and the money, most of all. Not the blood and bone. Not the pleasure or the pain. The depth. Nothing about the reality of who I am.

None of which bothered me at all. Yesterday.

Today it does.

It bothers me a whole lot.

Because the difference this girl is providing, despite the fact that she's basically a total stranger, is somehow rocking my goddamn world.

I don't know how. Or why.

All I know is that I want to find out. I want to dig deeper and connect with the enigma of her because it feels better than anything has in a long time.

She's so different to everyone I know.

There's a quietness. A feisty, assured kindness. Like she knows more about what's good for you than you do. I don't quite get it or know what to make of her yet, but I'm already addicted to this mysterious draw she has. The deep well of *understanding* behind her eyes that's one of the most riveting things that's ever happened to me.

I sit next to her as the helicopter starts to lift.

She's watching the crowd wave at us as we rise above them. She waves back. The guy in the yellow shirt has his hands shoved into his pockets dejectedly.

She was always way out of your league, bro.

She's mine now.

The twist of my thoughts is fucked up. I unfasten the fridge and pull a bottle of Moët out. I pop the cork and pour two glasses, handing one to her. She takes it and I clink my glass against hers. Our gazes meet and—*holy hell*—she's doing it again. That soothing calmness, like some kind of balm for my twisted soul.

I'm trying to figure out what I want so badly about this girl.

Aside from the fact that she's a walking wet dream, if I was going to be crude about it, which I don't want to be. Not this time.

She's still wearing her black-framed glasses and I'm almost glad for this. Without them it would feel like staring into a supernova. They provide an element of shade so it's almost bearable. Her face is unique, with those knowing, golden eyes, the perfect nose and her pink, full lips that are almost too bee-stung, giving her sexy cuteness a sultry edge she's completely unaware of, like a sex goddess is trapped underneath the innocent façade. *Which I plan on freeing at my very first opportunity.* Her hair hangs in long, thick, strawberry-blond waves over bare shoulders.

In jeans and a loose shirt, she was stunning. In her tight little white dress, which hugs every mind-blowing curve, she's a pure, lust-soaked dream. She's blasé about this. She's not working it, like every other woman I know does.

Gigi doesn't *need* to work it. The shape of her body is doing all the work that ever needed to be done in the history of my world.

Which sounds over the top even to me as I think the thoughts. But it's true. If I could have designed a woman to fit *me* and every detail I would wish for if I'd ever thought to wish for someone so ideal, she would have blown all those specs to smithereens with an insolent shrug of her smooth, angular shoulders.

Does she look this good to everyone? I have no way of knowing. The pure, forceful *allure* of her, though, feels wildly over the top, like she's my own personal brand of perfection. It's not just the shape of her lips and her body and her face, or the color of her hair, or the sound of her voice that meshes with all my most rabid desires, but the feel of her presence. She soothes me for no particular reason. She *fits* there, with her calming aura rubbing up against mine, like the blend of her pheromones with mine somehow completes me.

Which is fucked up.

And I haven't even tasted her yet.

No one has ever had this effect on me before. It's so immediate. So all-consuming. So goddamn addictive.

Her breasts are lush and high. Tipped with the sweet, subtle outline of her pert nipples. The anticipation is sort of excruciating. *I can almost taste them already. I can feel them in my mouth, my tongue swirling until they're hard little peaks. Sucking hungrily until she's moaning. I want to drink her and eat her. I want to feast on her gorgeousness.*

My mouth is literally watering.

At the same time, my cock surges hotly, now fully, painfully hard.

Her waist is slim and her stomach is flat but not completely. There's a light, natural feminine curve to her that's ten times sexier than any gym bunny. Her hips are flared, tapering down to her barely-covered thighs and her long, tanned legs.

I'm so fucked.

I want to kneel in front of her and push her legs wider. Lift her dress. Rip her panties off. Lick her sweet pussy, teasing her, sucking

*on her clit and feasting possessively until she's coming on my
tongue.*

"I've never had champagne before," she says.

"Try it. This one's my favorite."

She sips.

I drink most of mine in one long gulp.

Because I'm thirsty.

And because whatever's happening here is intense. I
feel, maybe for the first time in my life … sort of lost for
words. I don't want to fuck this up.

"I like it." Her eyes have all the starry zing of the
champagne.

"Told you."

She turns back toward the window and looks out.
"This is so amazing, Vaughn. Everything looks so small
from up here."

"Look, there's Travis's house."

"And the pond!" Her excitement makes me rock-hard.
Not that I wasn't already. If I could touch her, I could
come so easily. "There's your cabin. And my house. And
there's—" she turns to me. There's a note of fury in her
voice that's the cutest thing I've ever heard. "You bought
my mother a *yellow sports car?*"

"It's a Corvette."

Her light anger takes a turn. To disbelief. "Why?"

"It's fun to drive. I have one just like it, in red."

"But … that would have cost—"

"It was worth it."

"But she hardly even drives. Except to go to the supermarket and to go play bridge with her friends."

"Well, I guess the bridge club will have something to talk about then."

She's quiet for a few seconds. "Vaughn, it's way too much. You have to take it back."

"Not a chance, darlin'. I figure it's a fair trade for the pies she said she'd bake for me. She told me she'd bake me one every day when I get back."

Gigi smiles almost wistfully. "My mother has never had a new car before."

"Well, then, it's about time she did."

Her expression is gentler now as she watches me. "That was such a nice thing to do."

"It's nothing."

"*Crazy*, but nice." She takes another sip of her champagne.

The hem of her dress is high, revealing the lightly-tanned tops of her thighs. I have to physically restrain myself from sliding my fingers under that tantalizing line. *I want to feel her. I want to find out if she's wet. I bet she is. I bet her little white panties are damp. I bet she tastes like honey. I want to lick her everywhere and slide my tongue inside* ... "We can talk about what kind of car you want next."

"You're not buying me a car, Vaughn. And I'm not sure why you're doing all this. You don't need to."

"I want to."

She's quiet for a few seconds, watching my face. "Why?"

I think about this as she watches me. "Because I like the look in your eyes."

That little crinkle between her eyebrows quirks. "What look?"

"The kind one. The soulful one. The one that feels like a cool rain. The one that tells me that you get me—or you will, in time—like no one else could."

She smiles gently but the furrow between her eyebrows smooths away. "I don't know what you mean." But I think she does know. Because she's looking at me like that right now, and it fucking worries me.

Because I think I might already be hooked.

You know *you're hooked.*

Which was always going to be disastrous.

8

Gigi

"I WANT you to stay close to me tonight." Vaughn tops up my glass of champagne as I look out at the view. We can see everything. The towns and fields, the tiny cars moving in slow motion along the ribbon of freeway. "Things can get crazy sometimes."

I don't bother mentioning that I've never seen the world like I'm seeing it right now, from up above like we're on a magic carpet riding into the sunset. I think he already knows all this. He's watching me like he does, as though he can read every thought I've ever had. It's a little eerie, actually, how perceptive he seems. How *in tune* he already is with my mood, my emotions, the dreams I never thought to dream for, until right now.

"Good." That smirk could launch a thousand ships. Isn't that what they said about Helen of Troy? I remember reading the Iliad in high school. It was Helen's beauty that started the Trojan War. Vaughn's could do that too, I can't help thinking. Maybe in a more modern sense of the word. His beauty could launch a million album downloads, maybe. And already has. Beauty has a power to it. A force. Vaughn's is magnified because there are so many aspects of it. His face. His body. His voice. His size. His look. Most of all, him. The dark energy and the intensity of his allure.

The entire cocktail is sort of overwhelming me, up close and in this sealed bubble as we fly through the sky. It's all around me, burning into my senses and awakening me. I'm riding an adrenaline rush from the close contact to all that he is.

I take another sip of the delicious champagne. I like the taste and the zinging zest of it. It's like drinking liquid happiness. "I never imagined I'd fly to the city in a helicopter. Everything about this feels like a fairy tale, doesn't it?"

My excitement amuses him. "Yes. It does."

"I guess Ruby will have to get used to this kind of thing, the city lights and the travel. I know she'll love it. She was born for it."

His reply is soft. "What were *you* born for, Gigi Hayes?"

The question catches me off-guard. I don't really know how to answer it. I can hardly tell him about the butterfly wing and my quest to save people. It's not the kind of thing you can easily explain. But the champagne is already loosening my barriers. And it's Vaughn. The bond we share is so new, so untried, but it's growing. We both want it to, I can feel this even if I'm not sure why. Underneath his cool, masculine bravado, I can sense that he's already fully invested in whatever it is I'm about to say. "I think I was born to help someone change their future." It doesn't quite scratch the surface and it sounds weird, since everyone changes other people's futures, just by being alive. But at least it's honest.

He smiles like he likes what I've said, and gets it. And, strangely and almost against my will, it's this small detail —that he *gets* something about me that very few people do, or at least that he want*s* to—melts through my force-field like nothing else could. "Whose?"

"Whose what?"

"Whose future are you going to change?"

"I don't know yet. I guess I'll find out when I start working."

"When do you start?"

"I have another week of classes and then I get to sit in on my first case study soon after that. At a place near the hospital. They say it's the best rehab in Tennessee."

There's a sadness in his smile. The word is a trigger for him. I noticed it earlier, too, when I mentioned something about it in the kitchen. Then again, I guess "rehab" could be a trigger to anyone who sips whiskey from a flask before noon. I don't know what his story is or the extent of anything about him, but I get that pang again. Tiny, invisible strands of my soul want to reach out to him. *Maybe he needs me.*

"Such a noble, selfless aspiration. Helping people." His comment isn't mocking, just truthful.

"I don't know if it's selfless. Or noble. I think everyone helps people in their own ways. You help people. With your music. Music can help more than anything."

"You think so?" The quietness of him as he watches me is another side to him. I can guess that this is a piece of himself he doesn't often reveal. His public persona is all about the larger-than-life rock star. This contemplative, stoic side to him is one I can relate to. The threads of his pain show more clearly and are digging in to every protective and compassionate instinct I possess. Which, for better or worse, own the lion's share of my psyche. I want to know what hurts him.

"Definitely. I listen to your music all the time and it helps me. If I'm having a bad day for some reason, like if my sister is having a hard time with her new baby, or my other sister is crying over some boyfriend who never calls, or if my mother cries because she misses my father, it helps. It's steady and soothing and it's always there when you need it."

"What happened to your father?"

"He died, six years ago. From … a heart attack." I don't know why I pause before saying it. I never pause. It's on his death certificate and it's what we always say. It's what my mother and my sisters still believe.

"I'm sorry." He takes my hand in his and begins to play with my fingers. "It sounds like your problems are all about other people's problems."

Vaughn's hand is warm. And rough, with callouses. No doubt from all the drumming he does. I've often listened to his music and I've seen photos of them on the internet, but I've never watched them perform live or seen many of their music videos. I wonder what he's like when he's playing. The warmth and the grip and the rough textures of his touch feed tendrils of his allure directly into my bloodstream, warming me with his effect. Heat gathers and pools. In my heartbeat. And in secret places, where I can feel my pulse. "Well, they're my family. They sometimes rely on me to get them through things. You must do that too, for your family. You and your brothers seem close."

"We are. But my brothers punch me more often than they cry on my shoulder."

"Maybe because you spend so much time together. And you're in a band. I bet that can cause friction when relationships are that intense."

"Yeah. It does. But mainly, we're good. We're there for each other when it counts."

It's dusk now and we can see the skyline of the city, the lights of the skyscrapers and the pointed peaks of the Batman Building. I'm high from the champagne and the flight and most of all him. "Thank you for kidnapping me."

"Rescuing you, more like it." He bumps his shoulder gently against mine. "From nerd boy."

"Getting my halo dirty is more fun than I expected," I joke.

His eyes glow a brilliant, fiery blue from under the thick fall of his black-silk hair. He contemplates me through dark lashes and his voice is low. "We haven't even gotten started with that one yet, darlin'."

My face warms as our eyes meet, not in an embarrassed, innocent kind of way, more in a maybe-you-should-show-me-what-you-mean kind of way. Which is a new thing for me. Under his glow, the forcefield that guards my heart against meaningless connections is gone. Because nothing about him is meaningless. Even though I know the odds of Vaughn Tucker hurting me are sky high, there's a masculine tenderness to him that's burrowing into me. Loosening every barrier I've ever held close. "Do you like flying?"

"I don't mind it. People tend to either love flying or they hate it. Kade hates it. That's why we drive. He refuses to get on a plane."

"Why? Did something happen to him, to make him hate it that much?"

"He just says he prefers to stay on the ground. I guess we all have our phobias."

I almost don't ask it but it tumbles out. "What are yours?" I ask softly. "What's Vaughn Tucker scared of?"

He's sitting very close to me. His warm, jean-clad

thigh is resting against my bare skin. His blue eyes are bright, as though he's feeling this same ephemeral lightness and tuning into the connectivity of it, like somewhere, stars are aligning. "You."

I smile. He's playing with me again. "There's nothing scary about me. I'm about as harmless as a girl can be."

"Wrong. You're the most dangerous girl I've ever met."

The orange light of sunset tints the perfectly put-together planes and valleys of his face and the contours of his square jaw, like a masterpiece. He's mind-numbingly handsome. "I promise to be nice to you."

"How nice?" His low question is playful but has a filthy spin to it.

I meet his challenge quietly. "Very nice."

He grins darkly but we're in the city now and the helicopter is starting to slow and hover. "I'll hold you to that promise," he says, lacing his fingers through mine.

We land on a helipad on top of one of Nashville's tallest buildings. Once the propellers come to a stop, a man opens the door for us, dressed in a uniform and flanked by three extremely large security guards.

Whoa. "What are they here for?"

"The place we're going to has some strict security measures. A lot of the clientele demand security at every entrance. So we don't get mobbed."

Wow.

We're led across the roof to a door, which opens into

a spacious glass elevator with spectacular views of the sunset over Nashville. The uniformed man gets in with us, pushing the button.

This whole scenario is so over the top. The flying and the new car. The uniformed butler and the beefed-up security guards.

He's so famous he doesn't even have to push his own elevator buttons.

Vaughn smiles at my awe. He's a free spirit, but under all that I notice again a gravity there too. It's easy to see that there are a lot of broiling emotions lurking underneath his expression, which gives his roguishness an aggressive edge. The more time I spend with him, the more I see of this side of him. It doesn't detract from his easy-going charm, though. Instead, it sort of enhances it, fascinating me.

I think of the butterfly wing again. The ripples of the universe that'll be influenced by his volatility. Or by the soothing of all that storminess.

The differences between the two futures.

I *could*, I find myself thinking.

I could soothe whatever it is that hurts him, I can already feel that.

But it's a ridiculous idea. He's hardly my pet project. He's a world famous drummer with legions of fans and most likely dozens of girlfriends. He probably takes women on helicopter rides every night of the week.

I might be a small-town girl but I'm not *that* naïve, to think that this is something unique or special.

I wonder if he buys cars for all their mothers.

The elevator descends silently, the city sprawling out below us.

"I meant what I said. Stay close to me tonight." He holds my hand more tightly.

It's an intimate thing, holding hands. The contact causes my heart to beat faster. My blood feels hotter. I'm aware, again, of a pulsing warmth between my legs. There's a light, tingling ache to it. A low excitement that's needy and slippery and restless.

My sisters say they see it in me: a spark. Like my father, I'm steady. Reliable. I always do what's expected of me and I mostly follow the rules, much more than any of my sisters. But under the smooth surface of my personality, I can't deny that every now and then I can feel an unexplored recklessness simmering there, waiting for its moment.

My father's wild side cost him his life. I don't think mine will, but I have no idea what it *will* do, or in what directions it might lead me.

What I'm realizing is that Vaughn Tucker is honing in on that spark. He's feeding it and firing it up. He's lighting its fuse.

And I'm not sure I want him to.

At the same time, though, it feels *good*, to lean into his influence. It feels like freedom, like danger, like fun, all mixed together in a dizzying cocktail. It feels like he could talk me into walking through fire with his blue eyes and his warm, rough, calloused hands.

Trouble was my very first thought when I saw him standing there, shirtless and unzipped and about as free-wheeling and sure of himself as a man can be. I can feel it happening already. The vines of his energetic life-force are coiling themselves around me. Around my body, touching me intimately. Around my heart, which is usually so easy to protect.

I could love him, is what I find myself thinking. I could fall in love with Vaughn Tucker as easily as falling off the edge of the building we just landed on.

I don't want to get too close to the edge.

Then again, maybe I do. Maybe I want to see where it takes me.

Straight to his bed, that's where it'll take you. He's radiating sex. It's steaming off his body and beaming out of his eyes. He'll be a beast once he gets you there. He'll enlighten the hell out you in a thousand earth-shattering ways.

And then he'll be gone by morning.

Is that such a bad thing?

My two older sisters have slept with men they didn't love, knowing full well that it was all about the physical rush and nothing more. They didn't care that it was only one night. They *wanted* it to be only one night.

Why can't I just loosen up and go with it, for once in my life?

Because if you love him a little already, going to bed with him will only make it ten times worse. Then he'll break your heart and ruin you for anyone else. He's a stranger. A superstar. A player. A sex god. Have dinner with him and then run for the hills with your soul still intact, girl.

I'm not a coward but I am a survivalist.

The elevator door pings and slides open. We're led down a marble hallway to another elevator. It's one of those ultra-modern ones that swooshes silently and so quickly you get a slight wave of vertigo, but within a few seconds we're already there. I'm glad I'm holding onto Vaughn's hand. Between the rock god vibes, the champagne and the elevator ride, my equilibrium is off.

The door slides open to a large foyer area which is full of young, gorgeous, hip-looking people. Through a large doorway is an expansive restaurant with low ceilings and walls of windows, looking out to the twinkling lights of Nashville. The dusky skyline takes on shades of lavender and gold. Neon letters over the door glow blue. *Speakeasy.*

It's loud, with live, modern-sounding country music and the laughter and conversation of several hundred people.

Another brigade of giant bouncers are guarding the door.

"Vaughn!" screams a girl dressed in a fur coat and not much else. She teeters over to him on sky-high heels. Two more impossibly beautiful women follow her and they're all gathering around him. And, since he's still holding my hand, they're gathering around me too.

"Hey," he says to them, but he barely even acknowledges them. He's pulling me toward the entrance of the restaurant.

One of the bouncers pats him on the back. "Vaughn, man," he smiles, shaking Vaughn's hand. He checks me out, lingering for a few seconds on my face. But he doesn't card me. I'm with Vaughn. I get a free pass to the universe. He motions for us to go through.

The place has an open-air feel and a spectacular view.

A maître d' comes over. "Mr. Tucker, allow me to show you and your guest to your table."

Vaughn pulls me through the crowd. Everyone knows him. People call out to him. Some of them slap him on the back as we walk past, eyeing me curiously. They *all* want a piece of him. He introduces me briefly to a few people as we make our way through.

This is Nashville's glitterati. A slice of America's A-list.

I recognize a famous singer and her actor boyfriend. A movie star. A Victoria's Secret supermodel with her rock 'n roll singer husband. A couple of Nashville influencers. A Super Bowl-winning quarterback and his wife, who's the face of several major cosmetics lines.

The singer on stage is Jake Bodine and his band, whose song is currently number four on the charts. I usually check the billboard charts each week, just because

I've gotten into the habit. So I happen to know that the top three songs right now are Lonesome Blues, Hot Summer Night and Take Me Home, by—you guessed it—The Tucker Brothers Band.

"They're staring at us," I tell him.

"They're staring at you, darlin'."

He's right. They are staring at me. Pointing. Having hushed conversations. Wondering who Vaughn Tucker's flavor of the evening is. They don't recognize me. I'm not a part of their usual scene.

The table is—of course—the best one in the house. It's a swanky booth in its own little nook with a view of both the city and the band. I climb in and Vaughn slides close, touching me again with his warmth and his stardust.

"Can I get you a drink, Mr. Tucker?" asks the maître d'. "Miss?"

"A bottle of Moët and two Jack Daniels on ice," Vaughn tells him and the man rushes off to serve us. "You okay, Gi? Your tiger eyes are all swallowed up by your pupils right now."

"My tiger eyes?"

"They're almost striped, with starbursts of different shades of dark and light gold, did you know that?" He leans closer and takes the rim of my glasses between his fingers. "Can I take these off for a second? I want to see you without them."

"Um … okay."

He slides my glasses off and sets them on the table. I put them into my bag. I don't actually need them. I wear them because I used to think they'd make me look more sophisticated, which is almost embarrassing to admit even to myself. I also wore them so I wouldn't get … noticed so often, maybe. Hit on. Asked out. By one guy after another who didn't stack up, for whatever reason. Another part of my shield. The one Vaughn seems determined to—and very good at—breaking through.

Vaughn rubs his jaw as he smiles at me in a way that's … I don't know how to describe it. Like he's mirroring the thoughts I've been having. Like he's bemused and also … riveted. Maybe even … hooked.

Like I feel hooked.

"You're so damn pretty." His voice is softly gruff. "I've never in my life seen anyone so beautiful."

It's possibly the nicest thing anyone has ever said to me. And also sort of hard to believe, considering all the people in this room.

"I haven't even known you for an entire day and you already feel like the sun."

Wow. "Vaughn. You hardly know me."

"I know. Imagine how it's going to feel when I do."

Who knew the bad boy superstar would turn out to be a romantic. "What if you don't like what you find?"

"I think that would be impossible. You're already the nicest person I've ever met. And also the wildest."

This makes me laugh. As if. "Wildest?"

"Yeah. You just don't know it yet."

He knows. He can already see that side to me my sisters are always going on about. The one I've never indulged or given much time to. It freaks me out a little that it feels like this hidden spark is linked to *him*. Like Vaughn Tucker somehow *owns* it. Which is not a good thing.

The waiter arrives with our drinks. He places two tumblers of whiskey on the table, along with some menus, then makes a spectacle out of popping the cork of the champagne and filling our glasses, placing the bottle into the ice bucket. He bows and disappears into the crowd.

Vaughn clinks his whiskey glass against mine. "To changing the future."

He tips his back.

I take a sip. It burns lightly as it goes down but I like the taste. It reminds me of autumn days in my Daddy's shed, when he'd be tinkering under the hood of his pick-up truck with the radio playing and a bottle of whiskey on the workbench.

We order our food and we listen to the band as Vaughn tells me about some of the people he knows in this room. Jake Bodine, who's singing, is an old friend from their early days. The quarterback went to the same high school; he was Kade's year. The supermodel briefly dated his cousin.

A non-stop parade of women wave to Vaughn, blowing him kisses, trying to get his attention. They don't come over. His body language isn't inviting them. I'm not entirely sure why he would be, but he's fully focused on me.

The dance floor is crowded with people. I drink more of the whiskey and sip the champagne slowly. The night takes on a starry edge.

Vaughn is relaxed and attentive and funny. We're served courses of small plates of the most exotic food I've ever eaten. Bites of lobster roll with caviar and tarragon. Scallops served in a butter and wine sauce. Seafood ravioli with truffle sauce. Sliced filet mignon with horse-radish marinade. It's all new to me, and delicious.

The band comes back on after taking an intermission and Jake Bodine drawls into the microphone. "Vaughn Tucker, we want you to come up here and sing that new song of yours everyone's playing non-stop. The one that's in my way of getting to number one. Along with those other two. Come on, man. Come on up here."

"Shit," Vaughn says. "Do you mind me leaving you for a few minutes, honey?" For all his reputation as a rebel and a playboy, I'm learning that, at heart, Vaughn is a good person. He's a rough-edged, restless soul, but he's kind. I haven't asked him again about his parents, after he told me about the tattoo of his mother's name. Whoever she is—or was, by the sound of the way he reacted—she must have raised her boys right. Somewhere along the line—despite the mayhem and superstardom of their lifestyle, the money on tap and the women on call—it stuck. Or at least some of it did.

It doesn't mean he won't break your heart, though. Only that he might feel a millisecond of remorse about it somewhere down the line. "Go ahead. I want to hear you sing."

He stands up and the whole restaurant erupts in howls and applause. They cheer as he walks up onto the stage.

They *love* him. And who can blame them.

On stage, he's totally in his element. You can't help but be captivated. He takes his time, all cool masculinity and sure-footed talent. Under the spotlight, his hair is gold-tipped. The loose neck of his shirt shows off his rosewood skin and the inked designs along his broad shoulders and muscled arms. He couldn't be any more beautiful.

"This is our newest single," he says. "It's called Lonesome Blues."

The crowd cheers and claps.

The band strums the acoustic opening and Vaughn starts to sing.

His voice is quite literally to die for. On the radio it sounds soulful and deep. Live, he takes it to a whole different level. You can feel the resonating emotion in his edgy, husked voice.

On those days when I think the world has come right and the sun will shine bright, you're still gone. On those days when I know the rain's gonna clear and the moon's on the rise, you're still gone. The loneliness you've left behind, it cuts deep. It bleeds red. All that's left now is the sound of your voice and the songs in my head. But you're gone, still gone, always gone, forever gone.

The few times I've heard it, I never really listened to the lyrics of that song. But I can feel the pain behind the words he's written. Something in his life hurts deep.

He does need me.

It's a feeling I can't shake.

Just then, as Vaughn starts singing the last verse, someone slides in to the booth next to me. I vaguely recognize him, from an article I read recently in the Nashville news. I can't remember his name. He's an up-and-coming local actor who's starting to get noticed in Hollywood. He's had a few bit parts in some big-budget movies.

"Hi," he says, sliding closer. He has dirty-blond hair and brown eyes. He's wearing the Tennessee homeboy uniform of a plaid shirt, faded jeans and cowboy boots.

Abruptly, Vaughn stops singing.

The room goes quiet.

"Hey. Wade Sullivan," Vaughn says, into the microphone.

Everyone in the room turns to stare at Wade Sullivan. And at me.

"I don't want to have to ruin your night, Wade. So I'm asking you to slide yourself out of that booth and go back to your seat," Vaughn continues. "Right now."

"Come on, man," Wade yells back. "I was just being friendly."

"If you don't want my fist getting *extremely* fucking friendly with your face, then move."

The crowd murmurs. A few people cheer. Someone whistles. *What the hell?*

Wade slowly starts to move. But as he does this, he holds out his hand to me. "I'm Wade, by the way." Lowering his voice: "And you're gorgeous."

There's a sound of a microphone being dropped.

Wade scrambles out of the booth when he sees Vaughn coming toward him, pushing through the crowd. Vaughn grabs Wade by the scruff of his shirt and punches him in the face.

Oh my God.

I can't believe this.

Wade swings at Vaughn, who ducks and slams Wade in the stomach. Wade grabs Vaughn's shirt and punches back. They're both throwing punches, landing a few. The crowd is gathering around, cheering them on. Wade's nose is bleeding.

I slide out of the booth to try to stop this but the men are being dragged apart now by the beefy bouncers. Both Vaughn and Wade are being held with their arms behind their backs.

"Let's all calm down now, folks," says Jake Bodine into the microphone. "Back to your seats, everyone. Just some friendly caveman testosterone being thrown around on a Thursday night, that's all. It happens. Wade, he did warn you. And you *did* make a move on his date, man. So you deserved that. Vaughn, bro, I've got to say this is a new look for you, but I can see why you'd go apeshit, just sayin'. Now we can all get back to the music and the dancing, am I right?"

Vaughn shakes off the bouncer. "Stay away from her," he growls at Wade.

"Chill, man. *Jesus*. You're crazy, you know that?" Wade wipes his shirt across his bloody nose and wanders off.

Vaughn turns, looking for me. Finding me. Wade got the worst of it but I can see Vaughn's bruise already. His other eye. Both his eyes will have shiners by morning.

Which makes me wonder if the other fight he got in earlier today was over some other girl.

"I can't believe you did that." The band starts up again and people go back to their tables and out onto the dance floor. Vaughn's arm gently circles my wrist and he pulls me back into our booth. I slide in but I'm pissed off, that he would hurt someone just for saying hello to me. First the sweeping me off my feet and practically kidnapping me—even if I *am* having more fun than I can ever remember having—and now this.

Despite all that, I'm worried about his bruise. I can't help myself: I use my napkin to make an ice pack out of some of the ice cubes in the champagne bucket. Carefully, I hold it against his cheekbone. "You've hurt yourself again. Why do you do it, Vaughn?"

"He tried to touch you." His eyes are dark and

volatile. The strong stripes of his eyebrows are furrowed in the middle. His energy is aggressive and very … *male*. Like a gorilla defending its territory or something. I spend most of my time in the company of my sisters, my mother and a few girlfriends. This is a whole new world.

"He offered to shake my hand. It was nothing. You're acting crazy."

"That's because I *am* crazy. Because of you." He leans closer and I can feel the warm strikes of his breath and his insanely tempting scent. Of smoky nights and wildfire. Of worn leather and hundred-proof lust.

"I'm not your property, Vaughn. I can shake a man's hand if I want to."

"And I can punch a man's face if I want to," he counters.

I glare at him, feeling flushed. And angry. *And turned on*. As pissed off as I might be over his fight, I have to admit there's something carnally triggering about his primal reactions. He was protecting me and staking some kind of claim.

Be careful, girl. This is how he'll trap you. By showing you he cares and then, as soon as you believe it, he'll walk away. "What kind of lunatic gets two shiners in one day?"

"A besotted one."

Not helping. "What does that even mean?"

He slides his warm palm around the nape of my neck, pulling me closer. Very, very softly, he brushes his lips against my cheek. "It means I'd kiss you right now the way I want to kiss you. But I know that when I taste you for the first time, we need to be somewhere other than in a crowded room. Because one kiss won't be enough. Not even close."

Everything about him is so fast and so furious. The only way I know how to handle him is by keeping him at an arm's length. If I let him in, he'll destroy me with his sweet words and his outrageous draw, and most of all with his absence tomorrow. "Who said I'd kiss you back?"

Burning me with those blue-ember eyes. "You'd kiss me back." Cocky, as usual. He glances over at the dance floor. "But first I promised you a night out. You want to dance with me, Gi?"

We had a teacher at my school who taught us everything from line dancing to the tango. Some of the head nuns scolded her for teaching us moves that were supposedly too risqué, but Sister Jacqueline said the dancing was good for our posture, our fitness and our sense of timing and poise. So they let her continue teaching us. But I've never really had a chance to dance since then. "As a matter of fact, I do."

Vaughn takes my hand and leads me up onto the crowded dance floor.

His arm is around my waist, his other hand holding my hand as he holds me close. I can feel all the hard, exhilarating textures of his body. He's tall and big and rock-hard. *Everywhere.* He's gazing down at me as I gaze right back at him, struggling to drink in not just his mind-numbing handsomeness but also the awe in him. *This can't be a look he shares with everyone he meets, can it?* The current of our connection feels hot and electric. The hidden depths of his eyes are mesmerizing. His mouth. The beat of his pulse at his throat.

If we were alone right now I *would* let him kiss me. *I'd let him do anything. I'd kiss that pulsing place at the base of his throat. I'd lick those perfect lips like I was licking his soul and healing his wounds.*

I'm almost relieved when the next song is an upbeat line dance and I laugh because he's a seriously good dancer.

We dance until late and it's a magical, beautiful night. It's a night I'll never forget.

Later, when the band starts winding down and the color of the sky out the wall of windows is purple along the horizon line, Vaughn makes a call. We're escorted by security to another elevator, which takes us down to a parking garage where a limo is parked. We slide into its cool interior and the driver closes the door behind us.

There's more champagne on ice and an opaque glass partition between the driver's area and the seats, which are as big as two plush, face-to-face couches.

"Do you always have champagne wherever you go?"

"Sure. Everyone likes it."

Everyone. All his women. It helps loosen them up, no doubt.

He sits close to me, slinging his arm around me. I'm

euphoric from the dancing and the night. The contact of his body feeds its warmth into me. Little currents of it, barbed with his lusty energy, funnel into me. The colors of the night play across his face.

The limo pulls out of the underground parking garage onto the street. I can see through the tinted windows that it's almost dawn. We've been dancing all night.

And we're alone now.

The air is charged with … what's about to happen.

How far will I go?

I already know how far he'll go. As far as it's possible to go. He gives off that vibe: that he has no limits.

"How many times has Gigi Hayes been kissed?" he asks in a lazy drawl. Like he can guess that I'm not very experienced.

In a saner moment, I'd never admit it. But I'm a little drunk. Okay, more than a little. I never realized alcohol is basically a truth serum and I find myself admitting things I've never told anyone except my sisters. "Three times. Once on a middle school bus trip, for a dare. Once in a movie theatre. And once at a party." I fully realize how pathetic it sounds, laid out like that in all its unimpressive glory. They were hardly even kisses at all. Just a press of the lips in a cautious, curious game that was never intended to go further.

"You mean to tell me you've only been kissed three

times in your whole life? And one of those times was in *middle* school?"

"I'm not exactly proud of it. But it's not entirely my fault. After my Daddy died, Momma did everything she could think of to keep the four of us from getting into trouble. She said each of us had a twinkle in our eye, was how she put it, and no father to look out for us. She wasn't ready to wave his sawed-off shotgun around at every boy who happened to stop by. And there were a lot of them. So she spent the last of the insurance money and sent us all to a strict Catholic boarding school. During high school, we didn't even get much of a summer vacation, just a few days or a long weekend here and there. The rest of the time they kept us busy with community service, extra study and prayer."

Vaughn mutters a low oath under his breath, maybe in sympathy. "What did you pray for?"

"The usual stuff. The health and happiness of the people I love. World peace. Eternal salvation. That kind of thing."

"Shit." Like he can't relate. "What even is eternal salvation?"

"It means you go to heaven instead of hell."

He fills our glasses. "What if hell is more fun?"

"I guess you'll find out."

Vaughn laughs. *Damn him. I love the sound of it.*

"Champagne for breakfast?"

"It's the best time to drink champagne. Besides, I'd

better enjoy myself if hell's all I've got to look forward to."

"I guess maybe you should."

He finds the topic funny, but I sense there's an edge to his amusement. "Can't I repent in my final hours and have everything forgiven?" He asks the question earnestly, almost insistently. I find myself wondering why.

"Well … technically, yes."

"Good." But he's not finished with his inquisition. "What about after high school? You said you're twenty. So you've had two years since then. You never met a guy between now and then that you wanted to kiss?"

"I've been on dates but they never go anywhere. Because of my rule."

He pins me with an alert glance. "What rule?"

"I made a pact with myself that I'd never have sex with someone I don't love. I don't even want to kiss anyone I couldn't love because … well, what's the point of kissing someone if you're not going to … you know."

The look in his eyes is intense. But his voice is soft. "You're right. There isn't one."

"That's what I thought too."

"Unless you just really want to kiss that person." As he says this, he lightly brushes his thumb along my cheekbone.

His touch, like always, makes my heart beat faster, surging with two conflicting emotions. The very beginnings of something I can clearly identify as love. And the very beginnings of something else that's *just* as easy to identify. Heartbreak. "I never did."

"Then why did you agree to go out to dinner with the dweeb?"

"Oh, you mean Dylan? Well, because … just today, in fact, I was starting to think that maybe my rule is stupid, and pointless. What if I *never* find anyone I could love? I mean, I haven't yet, so maybe I just … won't. And what if I go my whole life never knowing what it feels like to be with someone just because my standards are too high? I realized that maybe I need to lower them. Like other people seem to do."

"No." Gruffly. Like I've offended him. "You should never do that."

"I shouldn't?"

"Absolutely not."

"*You* don't love everyone you've been with." He couldn't possibly.

"I haven't loved anyone I've been with."

I don't know why, but this shocks me. "Really?"

"No."

"You don't mind that?"

"I love one thing about them in that moment. Sometimes it's enough."

"It must always be enough, if you've never loved *any* of them."

"I guess it was always about me. It wasn't really about them."

I think about this. "Maybe that's what I need to do. Maybe it's time for me to change my rule."

"I don't think so," he whispers. His finger lightly twirls an end strand of my hair. "Let me ask you this: what would make you love someone?"

"I don't know. I guess I would expect to feel something different and profound. Something I could recognize for what it is. My mother told me that when she met my father, she knew within five minutes she'd marry him. She said he stood out like a king among thieves. That's how she put it, which I still remember. I'd never heard her say anything so … poetic before. He was taller and more colorful and so much more handsome than anyone else, she said. She fell in love with him on the spot. She knew he was the one from that very first day."

"Wow."

"Yeah. It's so romantic."

He tucks a strand of my hair behind my ear. It's an intimate gesture. "Does that mean you believe in love at first sight?"

"Yes. I have to, because of them. Do you?"

His pause feels heavy with sincerity. "I didn't, before. But now I do."

"Before what?"

Vaughn doesn't answer my question. "Just to clarify, does everything you just said about only being kissed three times and not wanting to have sex with someone you don't love mean …?" He pauses and there's a hopefulness to him. Like my virginity is something to be marveled at.

I don't happen to find anything marvelous about it. "Yes. "

"Really?" His breath becomes heavier. Then, like he doesn't believe me. "Not at all?"

"Not even a little. I don't even know what it feels like to …" This is embarrassing.

"To …?"

"I've never even …"

His eyebrows lift. "You've never had an orgasm?"

I hate that this makes me blush. Again. I'm not used to talking about it. "No."

"Ever?" Shocked, as though this is the most outrageous thing he's ever heard.

"No. Not once." I bite my lip. I don't mention that I *have* tried, a few times in the dark of night. To touch myself when the urges rise up like a fever. But I've never been able to do it. To *get myself off*, as Rose puts it. And now I hate that I'm so naïve and he's so … not.

"Poor little Gi," he says softly. Reading my expression, he touches two fingers under my chin, until I'm looking into the dark, fathomless pools of his violet eyes. "That's good, you know why?"

"Why?"

"It's good you waited. Because this is perfect. It was always supposed to be me."

Damn him. It's almost like … he's right. It's also like he just casually and outrightly offered to *give me an orgasm.*

I do my best to breeze past my inhibitions. Tonight is sprinkled in fairy dust, in so many ways. And I make my decision. If Vaughn Tucker is offering what I think he's offering … *I'm going to let him.* "My sisters describe things."

"What kind of things?" He leans closer, tilting his head, almost touching his mouth to mine. Teasing me now, like he can see my decision in the depths of my eyes.

"What … different things … feel like."

There's a playfulness to him, and a certainty. *It was always supposed to be me.* Slowly, he plants a soft kiss on my neck, lingering there. His body is unbelievably hard but his lips are the softest thing. I feel the touch of his tongue, which sends a dart of pleasure to my core. His voice is low and smoky, his words slow and soft. "Did they tell you what it feels like to have your dress peeled down and your nipples sucked on like two sweet, ripe cherries until they're sore and hard and so sensitive it makes you moan and beg for more?"

Oh my God. "No," I whisper.

Very gently, Vaughn brushes his lips across mine. The light, erotic contact sends another zing of his dazzling heat to the tips of my nipples, to the low pit of my stomach, to my pussy, which feels warm. He slides the capped sleeves of my dress over my shoulders. "Did they tell you how good it's going to feel when I rip off your panties and eat your pink, juicy pussy like a ripe peach, dipping my tongue inside because I'm starved for you and there's nothing I wouldn't do to get you hot and wet and ready for me?"

God. "No," I gasp.

He touches his tongue to my plump bottom lip. "What about how good it's going to feel when I slide two fingers around your clit and suck the top nice and slow until you come in my mouth? Until your honey is all over my tongue?"

My clit is pulsing gently. My panties, all of a sudden, are saturated.

"You want me to show you what all that feels like, don't you, darlin'?"

Yes.

He eases my dress lower, over my full breasts, freeing them with a gentle bounce. My nipples tighten in the cool air of the air-conditioned limo. He makes a sound, like a growl. "*Gi.* Fuck. Look at you. You're so fucking gorgeous."

Vaughn palms my breasts in his warm hands almost worshipfully, his fingers roughly rolling my sensitive nipples. I moan because it feels *so good*.

"That's my girl. You like it rough, don't you, baby? You don't even *know* how dirty you like it. But I do. I can tell you're as wild as they come." His lips are close to mine. "Say it to me. Say *kiss me, Vaughn. Lick me. Eat my pussy real good. Do it rough and hot. Dirty me and make me come hard, like only you can.* Say it."

"*Kiss me, Vaughn,*" I whisper.

He takes my mouth in a drugging kiss, opening me, his tongue stroking mine hotly.

I don't really know how to kiss. But my instincts and my cravings guide me. He tastes too good. I open to his demand as he kisses me with long, lush ferocity until I'm beyond the threshold of rationality, existing in a different realm, of lust and beauty and needy, willing acceptance. Everything about him is so *addictive*. I writhe against him, wanting to get closer. Hungry for more of him, I suck on his tongue.

He groans deeply. "*Gi.* I'm so damn *hot* for you, darlin'. I could come right now."

I want to provoke him. I curl my hands around his neck into his thick, silky hair, holding him close as he kisses me, his tongue pushing into my mouth greedily, in and out.

Still kissing me, Vaughn lays me back. He kisses my neck, moving lower to lick my nipple. He takes one of the tight buds between his teeth and bites softly until I squirm. Then he draws it into his mouth and sucks deep, laving his tongue over the underside of the tip until it's rosy and wet.

"This is what I'm going to do to your clit, baby, just like this." He sucks harder. I feel each volt of greedy suction in my pussy, which tingles with a sweet, silky ache. "I'm about to make you come so hard it's going to change your life, Gi. I'm going to blow your mind with pleasure and ruin you for anyone else."

I don't bother telling him he already has.

He takes his time, working my slippery nipples, letting one slide from his mouth only to rub and squeeze the tight peak with this fingers as he takes the other. "Mine," he growls.

I'm already getting close. To something. To the most profound thing that's ever happened to me. "*Vaughn.*"

"If I reach down into your panties right now and rub my fingers like this—" He rubs and squeezes one nipple as he sucks the other and, *oh my god, something's happening*— "over your little pink clit, you'd come, wouldn't you, darlin'? You're so close. You want me to do it so bad."

All I can do is moan because *yes*.

"You ready for me to kiss you, baby? I need to see you." He unzips my dress. The elastic of the fabric allows him to peel it over my hips. His thumb catches my panties and before I know it all I'm wearing is my heeled sandals.

Vaughn pauses to look at me, breathing hard, like he's starstruck. "What are you doing to me, Gi? *Look* at you. Christ Almighty. You're so fucking sweet. My strawberry blond girl, so wet for me. I'm going to taste every perfect inch of you."

Vaughn pulls his shirt over his head and tosses it aside. His muscles are bunched and coiled with his movement as he prepares to do … whatever he's going to do. His face, the mane of his hair, the outline of his broad, muscled, inked shoulders. The man is an absolute specimen of masculine magnificence, all sculpted and dominating and blue-eyed. *I want all of it.*

His hands are on me as his tongue dips into my navel, making me squirm, but he won't let me move. "When I first saw you, I couldn't believe you were real. I didn't know anyone could be so flawless. And it's *this* spot right here I knew I had to taste." He kisses and licks the smooth skin of my stomach. "Damn, you drive me crazy."

He moves lower, holding me down with his rough, iron-strong hands. And it's then that Vaughn kisses me *there*, touching his tongue lightly to my pussy. I wind my fingers through his hair because I need to hold onto him. I need an anchor. And I need him to stay there, and get closer. To give me more. He's gentle at first, licking and murmuring against my tender skin. *Your pussy is the sweetest thing I ever tasted, Gi. Like the most exotic, juicy, perfect fruit. God help me, you're so beautiful. You taste so fucking good.*

His tongue begins to lick, burrowing and exploring. He takes his time. Opening me, licking with open-mouthed gusto, wetting his face. Little starry jolts of pleasure vibrate through my body at the lewd, flicking touch. His fingers slide as his lips close over the tiny nub of my clit, licking and sucking that acutely sensitive peak into his mouth. With careful insistence, he sucks in furtive pulls as his tongue flicks and delves.

The pleasure begins in my belly, rushing up in a building, excruciating surge that consumes me in dazzling bursts. My pussy spasms and clenches around his invading tongue. He keeps it there, *tasting* my pleasure. *Drinking* it.

After a while, the ripples begin to ease. "*Vaughn.*"

"Shh, I'm in heaven. And just getting started. I need more. I'm addicted, darlin'. There's no escaping me now."

He takes my hips in his hands and twists my body slightly so my legs are spread wider, with one knee wrapped around his neck. I'm naked, trembling, with the aftershocks of pleasure still radiating through my body. I'm being held aggressively in place, even more open to his hungry, feasting mouth. The silk of his hair tickles the soft skin of my inner thighs. The stubble of his beard scratches against my sensitive flesh. His fingers slide through the moisture, circling, rubbing my clit in careful circles, and I can feel the bliss begin all over again.

He eats me in lusty mouthfuls, licking me *everywhere*. His tongue pushes into a *very* intimate place, playing me there as his fingers skate over my clit. I moan because my next orgasm is waiting there, the pleasure being drawn from my body by the unrelenting hunger of his mouth. "You like it dirty, baby. You're a wild little thing, aren't you? You want everything."

I do. I'll go to hell with him if it feels this good.

I feel lust-drunk. Sprung tight with need. The pleasure is a tidal wave, building, even higher than it was before. I sway against him, in tune with the rhythm of his filthy mouth and his sublime, slippery fingers.

"You ready, darlin'? You want me to take you higher than you've ever been?"

He already is. I'm on some kind of crazy precipice of pleasure that might just tip me over the edge of sanity. *"Please, Vaughn."*

He breathes his hot breath on my wet, swollen pussy, blowing on my clit. Then he slides his tongue into me, in and out, in and out, stroking the wave higher. And higher. He replaces this movement with his fingers as he, very lightly, draws the center of my universe into his mouth, milking it in greedy pulls.

The wave crashes through my body in mind-blowing clenches that wrack through my core, sending zinging jolts through my entire being. My pussy clenches tightly around Vaughn's fingers, over and over. I cry out as my body spasms and quivers with the overload of pleasure.

It lasts a long time. Vaughn licks me gently, spinning the ripples further, feasting devoutly on my pleasure and my essence like I'm made of nectar.

"Vaughn."

"Right here, baby." He kisses my clit slowly.

"Come here." I gently tug on his hair and he moves up my body lays himself over me. As he does this he wipes his muscular forearm across his mouth. Which for some reason is the sexiest thing I've ever seen.

He stares deeply into my eyes and I know in that

moment, I do: *I love him.* I love what he just did to me. And the way he did it, so lustily and hungrily, like only he would have. No one ever tells you it changes your life.

"You all right, darlin'?" he drawls. He's hot as hell—and so rock-hard it hurts, pressed against me—but there's a lazy satisfaction to his question. The alpha male in him has given me more pleasure than I've ever had and I know for sure that what he just did to me was extraordinary, as these things go. He knows that too.

I kiss his lips, tasting *myself* as my pussy pulses with the lingering ripples, like I'm still coming a little. "I want to taste *you.*"

He grins, laughing lightly, but his eyes are wild. "I'm yours to do whatever you want with. Just name it."

In answer, I sit up and I push at his big body until he lays back. He lets me do this and I climb onto him. Something about back-to-back stellar orgasms brings out every primal urge I've ever had—and then some. I don't care that I'm naked. I'm *glad.* I like the way his eyes darkly rove the curves of my body. My breasts feel full. My nipples are sore from his rough beard. My pussy is wet and still pulsing with the after-effects of his greedy mouth.

I run my fingers over the dusting of hair on his inked chest. Tracing the lines of one of his tattoos, a beautifully-drawn snake that winds over his shoulder, I love the feel of his warm skin. I kiss the rose on his chest. Then I run my tongue over his nipple, playing with the small ring piercing he has.

He laughs. "You're going to make me blow before you even reach the bullseye, honey."

I know what he means. My sisters have told me, of course. "Not yet." I don't know where this is coming from but I can't help it. My wild thing isn't just loose, she's *hungry*. "I want to lick you and suck on you."

His pupils swallow up most of the blue of his irises, making him look dangerous. "I bet you do, you sweet, dirty girl. I bet you want me to cover you all over in my cum."

I can control him with my touch. "I do. I want to feel you."

"Put your sweet mouth on me, baby."

I let my fingers rove over the defined six-pack of his abs, fascinated by the quilted muscles and the arrow line of dark hair.

Carefully, I ease his zipper lower. It's hard to do because his jeans are practically bursting. The hard ridge of him underneath the layer of denim is freaking *huge*. He helps me, unfastening and easing his jeans lower. He reaches in and frees himself. His cock springs out and ... *holy fuck*.

I don't usually swear, even in my own thoughts, but *come on*.

I knew what to expect ... but not the *size* of it. The thick, hard, veiny, beautiful length. It's engorged and hot-looking.

I never expected it to be so ... appealing. So carnally

freaking addictive. *I want to rub myself against it and take it into my mouth.*

I want to play. To taste. To feel.

I take his huge shaft in my hands and he groans in a rough-edged sigh.

This is it. My sisters have described so much about the male anatomy and what happens to it when you … do certain things. But nothing really prepares you for the reality.

It's different than I thought it would be. His cock is heavy and outrageously hard. It's silky and hot to the touch. A pearl of moisture seeps from the slit.

Gently, I lean down and touch my tongue to the pearl, lapping lightly. The salty milkiness is earthy and male. I feel changed by him already. Here's my elixir. *Here's* my wild side, right here. *This* is my trigger. Vaughn Tucker's sinful mouth and his huge, perfect cock.

I take the broad head between my lips, sucking gently, licking him with my tongue.

"Oh, fuck."

One of my sisters once said to me, *a man will fall in love with you if you suck his cock. And if you drink him, he'll marry you.*

Anyway, I'm not looking to marry Vaughn Tucker.

But I do want to drink him.

I want to make him feel good.

I want him to feed me with his wild, gushing rush.

I've never had thoughts or cravings like this before.

With Vaughn, I'm not myself. Either that, or I'm more myself than I've ever been.

My fingers explore as my tongue licks, swirling the moisture. I squeeze him carefully as I rub my fist along his length. I take him deeper, sucking more hungrily now, taking as much as I can.

His answering groan adds fuel to my fire. It's the hottest sound I've ever heard. A sort of deep, animal growl. A surrender.

There's a feminine power to this I wasn't expecting. He's completely at my mercy in this moment. The world famous rock god is under my loving spell. He's *mine* and I *love* this. The realization makes me greedier and I suck him more strongly. I want him to lose control. I want to overwhelm him with pleasure.

I've never done this before but I feel like I have a knack when it comes to Vaughn Tucker. I can read his pleasure. I can tell what he likes.

The string of oaths he groans are the dirtiest I've ever heard.

His cock surges in my mouth and I can feel in my hands the pumping gush as he floods my mouth with his cum. Wave after wave of warm, milky liquid. I swallow as much as I can but there's too much. It spills, wetting my face and my breasts.

And he's still coming.

The ripples calm and I drink the last surges of his release, taking my time, licking him tenderly. Taking more. I can feel his seedy life force inside me. I'm full of it. It's all over me. I'm anointed with his perfection. I feel golden and sticky and blessed. I kiss his wet, still-pulsing length. It's softer now but not completely. I love the weighted bulk of it in my hands.

"Gi," he rasps. "Come here, baby."

I climb up his body and he takes me in his arms, staring at me like I'm a vision he can't believe. He smooths my hair. He takes my face in his warm hands and kisses my lips.

"Come on tour with me. Come with me."

His request breaks the trance slightly. When I'm sucking his cock I feel reckless and free, weirdly. When he's confronting me with the craziness of his lifestyle and the reality of all that comes with it, I'm unsteady. Of course it's best if we leave it like this. I already knew that when I let things get this out of hand. "No. I can't. I have classes and work and then an essay due——"

"Gi. *Please.*" There's an urgency in his voice that's new. "Can't you do all that online? Can't the dipshit take notes for you?"

The limo is slowing down and I look out the tinted windows to see the familiar landscape of the road I live on. Our mailbox. We're turning into my driveway.

The magic bubble we've been living in for the past few hours bursts, sort of suddenly and heart-breakingly. I can't go on *tour* with him. That's crazy. "I'll see you after the tour, maybe. If you still want to."

He sits us up and he's still holding my face between his hands. "If I *want* to? Of course I want to. Doesn't what we've just done mean anything to you?"

I'm a little taken aback by his intensity. "Of course it does. It means everything."

He's quiet for a few seconds as the gravity of what I just said hangs in the air. "Then come with me."

How do I tell him what I'm thinking? That even though it's true, that this *did* mean everything—to me, at least—I also know there will be a long line of girls outside Vaughn's door tonight offering to do everything I've just done. And more. A lot more. Because we haven't really even gotten started. And he'll be everything to them too. "I can't, Vaughn."

"Why not?"

"Because. I have things I need to do."

"Cancel them."

Of course they're not as important as the things *he* needs to do. "I can't *cancel* them."

"You can."

"I can't just pick up and leave, Vaughn."

"Why not?"

"Because. It doesn't work that way."

"It *does*. It could. We can *make* it work, Gi."

"No. I can't." *I'm falling. I'm falling.* And it's too fast.

We've pulled up in front of my house. I'm thankful the limo has tinted windows as I find my dress and pull it over my head. I see the curtain move at Rose's window. I texted her much earlier in the evening to let her know I would be out late. She has no idea who I've been with but she'll be curious. And she's a light sleeper.

Vaughn tilts my chin, forcing me to look at him. He wipes away some sticky moisture—some of him—with his thumb. "Gi. I *mean* it. I want you to come with me."

"Vaughn. My life isn't your life." I regret it as soon as it comes out: "But thank you for dinner. I had fun."

"*Fun?* For fuck's sake, Gi. We just got each other off like no one ever has and you drank my cum. You had more than *fun*. I *need* you. Come with me."

I need you.

Oh, no. Not that. Anything but that.

I touch my fingertips to his square jaw. Gently, I kiss his lips, summoning every ounce of strength I possess and willing myself not to break down or give in. I've already admitted to myself that I love him. Or at least that I could love him, in time.

No. You love him right now.

But he's Vaughn Tucker. *Everyone* loves him. What am I going to do, follow him around like a love-struck puppy while he tours? Like all the rest of them do? I've seen the videos of all his rabid fans, screaming and crying because they all want a piece of him. I've read the articles. Maybe he had moments like this with some of them too. Maybe that's why they're so desperate for more, who would know.

It's a scenario that's a perfect storm for heartbreak. The devastating kind. The kind you never really get over.

Besides, my life is here. "Goodnight, Vaughn. Don't follow me, okay? Don't try to change my mind."

Before I *do* change my mind, I grab my bag—not bothering to search for my long-lost panties—and open the car door.

"Have a good tour," I say, before walking away.

"Gi, for *fuck's sake*." He stuffs himself back into his jeans and zips up. He gets out of the limo but I turn to face him and raise my palm in a gesture to stop him as I take steps backwards.

His face is the most beautiful thing I've ever seen. Even though his expression is as devastated as I feel.

I blow him a kiss.

Then I turn and walk to my door.

9

VAUGHN

I TAKE a few steps toward her as she walks up the stairs of her porch. The curtain moves aside in an upstairs window.

Faintly, I can see Rose's face and her eyes are wide.

I'm shirtless. My jeans are mostly done up but I'm half-cocked again, even though I just came harder than I ever have in my life. There's cum on my stomach. *Even though she swallowed as much as she could.* There was too much. A whole evening of being close to her, grinding up against her on the dance floor, touching her. It was agonizing. The release was otherworldly. I'm still dazed from the magnitude of my orgasm and the rapture of her insanely beautiful touch.

I can't really go banging on her door like this. It might shock her mother.

Don't follow me, okay? Don't try to change my mind.

To hell with that.

My phone rings in my back pocket. I pull it out. Roxie. I don't answer because I know what she's going to say. I can already hear the mantra. *Where are you? Are you on your way? Don't be late. Don't hold up a sold-out show of 75,000.*

It stops ringing, but a few seconds later a text comes through.

> There's a private jet at the airport waiting
> for you. They said you haven't arrived yet.
> Please don't be late, Vaughn. I hope
> you're okay.

It's that last line that gets me. She cares. They all care. But I don't even feel like going on this tour. I need a break.

I need to be with Gigi.

I don't bother analyzing the spin of my thoughts or how deep my craving goes. I don't want one night. *I want all her nights.* I want to feast on that gorgeous girl with her candy-pink pussy and her mouth like the sweetest heaven every minute of every day for the rest of my goddamn life.

She's so insanely pure and at the same time hot as fuck.

God help me.

I need more of my golden girl. My Gi. Gigi Hayes. Mine.

Ginger Hayes Tucker has a nice ring to it.

WTF?

I don't care what I sound like.

Her eyes, all fiery with lust. *I want to lick you and suck on you.* Her mouth, wet and plump and shiny with my cum.

My cock is rock-hard and my heartbeat feels hot. I'm closer to the edge—of what, I'm not sure—than I've been before. Walking away from her feels wrong. It's too soon. It'll always be too soon.

Taking one last torment-filled glance at Gigi's now-closed red front door, I get back into the limo. I press the intercom button. "I need to get to the airport as fast as you can get me there."

We roll out and the curtain in the upstairs window is closed now. I take the bottle of champagne out of the ice bucket and chug the whole thing.

By the time we get to the airport, I'm already well on the way to being completely shitfaced. The private jet is waiting but there's some hold up and we wait on the tarmac for a while before we finally take off.

Why wouldn't she fucking come *with* me?

She'd rather sit through a few boring classes about learning how to *help* people than come with me on tour? What kind of insane logic is that?

Why is it that every woman I've ever met in my entire goddamn life would *kill* to come with me wherever I go … except the one woman I actually *want* to come with me wherever I go?

Approximately fifty-seven percent of the population of planet Earth would sell their soul for the offer I just gave her. They stalk me relentlessly. They cry with rapture when I touch them and beg me not to leave. They sneak into my hotel rooms and fangirl all over me every chance they get.

But not her.

Oh, no, not sweet, innocent little Gigi.

Sweet, delectable little Gigi, with her honey-sweet pussy and her silky, sun-bleached hair. With her cool, careful hands. With her deliciously perfect nipples and the soft moans she makes as she comes hard with my tongue inside her.

Goddamn it!

I grab a fistful of my hair, knocking my empty glass off the tray table where it rolls across the floor. The flight attendant comes over. "Is everything all right, Mr. Tucker?"

No. Everything is not all right. Not by a long shot. "Bring me another one."

I'm usually not this much of an asshole but today I don't care.

She hasn't even agreed to come to one of our shows.

How am I supposed to wait two and a half *weeks* before I can see her again?

What kind of twisted karma serves me up a slice of Ginger Hayes only to then *deny* me?

Fuck you, universe!

I get up out of my seat as the flight attendant hands me another drink. I tip the whole goddamn thing back and hand the glass back to him as he stares at me. "Can I bring you anything else, Mr. Tucker?"

You can turn this plane around and take me back to her. "You can bring the whole damn bottle."

Of course I can't let them all down. They'd have to cancel the shows and it would be my fault. As much as I'd like to quit the tour and head back to my cabin in the woods that's within an easy walk of the gorgeous small town goddess that for some reason has rocked my world off its axis with a sultry blink of her golden eyes, I'm not going to do that to my family.

I make my way back toward the luxury bedroom. The flight attendant hands me the bottle of Jack. I take it and I close the door behind me. There's a plush king-sized bed and a table with two reclining chairs by the window. I sit in one of them and drink some more of the whiskey. Maybe it'll help me.

If nothing else, it might dull the pain. The old pain. And the new.

It's times like these when the memories are hardest to bear. When I feel closest to him, like his weaknesses are tainting me. His blood is my blood. The tendencies are all there and I hate that part of myself.

I hate that I'm so much like my father.

Even more—much more—I hate that she went with him. I hate that I drove her straight into his downward spiral and it cost my mother her life.

My fault.

My biggest, most painfully horrible regret. The one that feels like a ball and chain around my heart. It'll never heal, either. It can't, because she's gone. They're both gone and I was a big part of what happened that night and I can't ever bring them back.

Maybe it's best this way.

Gigi doesn't deserve me. Look at me. I'm a mess. I'd ruin her life.

She's better off without me.

I'd only do what my father did to my mother.

The whiskey is providing a buffer. I drink more of it, washing down a couple of Xanax along with it, until my demons retreat. Until I almost feel like I can bear it.

I don't know how Gi managed to do what she did today.

So easily.

So instantly.

The softness of her glance. The sweet, gentle sassiness of her response to me was so damn *soothing*, somehow. A cool tonic to the hot fever of my own angst, like she was injecting calmness into my veins with her gentle presence and her peaceful understanding.

I want more of it. So much more.

I fucking need it.

I can't remember the schedule. Maybe there's a day off after the first or second show. I'll fly back to Tennessee mid-week if I get a chance.

Hell.

This is bad.

I don't have her cell phone number. I'm not going to call her landline because I know she wouldn't answer. Rose would. And Gigi would refuse to come to the phone.

I don't even have a photo of her.

I pull my phone out of my pocket and I google her.

But there's nothing.

I scroll further.

What kind of person doesn't have any kind of digital footprint at all?

A small town girl, that's what kind.

I try Ginger Hayes.

There's a Ginger Hayes who lives in Detroit, Michigan. She's a high school principal. Another in Oregon.

The boarding school must not have listed stats or achievements, like some schools do.

So I google Ruby.

There are articles about her upcoming tour with us.

A few photos from Ruby's press release that Roxie organized.

The marriage last year of Scarlett Eleanor Hayes to John James Williams, a mechanic from Knoxville. The bride in the photo looks enough like Gigi and Ruby to figure out that she's a sister. Must be the oldest. There's a birth announcement. Clementine Sophia Hayes Williams.

There's an obituary for Charles Joseph Hayes.

The address matches.

Her father. The obituary is brief. *Charlie was a skilled carpenter who ran a small farm. He leaves behind his loving wife Robin and his four daughters, Scarlett, Rose, Ginger and Ruby.*

Cause of death: a sudden illness.

Which usually means either a heart attack or a drug overdose. Gigi mentioned a heart attack. She paused before she said it, though. Which makes me wonder if she was hiding something.

Maybe Gigi Hayes has secrets of her own.

THE EFFECTS of the Xanax are starting to numb me.

I crawl onto the bed, letting my phone fall out of my hand. My head is spinning.

Visions of her beauty consume my brain. The feel of her touch overwhelms my memories. Her face. Her body. *Her mouth.*

I need her. She's the most potent addiction I've ever had.

Eventually, I fall into a fitful sleep.

Several hours later, I wake to a knock on the door. "Mr. Tucker?"

I groan. My hangover feels like someone has implanted a jackhammer into my brain.

"Mr. Tucker?" Another insistent knock. "We'll be landing in forty-five minutes. Your meal is waiting and we'll need you in your seat with your seatbelt fastened for landing."

"Give me ten minutes," I call out to him.

"Yes, sir."

I check my phone. It's 5:25 pm.

There are twelve messages from Roxie.

And none from Gigi.

I text Roxie and tell her I'll be on time or close to it. Then I peel off my clothes and stumble into the shower.

As I put on some clean clothes, I dig around in my bag. In the buttoned pocket of a denim shirt, where I stashed it, I find the small baggie of coke. I do a few lines, hoping it'll clear my head. Then I do a few more, hoping it'll make me feel like I'm not being crushed alive under the weight of my regrets, my brutal hangover, and the fact that I'm jonesing so bad for Gigi Hayes I think I might be about to lose my fucking mind.

The perks of a private jet.

By the time I leave the bedroom I'm almost feeling human again.

The guy serves me some breakfast. I'm not hungry but I drink a bottle of water and some coffee. I add a third of my flask to it, checking my phone again.

Nothing.

We land and a limo picks me up and takes me to the Coliseum. My head is buzzing and my heart is beating fast.

Shit, I might have done a line too many.

I hardly care.

When I get to our dressing room, Kade is strapping on his guitar and Ruby is sitting on Travis's lap in a chair in the corner. He's kissing her and I feel a pang. Of longing.

I want to be kissing my *girl.*

And she looks too much like her sister. A reminder that makes me feel like putting my fist through the nearest wall.

Roxie walks over to me. "Vaughn. *Jesus.* Where have you been?"

I smile at her. "Told you I'd be on time, sweetheart."

"You're not on time. You're late. Ruby finished her set twenty minutes ago."

"Yeah? How'd it go?"

Ruby looks up at me and she's all starry-eyed. "It was amazing."

"That's great, kid. Well done."

Roxie's checking out my new shiner. "Vaughn, what is this? You got into *another* fight? Where have you been?" she asks again.

"It was nothing. I went out. With a friend." I glance at Travis but he's too preoccupied with Ruby to be suspicious of anything. Which is good. I don't really feel like another punch-up.

I'm fucking *flying* right now.

Roxie's contemplating me, probably noticing how

dilated my pupils are. "Vaughn," she says softly. Like she's genuinely worried about me.

But I don't feel like being studied. Or scolded. Or worried about. "Are we ready to do this or what? Let's go."

We do our pre-show huddle like we always do. It's a good luck thing we've been doing since the beginning. After, Kade takes me aside and says it out of earshot to the others: "What are you doing, bud? You've been acting different the past couple days. I can tell by your eyes you're high as a damn kite."

How to explain? "It's nothing. I'm fine."

"You're taking it too far, brother. You're walking a fine line."

"I know. Between heaven and hell."

"Don't force us to check you into a goddamn rehab."

"Wouldn't dream of it."

He's not happy with me and neither is Roxie but it's showtime so I escape further lecturing. When we walk out onto the stage the entire stadium erupts in cheers and applause.

That shit never gets old.

75,000 screaming fans.

And one little country girl whose smile is the only balm to my battered soul … and who's a long way away tonight. Who refused to come with me. Who's inspiring thoughts I've never had before. Of gifts and weeks alone with her and happily ever afters.

I climb up into my drum set and pick up my sticks. Then I tap out a couple of beats and we're on.

I play my heart out. I'm so amped up I punish my drums like a maniac. An inspired one, who's been sprinkled with stardust. It might be the best I've ever played. A magical cocktail. The touch of a goddess mixed with an unprecedented longing, whiskey and several grams of cocaine lifts me into some plane I'm not sure I've ever occupied before. And I'm feeling it.

We play for three and a half hours and do three encores.

By the time we get back to the dressing room, the effects of the coke are long gone. The room is spinning and I hold onto the wall for support. It doesn't hold me up though and I end up on the ground. I close my eyes and wait for the spinning to stop.

That's when the world goes black.

I WAKE up in a hotel room. My family and some voices I don't recognize are talking and at one point someone's taking my blood pressure and pulse.

A while later, Travis and Roxie get up to leave. Travis pats me on the head carefully and replies to something Kade has said. "Yeah, I think so." Roxie kisses my cheek, "Love you, Vaughn."

"Love you too, honey." My whisper is hoarse.

As Travis and Roxie leave, I see that a crowd of groupies and fans are gathered outside my door trying to get in. The wall of security keeps them out.

I'm glad.

How could I ever have wanted to *be* with any of them? They're like faraway pinpricks of light next to Gigi's hot, giant star.

I miss her so much it hurts.

How the hell did she make me want her so damn much, and so easily? When so many women have tried and failed?

Kade sits silently in a chair for a while. We're alone now. The room is dark except for the glow of city lights outside the window. There's commotion in the hallway but after a while it quiets.

The quiet feels so damn good.

"What's going on with you, Vaughn?" My brother sounds strung out.

And I know him well enough to know that he'll sit here all night until he gets an answer. Kade has a calmness to him, a stoic steadiness that for some reason helps my state of mind right now.

I'm not really high anymore but the lingering effects still course through my veins. There's a lucidity in the aftermath. A clarity that can be hard to come by. "You know that night of the car crash?" I ask him.

It takes him a few seconds to answer. "Yeah." We all remember that night like it was yesterday. It's etched into our collective consciousness as though carved there by the devil's blowtorch.

"I argued with him."

"So did I."

I glance over at him. "Yeah?"

"Yeah." The pronouncement is a heavy one.

Maybe it wasn't entirely my fault. "What did you say?"

"I told him to sleep it off before he ended up killing himself. Or someone else." He exhales a humorless chuckle. "It didn't help, though, did it?" After another brief, contemplative silence, Kade asks me, "What did you say?"

"I told him he was dragging our mother down with him and that he didn't deserve her. I told him he should leave. So he did. And she refused to let him go without her."

He leans forward, letting his elbows rest on his knees. "Vaughn, it wasn't your fault he drank too much. It wasn't your fault he left that night. And it wasn't your fault she went with him. It was his fault. And hers. For loving him too much, despite everything."

My brother's words spear directly into the heart of my sorrow. Because he might be right, even though I've never seen it that way. "But if I hadn't said—"

"Or if *I* hadn't said what *I* said. Or if he hadn't done what he did. Or if she hadn't insisted on going down with his doomed ship. None of those ifs can change what happened that night. Or the years building up to that night. We probably never could have changed it. I wish their fate didn't feel like it was always pre-written. But it does. They made the choices they made because they were always going to. You have to let it go."

His words don't entirely convince me but I'm glad they're out there, hanging in the air like little lifeboats I can try to cling to. I realize I haven't really *looked* at Kade in a while and something about him catches me off guard. It's the sadness, under the cool force of his presence. "You should break up with her," I tell him.

"What?"

"You should break up with Carmen. She's not good for you."

He stares at me for a few seconds. Then he leans back in his chair. "You think?"

"Yeah. Get rid of her."

"She wants to get married."

"Hell, man, if you marry her you'll condemn yourself to a life of misery. Look at you. I've never seen you this unhappy."

His eyes are blue even in the darkness. "God knows she's doing everything she can to convince me it's the real thing. But you're right. Something's missing. Something that should be there just … isn't."

"*Fun* is missing. Laughter and joy and having a good fucking *time* is missing, bro. You've got to free yourself—ASAP—and find someone who makes you happy. Okay?"

"I'll think about it."

"What's there to think about, Kade? Make a clean break. Go and have some fun. You won't know yourself."

"I wonder if it's possible to actually *tell* if you're in love with someone," Kade says, sort of philosophically.

"It is. It absolutely is."

"How do you know?"

I don't answer and he tunes in to my silence, taking it as some kind of clue.

"Who is she?" Then, like something has clicked. "Is *that* what this bender is all about? A girl?"

"No." I'm not ready to talk about this. It feels too new and too sacred. I don't want to jinx it.

But my brother is freakishly perceptive. "Don't tell me it's Ruby's sister."

"No. I don't know what you're talking about."

And irritatingly savvy. "The one you met for five minutes in her mother's kitchen."

I exhale mockingly. "Her? As if."

"The studious one, with the glasses and the banging body."

I don't answer. *He noticed that?* I have to force myself not to react. To remain calm with the knowledge that *everyone* notices how gorgeous she is. All those people she sees on a daily basis and *I'm not there.*

"Is *that* why you jumped off the bus?"

"No."

"Hell, Vaughn."

"You're way off."

He laughs softly and stands up. "So that's why Travis went apeshit."

"Travis goes apeshit every five minutes. Hardly breaking news."

"Get some sleep." He goes to the door, adding on his way out, "Travis sent both sisters plane tickets and backstage passes, by the way. I'm not sure for which show. Apparently one of them might be too busy. But the other one is trying to talk her into it."

"And I should care because …?"

At least I've lightened his mood. "See you tomorrow, Vaughn."

"Not if I see you first. Hopefully you'll be single by then."

After he leaves, I reach for my phone. I don't keep it on me when I perform because it distracts me.

I fish it out of my bag and—

Holy fuck.

There's a message.

From her.

It's from two hours ago.

She's sent the photo of the painting I asked her for, along with a short message.

> I can't accept the car. You'll have to take it back. I had a good time last night. I hope the tour goes well. xo, Gigi

We've discussed this. You had two killer orgasms. You swallowed mouthfuls of my hot cum. You had more than a good time.

There's no mention about her wanting to see me again. Or about how she's pining for me as badly as I am for her.

I add her as a contact and press the call button.

It rings ten times. I know because I count each excruciating ring.

Come on, my little Gi, with the sunflower soul and the rock 'n roll eyes. Pick up.

No answer.

10

I CLOSE the door behind me and lean against it for a few seconds. Rose is coming down the stairs so I head for my room, hoping to escape her inquisition—even though there's not a snowball's chance in hell of that happening. "I don't feel like talking right now, Rose." But I was never going to get away from her that easily.

She follows me into my bedroom, closing the door behind us. Her eyes are wide with zealous excitement. "You were out with *Vaughn Tucker*? Are you *kidding* me? I thought you were going out with Dylan. What happened?"

She takes a long look at me, noticing my disheveled hair, my wrinkled dress, my swollen lips from his punishing kisses, and quite possibly the wild, I've-just-come-twice-and-it-was-the-most-intense-and-magical-thing-that's-ever-happened-in-my-life look in my eyes. *I hope his cum isn't still on my face or somehow still visible.*

"You had *sex* with him?"

"No." I go into the bathroom but she follows me in there. "*Rose.* Do you mind?"

She closes the toilet seat and sits on it. "Tell me everything."

I take a long look at myself in the mirror and I look … amazing. My cheeks are flushed and my eyes are bright. I look like I just had the best night of my damn life. He's right too: my eyes do have starbursts of different shades of gold. I'd never really noticed that before.

"Where did you go?" Rose asks. "How did you run into Vaughn? I thought they already left for their tour. Does Ruby know?"

"I need to get ready for my class."

"No way. There's no way in hell I'm letting you go anywhere until you tell me what happened. Where did you go?"

I relent, only because I'll be late if I don't. "To Nashville."

"In a limo?"

"In a helicopter. What time is it?" I squeeze some toothpaste onto my toothbrush and start brushing my teeth.

"A *helicopter?* It's nine-thirty."

"Shit." I wash my face. "I have a class at ten. Is

anyone using the car?" And then I remember. Vaughn bought Momma a new car.

"Which one?" Rose asks. "The minivan or the freaking *Corvette*?"

"I know. I can't believe that."

"Gi, you *have* to tell me what's going on. Is the Corvette from Vaughn? Or Travis? Momma said it's for her. I don't get it."

"Vaughn bought it for her because she gave him a nice meal and some pie."

Rose is uncharacteristically silent for a few seconds. "Pie?"

"Yes."

"If he gives out Corvettes for a slice of pie, I wonder what he's going to give *you*. You look like you just banged the Dallas Cowboys. First and second strings."

"Would you stop? I won't get to class on time if I don't leave within the next five minutes." I spray on some perfume and attempt to smooth my hair. "And I already told you. I didn't have sex with him."

"I told you it would happen."

"What would happen?"

"The bad boy who shows up out of the blue and sweeps you off your feet in a goddamn *helicopter*! It was always your destiny. I can't believe I totally predicted this!" She's much more excited than I feel.

I've had my one night. Or close to it. And I'm glad I

didn't have sex with Vaughn Tucker. Because the thing is, I might have. I might have just kept going and done it with him right there in his limo if our trip home had been longer.

I push past her to get to my closet. I let my dress fall to the floor before I realize I'm not wearing anything underneath it.

I didn't wear a bra because the dress had one sort of built into it. I pull a clean sundress over my head, sneaking a glance at her. "I lost my panties." Rose starts laughing, which sets me off too. I don't know why. *Because everything is crazy. I rode in a helicopter and danced all night with Vaughn Tucker who then proceeded to give me two mind-blowing orgasms that feel like they've changed the alchemy of my soul.*

She comes over to me and holds both my hands. "Gi. Are you sure you didn't … ?"

"Of course I'm sure." My sisters don't believe in the concept of kiss and don't tell. I know she won't leave me alone until I give her at least something to chew on.

"But did he—?"

"What do you want to know, Rose? Did he *get me off?* Yes."

She squeals with delight. "*Oh my God.* Gi! Was it good?" She laughs, and claps her hands together, looking up to toward the sky like she's thanking our lucky stars. "What am I saying? *Of course* it was good."

"It was … I can't describe it. It was the most beautiful thing that's ever happened to me."

Rose squeals even louder. She hugs me. "I'm *so* happy for you, honey. Now you *finally* know what all the fuss is about. Or at least part of it. When are you going to see him again?"

"I don't know. Never, maybe. Or after his tour."

"Wrong. Guess what Ruby sent us last night. Travis insisted, she said."

"What?"

"Two first class tickets to Seattle. Three, actually, but Momma's got her bridge tournament that night and she doesn't want to miss it. She said she wants to wait until Ruby performs in Nashville."

"What are you talking about?"

"Two front row seats to their Seattle show. Two VIP back stage passes. And a suite in a five-star hotel."

"What?"

"Yes. Two weeks from Saturday. We're going, Gi. We're absolutely going. Ruby keeps texting me. She really wants us to come."

Wow. "I'll think about it."

"What do you mean you'll *think* about it? You just said he gave you—"

"I don't know if I want to see him again. Especially not in his natural habitat. The one where he sleeps with three women every night."

"Who cares?" I already know my sister is all about instant gratification when it comes to men. "You don't have to have a *relationship* with him, Gi. This is *Vaughn*

Tucker we're talking about. Have a one night stand with him. Cash in that overdue V-card with the hottest man on the planet."

I pick up my bag. "Even if I did want to do that—which I don't—who says he would want to?"

"Are you *kidding* me, Gi? Have you looked in the mirror lately? You're literally the most beautiful person I know, inside and out. Plus I'm going to give you a makeover. Time for you to work your assets, girl. You're going to put all those groupies he hangs out with to shame."

"Rose, the very last thing I want to do is compete with his damn groupies." I head toward the door. "I'll see you later."

"Trust me. There'll be no competition."

I roll my eyes. "Bye, Rose."

I head out the door, walking straight past the Corvette to the old minivan. The last thing I need right now is to feel closer to Vaughn Tucker than I already do.

By the time I get to my class, it's 9:59. I slide into my seat, which happens to be right next to Dylan's.

"Hey, Gigi." Sort of coldly, like he's pissed off at me.

I'm surprisingly unaffected by this. Before—*before Vaughn*—I would have felt bad about whatever I might have done to upset him, or anyone else. Today I feel different. More powerful, weirdly. "Hi, Dylan."

"How was your night?"

"It was … good. How was yours?"

"Not great. I was disappointed you skipped out on our date like that."

I take in his pout, his offended irritation, his rude presumption that I owe him something. "It wasn't a date, Dylan. It was dinner. And I didn't skip out." *I was swept off my feet by a drop-dead gorgeous rock god. Which was obviously a much better offer*, I almost say. *And I'm glad. Because I can still feel the lingering effects of my endorphin rush. I came so hard. Twice. And then I … God, I'm still full from drinking his cum.*

"Whatever," he mutters. Then, amazingly: "Can I borrow your notes for the essay due next week? You always take such good notes."

I think about the butterfly wing again. How I was always scared that something I might do—if it wasn't the kindest thing I possibly could do—would influence the future negatively. But now I realize there's more to it. I'm important too. *My* future and my well-being are just as important as Dylan's. And who knows, maybe creating the most beautiful life I possibly can for *myself* will influence other people in beautiful ways too. The things I do right now will begin to affect that. In this moment, I feel the power of my own control.

I decide to start using that control.

"Actually, I think you should take your own notes, Dylan. And I think you should buy your own book."

He stares at me, hurt. Or *disappointed*. Again. His favorite emotion.

But I'm spared more of his disappointment because

Professor Tate comes in and starts handing out papers. She stands next to my desk and hands me mine. "I saw the helicopter yesterday afternoon," she says to me. "Was that *Vaughn Tucker*, by any chance?"

"Um … yes, Professor. Yes, it was."

She winks at me, maybe noticing the color in my cheeks at the mention of his name. "I'm a big fan." Her voice is low, out of earshot of most of the room, except maybe Dylan. "Lucky you," she says, before walking back up to the front of the room. She starts writing a few names on the white board, including mine, along with a date and time.

Dylan scowls, but I tune him out.

"Some of you," Professor Tate says, "will begin your field work soon and I'm going to be meeting with you individually next week to discuss your placements."

I try to listen to the lecture but my thoughts keep spinning back to the night before. The glittering lights of dusk from the helicopter window. The husky, soulful tone of Vaughn's voice as he sang. The way he punched Wade Sullivan just for saying hi to me. Dancing until dawn. The limo ride. His erotic, drugging kisses. *Coming hard with his tongue inside me. Sucking on his big, bursting cock. Drinking his cum like I was starved for it.*

Hell.

Thinking about it now, I hardly recognize myself. My wild side indeed. I've never in my life been so completely … abandoned. So in the moment. So crazily *turned on.*

I wonder what he's doing right now. If he's thinking about me. Or if he's already moved on to someone else.

The lecture ends and I vaguely say goodbye to Dylan before making my way to my next class. The enlightenment of the past twelve hours and the total lack of sleep have left me lucid but dreamy.

I miss him.

I hope he's okay.

After my second class ends, I drive to the library, where I have a four hour shift.

It's my job to check out the books as people come to the desk or to help them find something. I'm printing out the list of newly reserved books that I'll need to find and mark and stack on the shelf behind the desk when I notice someone standing there.

"Hi, Gigi."

"Oh. Hi, Troy." Troy is a cop in training, he told me. He looks like one too. Stocky, pumped-up and slightly intimidating. He comes in almost every shift I have. "Do you need help with something?"

"Yeah. I want to get some books out."

"Anything in particular?"

"Can you help me search for something?"

"What are you interested in?"

"I don't know." He checks me out in a way that makes me feel uneasy. It's exactly this kind of thing that led me to wear loose-fitting clothes and thick-framed glasses in the first place. To provide a buffer from men like Troy. "Football."

"The sports section is over there." I point in the general direction. "Just past that display. You can't miss it."

"I'm not sure where you mean. Can you show me?"

I sigh. Usually I'd humor him, but the last time he was here, he asked me to give him a tour of the nonfiction section and then he cornered me. He played with a long strand of my hair by the autobiographies, until I finally had to uncoil it from his finger and slide out from behind him so I could get on with my job. "I'm not really supposed to leave the desk unattended."

"Go out with me tonight."

He asks me this three times a week. Usually I make up excuses. Instead, I say, "I can't. I'm seeing someone. I have plans with him tonight."

It irritates me that he seems offended by this. "*Seeing someone? Who?*"

I'm not really in the mood for this. I'm tired and I feel a weird craving. For *him*. For my rock god, with his electric energy and his blue eyes. For the hair-dusted textures of his inked, sculpted chest. *For his big, hard cock. I want to suck on him again. I want more of his seedy essence.*

Holy hell. "That's not really any of your business, Troy. Please stop coming in here unless you actually want to read something. I'm not interested in going on a date with you. I'm sorry."

He scowls, exactly like Dylan did just a few hours ago. "Like … ever?"

"No. I'm with someone. I'm taken."

Taken?

I don't analyze it. I'm allowed to feel taken, at least for today. *I swallowed, for fuck's sake. He's still* in *me. His gift is nourishing me, body and soul.* I've put up with these games for too long, trying to feel something for these boys and men who don't interest me and never will.

Now I know what the difference feels like. Even if I can never have Vaughn for more than the one magical night I've already had, at least I know that much.

Troy shoves his hands into his pockets. "Well, if you ever change your mind, can I at least call you sometimes?"

"If that happens, I'll call you. But I don't think it will, Troy. You're better off finding someone else. I'm sure you won't have any trouble."

He's miffed, but he finally takes the hint. "Fine, then. See you around, Gigi."

"Yeah. See you around."

It feels good, as I watch him leave, to have finally discovered this hidden strength in myself.

I just said no.

To two of them. I never realized how much of a weight it is to string people along in a way that was always well-intentioned but also surprisingly draining.

Whatever it was—the crazy chemistry, the stellar

orgasms, the taste and feel of his life force as I drank him in thirsty mouthfuls—I feel free.

My shifts finally ends and as I'm leaving the library to head home, my phone pings. It's a reminder. *Message Vaughn Tucker re the painting in his cabin.*

I'd almost forgotten. My heart skips a beat at the thought. He wanted me to go to his cabin. He gave me his number. I scribbled it on a piece of paper that I must have left in the dining room, where our old landline phone still sits.

When I pull into our driveway, there are two unfamiliar cars in the driveway. A delivery van and a very fancy-looking silver sports car. Two men are talking to Momma. Rose comes out the screen door and stands at the top of the porch steps to see what's going on.

"Here's your delivery, ma'am," one of the men is saying.

"What delivery?" Momma asks.

The man checks a piece of paper he's holding. "This is a latest-model Porsche 718 Spyder." He reads off the form. "It says here the new owner is a Miss Ginger Hayes. Is there a person by that name at this address?"

I close the door of the minivan and walk over to him. "I'm Ginger Hayes."

"Could you sign here, miss?"

"But … who sent this?" But of course I already know.

"Doesn't say."

"I can't accept this."

Rose comes down the steps. She smiles sweetly. "Actually, sir, *I'm* Ginger Hayes." She takes the pen the man's holding out, elbowing me lightly as she does this, "Nice try, Rose." The man looks questioningly at me, then her, then shrugs. Rose signs the form, forging my signature perfectly.

"It's all yours, Miss Hayes. Here are your keys. The rest of the paperwork is in the glove compartment." Rose holds out her hand and he drops the keys into it. "Ya'll have a nice day now."

"Thank you," Rose beams at him. "You too."

The three of us stand there as the men get into their van and drive away.

"*Holy shit*," Rose gushes, running her fingers along the tops of the black leather seats of the convertible, which might as well be a spaceship. It's the fanciest car I've ever seen. "This car is *beautiful*. Do you know how much one of these *costs*?"

Momma doesn't even scold her for swearing. "Did Vaughn send you this, Gi? Why would he—"

"Let's take it for a spin, Gi. I want to ride in it."

"No. We're not keeping it." It's one thing to buy Momma a car. This is taking things way too far. "Do *not* drive it, Rose." I don't know why I'm angry about this. I don't want a car. Does he buy cars for all the legions of women he spends time with? Is that the deal?

Well, I don't want his gifts.

I want him.

So do all the others, of course. That's our curse.

"I'll be back later."

I leave them there as they fawn over the ridiculously expensive gift.

"I'm just going to sit in it, Gi," Rose calls after me as I go into the house. "I won't start it."

I check the side table in the dining room for the scrap of paper with Vaughn's phone number. I'm relieved to find it's still there.

I key his number into my phone and I make my way out the back door, over the fence, across the field. To his cabin.

As he said it would be, the door is unlocked.

Cautiously—because it does sort of feel like breaking and entering—I go inside.

The cabin is sublime.

It's dusty from being empty for so many years but everything else about it is picture-perfect. Inside the front door, there's a sitting area, with a cushioned window seat, several comfortable-looking chairs and a coffee table made out of a smoothed piece of wood sliced directly from a tree trunk.

The cabin is much bigger than it looks from the outside.

The walls, floors and ceilings are all made of wood. The sitting area opens out into a living room with huge windows with a view to the field and down to the pond. There's a free-standing log-burner in the corner of the room. Three enormous leather couches create another sitting area next to a stone fireplace. A swing in the shape of a deep, comfortable rope chair hangs between the two areas, giving the place a whimsical feel. Decorative lampshades and tasteful rugs add pops of warmth and color. There's a bar with stools and an open-plan, state-of-the-art kitchen. Chunky glass pendant lights hang over the bar. There's a dining table on the other side of the kitchen with French doors leading out to an outdoor table and a fire pit. And there, on the far wall above the table, is the painting Vaughn described.

Black and white geometrical shapes. It almost looks out of place in the rustic space, but the patterns are organic and mesmerizing after a while. It grows on you.

I peek into the bedroom, which is spacious and light-filled, with a huge bed. There's a stone wall with a fireplace and a desk with a lamp. There are two sash windows on either side of another set of French doors. I can't help exploring further. A second door in the bedroom leads into a luxurious bathroom complete with a jacuzzi bath.

Wow.

I love everything about this place.

I could live here.

With him.

We could spend all day in his bed, doing all the things we did in the limo. And more. Much, much more. He could be my first everything.

Dragging my mind back to reality, I walk over to the painting. I take a few photos of it.

Then I go into the living area and sit on one of the couches. There's a throw blanket I pull over myself because the air is cooler tonight. I send the photos to Vaughn, along with a text.

The past twenty-four hours are catching up with me. I didn't sleep at all last night and it's been a busy day.

I'll just rest my eyes for a few minutes.

As soon as my eyes close, I see him in my memories. All blue-eyed and beautiful.

Maybe Rose is right.

Maybe I should just do it. I could go to Seattle with Rose and we could see Ruby perform—which I would absolutely love to do. We could spend time with her and celebrate her new success. I haven't talked to her much lately because she's been so busy and I miss her.

Then … I could see how it goes.

If *his* rule is one night, and *my* rule is not to have sex with someone I don't love, maybe we can both get what we want. My rule *could* happen in one night.

If I have sex with Vaughn Tucker for one night and one night only, I haven't broken my rule. Because I do love him.

Everything I know about him so far, I love.

Except for one thing. That small detail about him being a playboy from hell.

I'll have no delusions about riding off into the sunset with him, because I know it won't happen that way.

I don't care.

I'll make love to Vaughn Tucker once. I'll cash in my damn V-card. Finally.

And then I'll let him go.

11

VAUGHN

I'M in our old house in Nashville, the one I was born and raised in until the day I graduated from high school, which was only a few months after the accident happened. We sold the house, gave most of the small amount of money to Roxie, who moved in with a friend for the last two years of high school. Then we took off on tour and never looked back.

In my dream, the house is different, though. There are caves inside, where the bedrooms used to be, with dark shadows lurking in hidden corners.

My father is in the kitchen, his face still dirty with soot from a call-out he's been on. His fire fighter's hat hangs on a hook by the door. In my dream, he's on fire. But he doesn't seem to notice this. There's a glass of neat whiskey in his hand.

I remember the night so clearly.

I knew why he drank. His own father was a mean drunk who hit first and asked questions later. He beat his wife and his two sons until the damage stacked up in ways my father has never been able to shake. Until my father ended up putting my grandfather in the hospital because one night he fought back.

My own father's triumph was that he broke the cycle of abuse. But it didn't mean he drank any less. He wasn't a mean drunk but he was a tormented one. Angry at himself, although I never entirely understood why he would be. Old scars I didn't fully understand. He wasn't the kind of man to talk about things like that.

I think he broke the cycle through grit and because he was so in love with my mother. Everyone was. She was that kind of a person. You couldn't help but fall in love with her. And they had four kids who, even though we weren't perfect, at least had our own talents and managed to stay out of the worst kinds of trouble.

But for him, it never seemed like enough. He was still tormented. I resented him for that, which compounded itself over time. Why weren't we enough? In my dream, I ask him this question. Instead of answering me, his fire burns and he pours himself another drink.

My mother's twin sister was married to a genius investment guru who had more money than he knew what to do with. Tens of millions of dollars. Maybe even hundreds. It seemed to come so easily for him. They traveled the world. My uncle built my aunt a castle. He bought her a boat and diamond jewelry. My aunt could design clothes as a hobby when she felt like it while she stayed home with her three sons, had the help of nannies and housekeepers, and lunched at the club.

My mother, meanwhile, worked odd jobs as a cleaner, or bagging groceries at the supermarket. Eventually she got an associates degree by studying at night after her shifts ended and got a job as an assistant in an insurance office.

Money was always tight.

We bought our clothes at thrift stores. All three of us boys shared a bedroom our entire childhood. We drove old cars that always needed fixing. The roof leaked. We complained about being hungry, which we learned not to do.

It only made things worse. My father's fire has completely consumed him now but he's used to it. He lives his life that way.

My mother would listen to her sister's stories over the phone about their trips to Paris and Rome, the new ruby bracelet her husband had bought her on a whim in New York City, where they'd seen the latest show on Broadway. Or the new car he'd surprised her with.

My mother soaked in those stories each day like she couldn't get enough of the fantasy. She hid the hardships of her own family from her sister. Which, in my dream, makes my own fire burn. I'm on fire too now. His sorrow consumes us both. When I was young, I couldn't understand why she wasn't honest about who and what we were. Every summer we'd go to their house in Ann Arbor for a week and it was like stepping into another world. My mother would buy us special clothes for our visits and made sure we got haircuts.

None of it mattered to her, she insisted. She adored my father. He was 6'4" and handsome and the bravest person she knew, she used to say.

And he worshipped the ground she walked on, we all knew that.

But my father took our hardships personally. Every second-hand shirt and every overdue bill: his fault. Every fire that burned too high: his fault. Every soul they couldn't quite save: his fault. And even though he worked his way up to chief of his fire brigade, which I always thought was a wildly impressive thing to do, it still didn't mean we could take trips to Rome or buy new cars.

He loved my mother to the point of madness, he once told me. And it was his fault she couldn't have a life like she deserved.

Our life was just as good, I tell him in my dream. It's just a different kind of good.

I'd try to talk to him about it, to get him to listen or notice me. But he never really did. He was too stoic. Too damaged, maybe. Too complicated and too sad. His regrets were too layered and too deep, reaching all the way back into his own turbulent past.

Let it go, I tell him. The past is full of shadows, but only if you feed it dark things. Those things happened once but they're not happening now.

But my words are only wood chips that feed his fire higher.

As always, his self-imposed regrets took their toll.

He drank more. Until it became the biggest thing about him.

That night he was very drunk.

And I was tired of his sorrow. I wanted to rile him out of his own misery.

So I took his glass of whiskey and chugged the entire thing.

Pissed off, he poured himself another. I drank that one too.

He grabbed me by the scruff of my shirt and shoved me backwards.

Why aren't we enough, Dad? I remember saying. Why don't you just appreciate the good stuff once in a while?

When you're the son of an alcoholic—like he was—and like I

am, even though he saved us from the worst of his own experience, reality gets skewed. Things that are hard feel ten times worse. Sadness is heavy and anger ignites into rage like the wildfire it is.

I punched at him, but I was no match for my father in those days. I had just turned eighteen and he was a built-as-fuck firefighter who was as tough as they came.

You're a punk, you know that? he'd said. You don't know anything.

Then tell me, Dad. Tell me.

My mother heard the commotion and came into the kitchen to find us fighting. Our fire spread to her. She would burn with us. She pleaded with him to stop, and he did. He grabbed his keys as he walked out.

I tried to stop her from following him. But I couldn't.

I love you, Vaughn.

That's what she said to me as she climbed into his truck that night.

She loved him more.

The tail lights of his Dodge glowed red as they drove away.

In my dream I'm there with them as they hit the tree.

I bleed with them.

I burn with them.

I die with them.

I wake with a start.

It takes me a few minutes to figure out where I am.

A hotel.

I'm in L.A.

We're on tour.

Fuck. My nightmare is still pummeling through my brain. My heart is beating fast.

That's all it was: a nightmare. The thing is, I remember my childhood as a beautiful one. We ran wild. Our days were full of laughter and family. All the details of my nightmare were the worst of it. We never considered ourselves poor, and we weren't. We always had enough of what we needed.

Maybe it was my conversation with Kade that kicked up those old memories. I read somewhere that dreams are our brain's way of processing the day's thoughts, sorting them into compartments of memories. Whatever compartment my nightmare came out of was all the hardest things, weaved together into one dystopian back-story. Snippets of the dark side of our lives that led to one pivotal moment which changed everything. But it's not the way I remember it.

I reach for my phone, which is next to me. I want to talk to someone.

And I remember now: I got a text from Gigi last night.

Which means I have her number.

I call her.

On the eighth ring, she picks up.

"Hello?" She sounds soft and tired, like I just woke her up.

"Gi? It's Vaughn."

"Oh. Hi." There's a pause. "Oh my gosh. I'm still in your cabin. I fell asleep here last night."

"Yeah?" This makes me happy and it's a visceral thing. Splicing through the sorrow that's etched so deeply into my soul, all refreshed now and cold as ice after my nightmare. "Are you in my bed?"

"I'm on the couch. It's so comfortable. How's the tour going?"

"It would be better if you were here."

I can hear rustling, like she's getting up. "Vaughn, you know I can't accept that car. I don't know why you keep doing that. You have to take it back."

"If you send it back I'll just buy you another one."

I can hear in her silence that she's mildly pissed off and I *love* this. I crave her with everything I have. I can picture the little furrow between her strawberry eyebrows. The light exasperation in her kaleidoscope eyes. "I don't want it."

"You don't like the Porsche? Maybe you'd prefer a Mustang. Or I could get you a Maserati. Or another Corvette."

"I don't want you to buy me *any* kind of car, Vaughn. I mean it."

"Too late, baby." I can picture the soft pout of her pink lips at my endearment. *She didn't mind me calling her baby as I was eating her pussy, so she better get used to it. Because I haven't even gotten started.*

"I'm not keeping it."

"Then sell it and donate the money to charity. But I'll buy you three more if you do that. A Mustang, a Maserati *and* a Corvette."

"I don't want you buying me gifts, Vaughn."

My nightmare has added a clarity to my angst that's new. I was young when my parents died. Clueless, in many ways. Now, with some distance, I can see that I was just trying to get through to them. Because I loved them.

I'm sure they knew that but, thinking about it now, I don't know if I ever said those words to my father. I don't want to make those same mistakes again. "Well, that's just too damn bad, darlin'. Because you deserve gifts. And I'm planning on giving you a lot of them. Starting with a plane ticket."

A huff of gentle laughter, which makes my cock harden and throb. "To where?"

"To wherever I am. Which happens to be L.A. We have another show here tonight. Then San Diego. Then Vegas. Then Sacramento. And so on."

"That's so busy."

"Yeah. My sister is a sadist. We have twelve shows in fourteen days."

"Wow. Hang on a second." I hear her close the door of the cabin. "I'm walking back to my house. I have a class at nine." I'll take anything I can get from this girl, my dream girl, who stormed into my life at a time I'm now suspecting I most need her. I'm not usually the kind of person who gets hung up on things like fate or destiny, but it almost feels like she was planted here just for me. I can't take that lightly. I don't *want* to take it lightly. She's mine and I'll do whatever it takes to have her and to keep her. "Did you get the photos I sent?"

"Yeah. Thanks." I can picture her walking across the field in the morning sun, all golden and sleep-tousled. I have this wild urge to love her so insanely *hard* it's making me crazy. Like everything else I've done in my life, loving this girl is something I'm falling—or diving—head-first into. I can't control it. I don't want to control it. I want to grab it with both hands. "So, what do you say?"

"I told you. I can't just take off like that. It's my last week of classes. Next week I have two exams. Then the week after that I start my field work. This is what I've been working toward for two years."

Her voice is so soothing to me. I want her to keep talking. "If you could go anywhere in the world, where would it be?"

I can hear the smile in her voice at my change of subject. I'm not ready to let her hang up. "Anywhere?"

"In the whole world."

"Hmm ..." She thinks about it for a few seconds. "The Bahamas."

"Really? Why?"

"I don't know. I saw a show about it once and it looks so beautiful. I've never seen the ocean and this house they were showing had views from every window. The water was so blue and clear. I think about it all the time."

"You've never seen the ocean?"

"No. Never." I hear a screen door swing closed and kitchen sounds in the background. She's home now.

"Gi, I'm going to take you there. Just as soon as I'm done with this tour and you have some time off. We're going to spend a month in a house by the beach, just you and me."

"That sounds … expensive." She laughs, like she doesn't believe me.

"Good. Because all this money is burning a hole in my pocket. My cousin invests it for me and he's some kind of genius or something. Every time he sends me the numbers, they've tripled."

"Wow. Listen, I need to get ready. But I hope you—"

"Gi?"

"Yeah?"

"Tell me again about your hopes and dreams."

I hear a door close, and it's quiet. She might be in her bedroom now. "I told you. Helping people. That's my dream."

"Help me, then."

That careful patience spears me right through my heart. I've never needed anyone to be patient with me before. They always fall all over themselves to do whatever I want. With Gigi, I have to earn her time. "What do you need help with, Vaughn?"

"My new addiction."

Carefully, she says, "What … new addiction?"

"Your perfect pink pussy."

"Vaughn," she whispers, scolding me. I'd pay a million dollars to see her blush and squirm right now.

"The taste of you on my tongue."

A soft exhale.

"You loved it, didn't you, baby?" I want to rile her. I want her to remember how good I felt. "You *loved* when I sucked on your clit and made you come. You were so damn *hot* for me, Gi. But it wasn't enough, was it? You want me to do it again, don't you, darlin'? Except next time, it won't be my tongue—"

"Vaughn," she whispers. She's not used to phone sex. Neither am I, come to think of it. I don't know if I've ever actually talked to a girl on the phone before.

But I'm not that easy to dissuade. "There's no stopping me now, honey. Especially not after the way you *felt*, Gi. Your sweet, greedy little *mouth*. You're a dirty, thirsty girl. I want to give you more."

A huff of shy laughter. "God. Vaughn."

"You're so fucking *beautiful*, Gi."

She's quiet but I can feel her. She's remembering, retracing all the details of the ferocity of our connection. "So are you," she says, and her soft reply that's under-scored with longing gets me hotter and more manic than anything ever has. Her innocence, entwined as it is with a raw, blooming lust just totally slays me. She may as well have reached into my chest and gripped my heart in her cool hand while holding my hot, engorged cock in the other. I'm lost. I'm burning up. I need her more than I've ever needed anything.

"Let me fly you out here, Gi. Come tonight."

"I'm going to be late, Vaughn. I really have to go."

"All right. We'll talk later, though, okay? The car is yours. We've got a trip to the Bahamas coming up. And I'm already addicted to everything about you. So pick up when I call you."

"I'll try to."

"Don't make me have to jump off the tour bus again, baby. My family would be very unhappy with me if I fuck up this tour."

"*Okay*, Vaughn. I'll pick up. I promise."

"Gi?"

"Yeah?"

"It was always supposed to be me."

12

I say goodbye to him and end the call.

It was always supposed to be me. "I know," I whisper.

I would, if I could. I'd take his plane ticket and I'd go on tour with him. I'd soothe him and kiss him. I'd do anything he wanted.

That's what scares me the most.

But I'm running late and the rest of the day is a blur of classes, studying and another shift at my job. I'm glad for the distractions.

When I finally get home it's after ten. I take a long shower and get into bed. I talk to Scarlett for a while. The baby is finally starting to settle and my sister sounds better. At least she wasn't crying the whole time. I send a text to Ruby, telling her I'm thinking of her and hope her show went well tonight. It's still hard to believe she's touring with the biggest band in the country right now. And dating the lead singer.

And that I … happen to know one of them too.

It's almost midnight. I set my alarm for 7 a.m.

And as I lay quietly in my bed, I think about the way he felt. *The way he tasted.* My phone starts buzzing.

The screen has lit up with his name. *Vaughn.*

I get this sixth sense that he needs me to answer. "Hi."

"Hi." His voice sounds strained. Just with that one word I can read the tone of his mood. He sounds strung out.

"Is everything okay?"

"It is now."

"How was the show?"

"Good." He's uncharacteristically abrupt.

"Where are you?"

"In my room."

I can hear pounding in the background. Vaughn is quiet for a few seconds and the pounding gets louder. "Who's banging?"

"People."

"What people?"

"People outside my door. They're trying to get in."

"Oh." His groupies. Wanting a piece of him. It never really occurred to me that maybe it's not always fun to be hounded and pursued by rabid mobs. I wonder if it ever feels oppressive. Or scary, even. It sounds scary to me. *I'd be scared.* "Are you okay, Vaughn? Is there anyone …

with you?" He seems uneasy, like maybe he shouldn't be alone right now.

"No."

"Are you okay?"

"I hate that you're so far away." His voice is rasped tonight. Maybe from singing. I wonder if he's tired or if there's more to it. He doesn't sound drunk, but something's different. I wonder if he's on something. The thought makes my throat sort of ache. With a longing and a realization.

Maybe he really is the one. Maybe it really is meant to be him.

By the time I found out my daddy needed help, he was already too far gone. Vaughn isn't too far gone. Not yet. But for some reason, he's medicating. If I can find out what those reasons are, I might be able to save him from himself. "I'm not far away. I'm right here."

"Talk to me, Gi. Tell me about your day."

Scarlett just asked me to do the same thing. She likes to hear me describe the familiar, predictable rhythm of my life. With all the new things going on in hers, like a demanding (in mostly a good way, she always insists) husband and a fussy new baby, the routine stuff comforts her. I've found that when my sisters are worked up for whatever reason, just talking to them in a soothing, easy kind of way usually calms them. "Well, my first class this morning was Introduction to Social Case Work. The professor is really good. She's a fan of yours, by the way. Then I had a meeting with her afterwards. She told me about what to expect when I start to work with patients. I'll have a supervisor who will take me with her on her rounds. Then I had another class that's a psychology class, about personality types, which is so interesting, I think. I'm what they call a Counselor, apparently, which is funny when you think about it because it's so accurate. I was thinking about you and my guess is that you'd be a—"

"You were thinking about me?"

"Yeah. I think you'd be the personality type that's called a Champion. Which means you like doing things your own way. You like company but only with people you choose. You're very perceptive and thoughtful but you hate living inside a box."

"That does sound like me."

He's quiet then so I keep rambling. "After that I wrote some of the essay that's due next week, then I had work for a few hours, which went fast today because it was busy. And then I went home and talked to Rose for a while. She's still upset because her boyfriend—well, *ex*-boyfriend now—cheated on her—"

"He's scum for doing that. I had no idea he was in a relationship with someone. He always told me he wasn't with anyone."

I'm almost surprised he would feel that way. His reputation, after all, is as a playboy of the highest order. "You don't … cheat?"

"I've never had anyone to cheat on."

No. I guess that's true. His rule and all that.

There's more pounding. His groupies are calling his name. "I'm sitting here in the dark," he says, his voice low, "looking out at the city at night. And all I can think about is you. That's it. I was even drumming my songs to you. All day, we had all these interviews and press conferences and I couldn't concentrate on any of it. You've taken over every thought I've had. Everything. Nothing else fits into my brain except you. I don't know how you've done it, baby, but it's a problem for me that I can't see you tonight."

It's … the sweetest thing I've ever heard.

"Do you ever feel like you're walking a fine line, Gi?"

"What to you mean?"

"Of your own sanity."

There he goes again. With every passing day it's become clearer and clearer. *He's my person. He's my dream.* "You're okay, Vaughn. You are. You just feel things deeply."

"I feel you so damn deeply I can't see straight." His breathing gets heavier. "Are you in bed, Gi?"

"Yes."

"What are you wearing?"

"Just … a tank top … and panties."

"Take them off." The aggression in his command—sort of crazily—makes me go instantly wet. My skin feels warm and my panties cling damply. I want to soothe him and I want to provoke him. I want him to open up and give me everything.

It's not like he hasn't already seen me naked. And much more than that.

I slide my panties off. Then I peel my tank top over my head.

"Are they off?"

"Yes."

"Everything?"

"Everything. Take yours off too. It's only fair."

I hear his zipper come down, then a low curse. "All I can think about is how fucking sweet you taste. I just want to lick that golden pussy until you're coming all over my tongue again." *Oh.* "I'm going crazy for you, baby girl. I want to bite your cherry-ripe nipples between my teeth again until you moan my name. Touch yourself, darlin'. Touch that little pink clit for me. Are you wet for me?"

My fingers slide over that sensitive bundle of nerves and I gasp.

"That's my girl. Slide your fingers just inside, where you're all slick for me. Where you wish my tongue was right now, licking and tasting and getting you all wet and ready for me."

"Vaughn."

"Right here, baby." I can hear the slippery sounds of his hand working his big, thick length.

"I wish I could touch you." My voice trembles. This is the side of me that's all Vaughn's. The part of me that will do anything he says, and more. "I wish I was sucking on you right now."

He groans. "*Hell, Gi,* you get me so fucking hard. You want me to lose control. You wish my big cock was pushing inside you where your fingers are. You want me to fuck you nice and deep and hard until that sweet pussy is coming all tight and juicy around me, don't you, sugar pie?"

"*Yes.*"

"Slide your wet fingers on either side of that pink clit, baby. Can you do that for me?"

I moan a soft reply as I do it. I feel desperate, so needy for him I'm in a haze of desire for his dirty words and his huge, spilling cock.

"Good girl. Now rub your fingers across the top of it, like my tongue would be doing right now, flicking it, working it nice and slow. That's it. Faster now."

My fingers move in time to the squelching sounds his hand is making as he strokes himself hard and fast. The rise of pleasure is astounding, like an explosion of bliss that starts in my clit and radiates through my entire body in electric jolts. My thighs are sticky and quivering, my pussy spasming tightly, over and over. I'm moaning his name and I love the grunting, desperate sounds he makes as he comes. *Oh hell yeah, baby. You're mine. Mine.*

"I'm yours," I whisper, because in this moment, it's just the damn truth. It hurts it's so true.

And after, as our breathing starts to slow, I miss him

even more. I want to hold him and kiss him. I want to show him how good he makes me feel.

"I miss you, darlin'," he murmurs.

"Miss you, too, Vaughn."

"You're my strawberry girl."

I hold the phone in my hand carefully. I like that I can hear the sound of his breathing. That I'm here if he needs me. It's like this that we fall asleep.

VAUGHN CALLS me four or five times a day. We have long conversations about every topic under the sun. He tells me about the songs he's writing, the tour, his excitement over finally having a break for a while after four solid months on the road. There's always a lot going on in the background of his calls. He never seems to be alone.

Except late at night, when he murmurs sweet, dirty words to me until we're both hot and wet and coming hard.

Every night.

Despite everything, I don't tell him I'm coming to see the last show of their tour.

I don't have any expectations. Except one. One night.

Our connection feels insanely real.

It also feels insanely fast. And more than a little complicated.

I don't know if Vaughn acts like this with all the

women he's been with. I mean, I don't *think* he does, but how can I know that for sure? Hundreds of articles have been written about his inability to commit. Legions of women have begged him for more, only to be disappointed.

So I force myself to recognize it for what it probably is: beautiful, but temporary.

If he's not busy on Saturday night, that is.

If he is, then it's a friendship that will begin to fade out on Sunday morning. I'll employ my brand new skill of saying no. I can't help him if he belongs to someone else. With him, it won't work that way. He can only be my person if he's mine. All mine. I'll get on with my life, my heart still intact, my V-card regrettably still in place.

Rose and I will go to Seattle. Beyond that, I can't think too much about what might or might not happen.

I want it to happen. Of course I do.

The more I talk to him, the more deeply I fall for him. He's funny and smart and has a crude but infectious sense of humor. He's a deep soul, sometimes coming across as tough and untouchable, but at other times, the hidden cloisters of his pain are almost breathtaking.

He's rough-edged and unapologetically masculine as all hell, but he also has the softest heart under all those big muscles of anyone I've ever met. He can be so sweetly tender, asking questions no one's ever asked me before. *What's the last thing that made you cry? Do you ever feel lonely? What does your perfect day look like?* Until I'm telling Vaughn

Tucker things I've never told anyone. He has a way of reaching around corners I didn't even know existed.

Time passes quickly and before I know it, it's Saturday morning. Rose and I are getting ready to catch our flight to Seattle. As we leave, I don't know why I do it, but I reach for the gold rosary that hangs on a hook next to my bed. My daddy gave it to me for my tenth birthday. I don't really use it all that often but it's always given me a quiet strength on the more emotional days of my life.

I slip it over my head.

I feel like I'm going to need it.

Rose and I board the airplane and the flight attendant shows us to our seats at the front. The morning feels dusted with magic. Through the airwaves or whatever it is, I can feel him already. I'm getting closer and his energy is stronger now, infusing me with a starry restlessness.

I told Ruby to keep it top secret, even from Travis, that we were coming tonight. I didn't want to give Vaughn warning. I'm not sure why. I want to both surprise him and test him. If he's there for me, if his reaction is true to the words he whispers to me late at night as we fall asleep together, our phones on and connecting us like there's no distance between us, it'll add a deeper layer to what's about to happen, that's what it feels like. Of realness.

He can earn what I'm about to give him, by being available. By wanting to take it.

If not, then I'll deal with the devastation and the broken heart in whatever way I can. Somewhere at the back of my mind, I've prepared for that all along. From that very first time I saw him. I knew I would fall in love with him. And I knew he would kill me with either agony or ecstasy.

I'm willing to risk the agony, because the small taste of ecstasy he's given me so far is too damn sweet not to take a chance.

A limo picks us up at the airport and takes us to our hotel, where we drink champagne in our five-star hotel suite. Rose turns the music up and helps me put on the dress she chose, which is a pale pink silk with spaghetti string straps and a short little swing skirt. It hugs every one of my curves in a sexy but flattering way. "Remember, Gi. Rock stars are incapable of being faithful. Look what happened to me. My advice is to do him, have the best sex out there but do it with the realization that it's just sex and nothing more. Go in with your eyes wide open. What I'm saying is to have fun but don't even *dream* of getting attached."

"I won't," I assure her.

Too late.

"You look so drop-dead gorgeous I can't handle it," she says, standing back to admire her work. My hair is down, hanging almost to my waist. Rose has blow-waved it, so it's shiny and smooth. I'm wearing more make-up than I ever have, but it's natural-looking and understated, except for my eyes, which are rimmed with a light kohl. My eyelashes are long and dark with mascara. My lipstick is pink. She vetoed the glasses but let me keep the rosary on, since it's real gold. "You look like *you're* made of gold, Gi. Your hair and your skin and your eyes are all golden." On my feet I'm even wearing gold high-heeled sandals. "Vaughn Tucker isn't going to know what hit him."

A car takes us to the stadium, which is massive and already filling with people. I can't believe this is where Ruby will be performing to a sold-out crowd.

We're shown to a dressing room. The security guard tells us to wait here. There are tables set up with food and drinks and Rose helps herself.

Ruby rushes into the room and the three of us hug and cry.

"Look at you. You're so beautiful," I tell her. She really is. She's wearing her stage make-up and a silver sequin dress. She looks like a movie star.

"So are you," she tells me, hugging me tight. "I've missed you so much, Gi."

When it's time for her to go on stage, we're shown to our VIP seats. Ruby walks out under a single spotlight and she sings the songs she wrote in our bedroom or on the bench under the old oak tree, where she used to sing them just for me. She's so good I have tears in my eyes but

Rose scolds me and tells me not to mess up my make-up any more than I already have.

Ruby's voice has always been something special but tonight its layered edge gives me goosebumps. Under Travis's wing, she's blossomed from a shy, innocent amateur to a shining star who can—and is—competing on the world stage.

As I watch her, it's enough: that Ruby has made it to exactly where she always wanted to be. If I had anything to do with it, I almost feel like I've already accomplished everything I ever dreamed of. Our daddy would be so proud of her.

And then it's time for the main act.

The Tucker brothers walk out onto the stage and the entire stadium erupts in cheers and applause. It's breath-taking and at the same time eye-opening.

Why did I ever think he could be mine? And only mine?

This is a sold out show of 70,000 or more people. At least half of them are as in love with at least one of the Tucker brothers as I am.

Girls are screaming and crying.

All three men are just … outstandingly beautiful. They were clearly born for this and it's an amazing thing to watch.

Travis's stage presence is mesmerizing. Kade might be a genius.

And Vaughn.

I fall cataclysmically in love with him. There's something both graceful and forceful about his talent. He plays those drums like he's possessed by the music. He's a poet and a powerhouse.

The band plays for three and half hours but it feels like it's over before it even began. They give the kind of performance you never want to end.

The cheers go on and on and they give three encores.

And then they take their final bow and it's time to meet Ruby in the VIP lounge, where the band gets together after the show.

I'm nervous.

And I'm prepared for anything.

Rose is practical and she reminds me what I need to expect. She's treating this whole thing like it's a tactical exercise. "Don't worry about it if he's surrounded by groupies. Act like you're not even interested. Flirt with one of the sound guys or something. Play it cool."

"Rose, would you stop? This probably isn't even going to happen so let's not overthink it." I'm starting to regret this whole thing. "Maybe we should just go back to the hotel and skip the after-party."

"Are you kidding me? You're not giving up that easily, honey. I won't let you. Now cowgirl up and let's do this."

I can't help smiling at her. She's a hundred percent dedicated to her mission of getting my V-card well and truly cashed in. And I'm emotional. That show was sort of ... life-changing. You can't help but be inspired after witnessing so much raw talent and alpha-freaking-masculinity. It stays with you. It makes you ache and yearn. I give her a hug. "You're a good sister."

"So are you, sweetie. The best."

We find our way to the performers' area and show our VIP passes to the security wall. They make us go through a metal detector and we're finally allowed through.

It's crowded. It was the last show of the tour and people are partying. There's an air of celebration. They must have a huge crew. And, of course, the entourage of everyone who's lucky enough to get close to them.

The VIP lounge looks like a nightclub. The music is loud. There's a bar at the far end. Ruby's there to meet us and we make our way through the crowd. A waitress takes our orders and asks Ruby for her autograph.

The brothers haven't arrived yet but the room is full of people, talking and mingling and waiting for the super-stars to arrive.

Rose is bubbly and fun and Ruby talks to the people who stop by our group to congratulate her. Ruby intro-duces us to Roxie, the brothers' manager and sister, who's petite and gorgeous. Her eyes are the exact same color as Vaughn's. She takes in my hair, my dress, studying me in a way that makes me think she knows something about my … connection with Vaughn, if you could call it that. She smiles at me almost ruefully. "Now I get it," she says, even though I have no idea what she's talking about. "He's been in an absolute bitch of a mood."

Before I can ask her what she means, an excited

murmur goes through the crowd and I glance over to see Travis and Kade walk in. Travis sees us and starts making his way through the crowd. Kade heads toward the bar.

My heart is beating fast.

Maybe he's not coming to the after-party.

Maybe he's already left with some other girl.

But then … there he is. All 6'3" of amped-up rock god perfection. His eyes are wild, his hair still damp with sweat. He's wearing black jeans and a black sleeveless t-shirt that shows off his muscular, inked arms. Moody aggression radiates off his wide shoulders as he pushes past several people to get to the bar. He seems impervious to the crowd of adoring fans surrounding him. A girl touches his arm but he turns away from her as the bartender serves him a drink. He tips it back.

He surveys the crowd, as though he's searching for someone.

It's at that moment that he sees me.

I can't even breathe.

His eyes widen and his gaze drags down to my high-heeled sandals and slowly back up again.

He starts walking over to me.

My pulse is rioting but I do my best to stay calm, and *not* melt into a puddle on the floor, of lust, love and heart-pounding anticipation.

Before, Vaughn always had a coolness to him, a cocky, laid-back arrogance that made him seem like nothing affected him too deeply.

That's gone.

The look in his eyes is feral and wrought.

He reaches me, and he glares down at me, like he's furious.

It never occurred to me that he might be angry that I've come here.

But then his warm, rough palm slides under my hair around the nape of my neck. Vaughn's mouth takes mine in a scorching kiss, his tongue touching mine. Right here. In front of his family and this crowd. He pulls back and there's a smug challenge in his eyes, like he's just made some kind of point. "I can guess why you wanted to surprise me. Did I pass your test?"

"It … it wasn't a test."

"I don't believe you." His fingers lace themselves through mine in a steel-strong grip. "And I need to talk to you. Alone."

He guides me through the room. I glance back to see Rose giving me a thumbs up. Travis looks pissed off. Roxie has her hand on his chest and Ruby is holding his arm, like they're restraining him.

I hear the murmurs of the people we pass. *Isn't that the same girl he was with at Speakeasy? Who is she?*

I can feel the ferocious tension in Vaughn's body as he keeps me close to him, until we're at the door, where several security guards take us to a limo.

We don't talk much on the way. Despite the erotic conversations we've been having until late into the nights, our relationship is too new. We've only spent a matter of hours in each other's company. His fierce energy isn't scaring me … in fact it's making me feel reckless because I know what he's going to *do* with all that pent-up temper. He's going to use it on me.

And I want him to. I want all of him.

We're taken to a hotel where we're escorted through a door to a private elevator. The doors close behind us and we're finally alone.

"Are you *trying* to drive me insane?" he seethes.

"What do you mean?"

"That dress."

I look down at my dress. "What, this? What's wrong with it?"

"Every man in that room was watching you."

"It's none of your business how I dress, Vaughn. I wasn't even going to wear this but Rose insisted on giving me a makeover."

"You're just as beautiful without any makeup at all. Even more beautiful, just as you are."

It's a nice thing to say but the delivery is just as grumpy as the rest of his mood. "I don't know why you're angry."

"I'm not angry."

The elevator pings and opens into a hallway with four doors leading off of it. Vaughn opens one and leads me into a huge hotel suite with views over Seattle at night. The sky is dark with gray storm clouds lit theatrically by a bright sliver of moon. "This is a nice room." It's like a fancy, modern apartment. I go over to the wall of windows to look out at the view of the city and the rippled, expanse of water beyond it. "Oh my God. *Look.* Vaughn. It's the ocean. It's so … vast. Like it goes on forever."

Vaughn comes up behind me. Very lightly, his rough fingers ease the strap of my dress over my shoulder. The warm scratch of his skin sends a warm current of simmering heat to the tightening peaks of my nipples and the damp softness between my thighs. "We can go look at it tomorrow. But I've got plans for you tonight, tiger-eyed girl."

"You're not mad at me? That I came here?"

"I'm mad you made me wait so long to see you again. I've almost jumped on a plane a hundred times over the past two weeks." He lowers the other strap of my dress, weaving my hair around his hand. Leaning closer, he kisses the curve of my neck. His tongue touches my sensitive skin, flicking in wet laves, and the soft pressure funnels directly to my pussy, pulsing there like a promise. Instinctively, I arch against the hard wall of his body. The oversized bulge rests against my backside and I can feel the throbbing heat of him through the layers of our clothing. He finds the zipper at the back of my dress, which he slowly unzips.

My dress drops to the floor.

All I'm wearing is a tiny thong (Rose's idea) and my heeled sandals.

Even though we haven't spent all that much time together, the time we have spent together has been searingly intimate. The ride home from Nashville in the limo and our erotic, late-night phone calls have stripped away any normal boundaries. We're too *hot* for each other for normal boundaries.

He turns me to face him and his aggression has an awed, tender edge. "And I'm mad at you for being so fucking gorgeous you've ruined me for anyone else. Are you ready for me, Gigi Hayes?"

"Are you ready for *me*, Vaughn Tucker," I say softly, because I can feel that sparking wild side taking hold again, the one directly linked to him and all his unruly, crazy appeal. I'm as hooked and desperate as he is. I want to do everything with him. My lust feels like fire in my blood.

He leans down and takes my nipple into his mouth. There's a savagery behind the tender pulls as he sucks on me that promises as much as I can handle. In the darkness, his shadowed face, his thick, dark hair and his taut, corded muscles make the danger of him so arousing it's almost uncomfortable. *Now* I get why the bad boys and the villains are what every woman secretly wants. The alphas who will kill you with pleasure because there's nothing they wouldn't do.

He stands, looming over me. Vaughn takes my mouth

in a lewd, hungry kiss as his fingers swirl the moisture he left with his mouth, teasing and pinching. I'm hypnotized by his touch and his alpha rock star scent, of adrenaline and smoke and decadent virility. Carefully, he takes the rosary from around my neck and places it around his. "I want you completely naked. There's nothing about you I'm not going to take tonight, darlin'."

Oh my God.

Vaughn lifts me like I weigh no more than a child. He carries me into the bedroom and lays me onto the king-sized bed. He kisses my lips. I open to him, drawing his tongue into my mouth, and his answering scorched-earth growl is depraved. He kisses his way down my body, feasting on my nipples, licking his way down my stomach. His tongue touches my clit through the thin, saturated sliver of fabric. "Now let me kiss you everywhere. Look how damn wet you are, baby. Your pussy's aching for me to touch you and eat you so good." Sliding the wet cotton to the side with rough fingers, his tongue licks and delves. "Ah, my *fix*, baby. You have no idea how much I missed this candy-sweet pussy." He rips my panties and discards the tiny shred, eating into me like he *is* addicted to me. I weave my fingers through his hair, to anchor myself. His mouth latches onto the hyper-sensitive nub and the insistent, greedy suction pulls the orgasm over its peak in a sudden, lush burst of euphoric lightning as I go pliant against him.

Vaughn feasts on my climax, spinning it further.

It's a long time before the ripples begin to calm.

I feel so vulnerable and exposed. My pussy is swollen and glistening from his mouth, my nipples flushed and sore. I'm still in the final lull of my orgasm. And he's still completely clothed.

The ridge inside his jeans is *gigantic*, like someone stuffed an anaconda down there. He pulls his shirt over his head. Unfastening his belt buckle, he unzips, releasing himself. *Holy hell.* It's daunting now, that I'm going to *take all that inside me.* The huge bulk of him is hot-looking, the broad tip seeping with creamy liquid. I reach for him, swirling the moisture. Then I touch my finger to my tongue, tasting his essence. "I want you," I whisper.

"Oh, you'll have me, baby. I'm going to take everything tonight. I'm taking you and I'm *keeping* you. I'm fucking *starving* for you, darlin'."

He steps out of his jeans and lays his big, hard body over me. He tips my face up, making me stare into his midnight-blue eyes, dark with intense desire.

The thick length of his colossal, perfect cock presses against my sensitive flesh and the hard, silky pressure grinds against my clit. I'm already starting to come again. The wave is building exponentially.

"Wrap your arms and legs around me, Gi. I'm going to take this as slow as I can. I'm going to try not to hurt you."

Hurt me. I don't care.

His kisses turn slippery and crazily erotic. He feeds his

taste into my mouth, getting me drunk with it. All my senses are captivated and obsessed. There's nothing but him and his mouth and his hands and his big cock that's all slick with my own desire. I *need* it.

I'm wrapped around him with his heavy weight on top of me and I give in completely to the carnal rush of my need for him. There's no room for modesty when the fever burns this bright. My legs are wrapped around him and my knees are fully bent. I suck gently on his tongue as I offer myself to him. I'm shameless and desperate and I don't care.

Vaughn stares into my eyes. "There can't be anything between us, baby. Not with you. I'm doing this bareback."

I'm so lust-dazed it takes me a second to realize his meaning. "It's okay."

"I've never done it without a condom before. But with you, I can't tolerate a barrier. I need to *feel* you, Gi. I want to feel everything."

I don't know why this surprises me. "Never?"

"Hell, no. Everyone wants my babies."

I'm sure that's true. And I feel a tiny fissure in my heart open to him. What he's saying sounds like … maybe there's more to his desire than one night. Maybe *much* more. "I'm on the pill, Vaughn."

"Yeah?"

"Yeah."

"You know the pill is only ninety percent effective."

"Really?"

"Yeah."

"Well, put one on if you want to."

"No. I'm going to fill you up and get you all blissed-out and juicy with my cum. I don't care if I get you pregnant. I *want* to make a baby in you, darlin'. Because you're mine. Every part of you belongs to me. I want to *worship* you and possess you, body and soul."

Wow. "Vaughn," I breathe. It's unlikely that would happen. But there's no denying that the animal, biological urge is a ridiculously strong one. The thought of his *seed* filling me up is enough to make a devil out of an angel. I understand my sisters just a little bit better all of a sudden.

Vaughn is only making it worse. "Tell me how much you want my big cock to fuck you nice and deep now, baby girl."

God. The hard ridge of his erection is low against my stomach. He slides it lower until the thick tip is resting wetly against my still-pulsing clit.

"Tell me."

"*Please*, Vaughn." I'm almost sobbing. "I need you so much."

I feel the thickness of him pressing against me. *Into* me. The heavy immensity of him is hot and insanely hard. The stretching sensation feeds a warmth to the lingering pulse of my earlier orgasm. Vaughn drags his mouth over my throat, breathing hotly against the trail. I can feel that he's burning with his need, as much as I am.

His fingers find my clit, gliding lightly as he pushes himself deeper, opening me with the force of his thick possession.

"This is going to bind us, baby girl. You're mine now. I'll give you everything I have. I'll make all your wildest dreams come true. I'll give you diamonds and houses. I'll take you to the fanciest restaurants and the nicest hotels. I'll treat you like the goddess you are. But every chance I get, I'm also going to fuck you nice and dirty just the way you like it until you're moaning my name and overflowing with my hot cum."

Oh my God. Even as my tight, quivering body resists him, his words and the insistent, circular rhythm of his fingers tips me over the edge of another lush lava flow of pleasure.

"Good girl. You're coming for me already. Damn, you're a hot little thing. Let me in, baby. All that tight, luscious perfection is *mine. Oh, hell, Gi.* You feel so fucking good."

I grip him, coming in jolting bursts, each wet compression drawing him deeper and deeper as he thrusts. There's pain as he breaks through the thin barrier of my virginity, sliding deep, until his massive arousal is fully rooted. The stretching totality of his slick, plunging depth caresses me as one gigantic trigger. *Is it supposed to feel this good the first time?* It hurts like hell, but the pleasure is bigger. The pain is *inside* the pleasure, compounding the tidal swell. I'm mindless with this jagged ecstasy. He's so big and *so* deep. The rolling surges of my body tug him strongly, milking him with soft, clamping adoration.

"*Holy fuck,*" he growls and I can feel the throb of his big cock as it bucks inside me, flooding me with wave after wave of lustrous heat.

We stay like that for a long time, locked intimately as the ripples fade. Moisture trickles down my thighs. I stare up into his fathomless eyes.

Vaughn smooths a strand of damp hair from my face. "We're bound now, Gi. You and me. This means everything. I don't ever want to pull out of you. I want to stay inside you forever."

He does stay inside me most of the night. He spills himself inside me many times, and each time I'm coming right along with him. It's like my body wants to take as much of him as he'll give, pulling his essence from him greedily. Working him until I'm so sore and sated, a deep exhaustion comes over me. I've lost count of how many times we've come together. I'm so full of his seed my thighs are sticky with it. My lips are swollen from his kisses. My nipples are pink and tender from his hungry mouth. My muscles are bruised from his grip and this new form of clenching, writhing exercise.

When we finally sleep, his big body is curled around mine possessively, his cock wedged deep inside me. He soothes the burning soreness with more of his warm cum and I love him.

WHEN I WAKE AGAIN, Vaughn's next to me, asleep on his side. I watch him sleep, awed by everything about him. His handsome face. With his eyes closed, hiding his stormy expressions, he looks younger. Peaceful. And so gorgeous it makes my throat feel tight.

God.

The things we did. The scorching intimacy.

Vaughn hasn't just filled my body with his life force, he's filled my heart with it too. He's spilled his essence into everything about me.

I don't want to think too much about how invested I am in this, in *him*, already.

It already feels painful, wondering how the next chapter will play out.

I get out of bed, carefully standing up. Gushes of milky liquid drip down my inner thighs. There's blood there too. My virgin blood.

Wow.

Gingerly, I make my way into the bathroom. I feel thoroughly used … and better than I ever have in my life. I finally understand so many things. Life, lust, biology, temptation. *What it feels like to be thoroughly, outstandingly made love to by a hot alpha hunk.* I take a shower and dry myself with one of the fluffy towels. I go and check my phone in the little clutch that's on the floor next to my dress.

There's a message from Rose.

We have to be down in the lobby at 11:15 for the limo shuttle to the airport. Meet me there. I'll bring your bag. Hope you had fun!!!!!!

And one from Ruby.

Travis had to go downstairs and deal with some logistics for the tour but he wants me to meet him down in the lobby at 11:00. Come see me before then! I'm in room 404, the one directly across the hall from Vaughn's.

The time is 9:52. I have time. I put my dress on and pull on my sandals. I go in and see if Vaughn's awake yet but he's still fast asleep. I figure he needs the rest after his grueling touring schedule so I find a notepad and write a quick note to him.

I'm across the hall visiting Ruby. I'll be back soon. G 🩶

I open the door of his hotel room and then decide I should probably prop it open with something so I don't have to knock and wake him up. So I wedge the doorstop into it to leave it open a crack.

I knock on Ruby's door and it swings open.

She looks as … well, as enlightened as I feel. She pulls me inside. "Tell me everything," she says. I can tell she's excited for me. She knows all about my rule and she can read in my eyes that I'm already … whatever the word is. Either about to embark on an epic, life-changing love affair … or setting myself up for the worse kind of fall.

We talk for a while until she gets a message from Travis. He wants her to meet him downstairs soon and I'm glad. I don't want Travis to see me this way. All fiery-eyed and buzzing from a marathon of endorphin rushes. I can guess by now what he and Vaughn fought about.

Giving Ruby a huge hug, I leave her to finish getting ready, closing her door behind me.

When I get back to Vaughn's room the door is closed.

Which seems strange. But maybe he woke up and closed it.

I knock quietly.

The door opens.

It's a girl.

A very beautiful girl. And she's not alone. There are two more of them who are just as stunning.

They keep the door mostly closed, like I'm encroaching on their territory and they're guarding it.

One of them walks over and hands me my note. She's not wearing a stitch of clothing. "Is this yours?" She crumples it in her hand and holds it out, dropping it on the floor.

They must have gotten through his security.

Because they know him.

They've been with him before.

"Let me in," I say. "I need to see Vaughn."

"No. He's ours."

He's ours?

"I need to see him," I say again.

"Sounds like you've already seen him. It's our turn now."

"It's important. Please. Let me in." I try to push the door open but I'm not stronger than all three of them. "You don't understand. I'm—"

"Let me guess," says the first one. She's dark-haired with bright green eyes. She could be a supermodel. "He told you you're the one. He promised you everything. He spouted lines about how you're the most beautiful girl in the world and you're not like all the others. Newsflash: we've *all* heard those lines before."

"Yeah," says the blonde. "You're no more to him than we are."

With that, they shut the door in my face.

13

———————

VAUGHN

I FEEL her slide into bed with me. I'm still half asleep and my eyes are closed but my cock is already brutally hard. I want to get back inside my nirvana girl. She'll be sore but I don't know how to love her small. She's too beautiful not to gorge myself on every quiver and every sigh.

Somewhere in the middle of coming hard inside her ludicrously luscious body for the fourth or fifth—or sixth —time, I realized something. Things I've thought were addictions in the past simply weren't. They were a desire to punish myself for things I regret. Or they were masks to hide the pain of those regrets. In the shadow of Gigi's blaze, I don't want any of them. I don't *need* them when I can lose myself in the snug, squeezing embrace of her perfection.

I already knew there was more to my connection with her than just lust. What I didn't realize was how *much* more. A whole *universe* of more. Because when I told her it was always supposed to be me, I meant it. I feel it. She's my star-crossed savior. I've fallen in love with the way the sun in her eyes lights up the moon in mine.

I've already decided that I can't let her leave me again. I'll convince her to spend the day in bed with me, then we'll fly back to Nashville together when we feel like it. We'll live in my cabin until she has time off, then I'll take her to the Bahamas. She deserves everything. She deserves a love that's gentle yet roaring. Her soft, caring understanding is the light in my darkness and the calm to my storm.

She's the one.

Mine.

Even half asleep, the thought of her leaving me feels more than unacceptable. It feels like it has the power to fuck me up. I've been lost in the desert and she's the rain. One night and I'm more than just obsessed, I'm deeply, devastatingly in love with her. As for the lust part of the equation, my craving is a beast I can't control. It's a raging inferno that's bigger than me. I need to be inside her. My heavy, rigid cock seeps with pre-cum in anticipation of the tight, slick beauty of my girl.

I reach for her and pull her close. My hand wanders over her front and I pinch her nipple between two fingers, hungry to kiss her. My rock-hard cock presses against her thigh, sliding closer to heaven on earth.

I can immediately sense a change in her. She's not as

fiery and horny-as-fuck for me as she was last night. Her breasts … aren't as lush and bouncy. Her scent has changed, to something foreign and odd. Her hair isn't as soft—

I open my eyes.

And I jump back as though scalded. "What the fuck—"

"Hi, Vaughn."

It's not Gi in my bed with me. It's those other chicks. *Three* of them. The ones from before. Some of the nameless, endless, meaningless ones that right now are infusing me with rage and disgust. "Where's Gi?"

"Who?" one asks coyly.

"What the fuck are you doing here? Where's Gigi?"

"Oh," says the dark-haired girl, who's name, I remember vaguely, is Amber. "She left."

"*Left?* What do you mean she left? You *saw* her?" Which means *she* also saw *them.*

"She had to go."

I jump up. I pull my jeans on, stuffing myself into them, and I grab my phone. I run out into the hallway and punch the button for the elevator. But I can't handle waiting so I find the door for the stairs and run down to the lobby.

I'm surprised to see Ruby waiting there. And Travis.

"Where is she?" I demand.

Travis is pissed off as hell. Ruby's eyes are red, like

she's been crying. "She's gone, Vaughn," she says. "They got on an earlier flight and they're already boarding. She told me to tell you that she doesn't want to see you again. At all. I'm sorry, but she doesn't want you to contact her. She really means it."

Travis, for all his asshole behavior over this whole thing, maybe can sense that my reaction isn't just stunned, it's deeper than that. It's a shift, somewhere behind my sanity. "But she's got it all wrong—"

"Vaughn." There's almost something worrying about the way Travis slings his arm around my shoulders instead of punching me. "She was upset and very clear about it. You need to respect her decision. I'm going to *help* you respect her decision. It's better this way. For her sake, you need to leave her alone."

If she's already boarding I might not be able to catch her. But I could get the private jet. If I leave now—

"Whatever you're thinking, stop," Travis says. "Let her go. She wants a clean break."

A clean break?

No! There's no such thing as a clean fucking break! I need her too much.

I need my Gi.

Travis leads me out the door of the hotel with Ruby sticking close to us. I allow this because my head is spinning. She's gone and I can't get my bearings. Our bus is waiting there. Travis tells one of the hotel people to go and get my bag. Then he pushes me forward, up the steps and into the bus. I'm still shirtless and barefoot, sort of reeling from the sudden absence of her. She lit everything with her sunny, beautiful aura. Without her, my world feels dismal. Empty. Unbearably bleak.

The bus rolls out and my family is careful with me, sensing I'm on the brink of something.

There's worry on their faces as they try to steer my thoughts in different directions but I'm strung out as fuck. I go into my room and shut the door.

I call her.

It goes straight to voicemail.

"Gi, you got it wrong back there. Completely, totally wrong. They were there when I woke up. I came running after you. *You.* You're the one I want to wake up with." This can't be the way this ends. It can't *end.* I won't let it end. "Come *on,* Gi. Pick up. We need to talk."

I send her a message.

> Pick up, Gi. You have to let me explain.
> They meant nothing to me. Please.

I wait for the three dots that mean she's reading it and replying to me.

Nothing.

I call her again.

And again.

The inside of my head is very, very dark. The ghouls that live in the caves at the back of my psyche creep out into the daylight, coloring everything with their sticky, black effect.

Like Travis said, it's better this way. For her sake, you need to leave her alone.

You're trouble.

You'll ruin her life. Maybe you already have.

You're the problem, like you always have been.

It was your fault they drove away that night.

It was your fault they crashed and burned.

You'll only destroy her. Just like you destroyed them.

She's much better off without you. Let her live a wholesome life with good people who don't wreak havoc on her body and soul.

It's too much. I need to escape the voices. Opening the top drawer of the built-in shelves next to the bed, I take out a bottle of pills. It's a mixture, a few extras from other stashes. There are seven of them. I have no idea what they are.

Washing them down with a half-full bottle of whiskey, I take them all.

TIME PASSES through a tunnel of nothingness. I hear sirens. People are crying. I recognize the voices of my family.

I feel pain. Sadness. Cravings that make me wish I was dead.

Darkness has never been *this* pitch black. I search for the light, and find it there, in the memory of her. That golden day when I walked with her along the trail by the pond. Following my sunny, star-crossed angel across the grassy field. I never believed, until then. She showed me on that very first day everything I never knew I'd been looking for.

I need to get back to her. So much.

The yearning stirs me. After what feels like several lifetimes, I surface.

My eyes open.

I blink a few times. I have no idea where I am.

In a white room.

Am I dead?

It's cold and sterile with a single window. It doesn't look nice enough to be heaven. Or feel hot enough to be hell.

There are people here. A man and a woman, dressed in white coats, standing over me.

"He's regaining consciousness," the man says.

I try to sit up but something stops me. My wrists are strapped to the bed. And so are my ankles. There's one across my chest. *Fuck! Am I in jail?*

I thrash against the restraints.

"Vaughn," the woman says, placing her hand on my arm as though to calm me.

But all it does is enrage me. "What is this?" My voice is hoarse and it takes effort to form the words. "Let me go."

"The restraints are in place to protect you."

I feel panicked. *Who are these people?* "From what?"

"From yourself. You've been very agitated. You've been sedated for four days."

Four days? "Where am I?"

"You're at the Summerview Rehabilitation Estate."

"What?"

"You're in rehab," says the man.

"Jesus Christ." I try to get up again, using all my strength to break the bonds, but I can't. "There's been a mistake. Undo these. I need to get out of here."

"I'm afraid we can't do that," says the man. "My name is Dr. Lopez. This is Dr. Clark. You were checked in by your family after you were released from the hospital. You had quite a cocktail of pharmaceuticals in your system. Not enough to kill you, fortunately, but enough to knock you out for quite a while. And enough to give your family a real scare."

Shit. I remember everything now.

Where's Gigi?

She left me.

"You'll be happy to know," says Dr. Lopez, "that we've been rated the top rehabilitation institute in the state of Tennessee for three years running. Our techniques are occasionally experimental and somewhat unorthodox but highly effective."

Holy hell. "Take these restraints off me, doc. I don't

need any of that shit. I've got somewhere I need to be. I'm okay now. Let me go."

"We can agree to remove the restraints if you can agree to remain calm, Vaughn. Can you do that?"

"Yeah. I can do that. Take them off."

The woman unlocks the padded metal cuffs at my wrists. Then she releases my ankles. Finally, the one across my chest. I'm dressed in some kind of hospital gown.

I sit up. Slowly, because I'm dizzy, I climb off the bed and walk toward the door. My head spins violently and I lean my hand against the wall for support. It takes me a few seconds to regain my equilibrium. I try the doorknob but the goddamn thing is locked. So I go over to the window. It's sealed shut. We're on what looks like the fourth floor. If I could break the window I could probably—

"The room is sealed for your own safety, Vaughn," says the woman. "That's reinforced, shatter-proof glass."

"Let me call my brother." *Those sadists.* I remember the echo of Roxie's concerned, sad warning. And Kade's. *Don't force us to check you into a goddamn rehab.*

"I'm afraid we can't do that, either. There's no contact with the family for two weeks, it's a requirement of our program." Dr. Lopez leafs through a page in the file he's holding. "I can show you your brother's signature if—"

"I don't care about that!" This is seriously testing the

limits of my patience. "I don't consent to this. Let me out."

Dr. Clark's voice is irritatingly calming, like she's talking to a wild horse she's trying to break in. "Your family has staged what we call an intervention. Which means—"

"I know what a fucking intervention is! I don't need an intervention! What I need is to get the hell out of this prison and go home. Open the door."

"I'm afraid we—"

"I'm serious, doc. I'll press charges. You can't keep me here."

"If your health is at risk, Vaughn, then your family is within their rights under the law to ensure your safety." The intentionally-hypnotic tone of her voice makes me want to smash something.

I take a deep breath and attempt to control my temper. "Please. Let's be reasonable. I'm fine now. There's something very important I need to take care of. Which means I need you to open this door and let me out of this room."

Dr. Lopez closes the folder he's holding. "There's actually a group session taking place in the community area right now. If you'd like to attend, we can escort you there. But you have to agree to do it calmly."

At least it'll get me out of his locked room. "Sure. Yes. I need all the therapy I can get," I bluff. "Obviously. Let's go."

Dr. Clark smiles at me, pleased with my progress, as Dr. Lopez takes the keys attached to his belt and unlocks the door.

I take my opportunity. I bolt, running down the hallway looking for the exit sign. There's a stairwell. I take the stairs in threes, reaching the first floor just as an alarm system goes off. I make my way down another hallway, into the reception area of the rehab. I'm woozy but it's no time to flake. Burly security guards dressed in white are already waiting for me. And the doctors have followed me down the stairs and are running after me.

I'm trapped.

I figure I have nothing to lose. I'm built. I can out-wrestle and out-run both of my brothers when I'm at the top of my game. I played some football in high school. So I try to ram through the wall of security to reach the door. Freedom is so close I can taste it.

But I'm no match for all six of them.

"I'll sue!" I yell as they get me to the ground. One's got me in a headlock. Four more are pinning me down, holding my arms and legs. "Get the fuck off me!"

There's a prick in my arm as one of them shoves a syringe into my vein. I feel the cool, numbing wash hit my bloodstream almost immediately.

"I need to see her," I murmur. Whatever they've given me is strong as fuck. Oblivion is closing in and I don't want it to. It's not right that they won't let me chase after her until she believes me.

The shiny marble floor and all the thugs are blurry now. And it just feels so damn wrong that I can't tell her how much I love her. She's in pain, somewhere out there, that *I* caused. My golden girl. And I didn't mean to hurt her.

It was the very last thing I ever wanted to do.

14

Gigi

No one tells you heartbreak is physical. It's not a metaphorical term at all. My heart *actually* feels broken, like there's a big black hole in the middle of it where all the things that brought me joy used to live.

I can't even be angry at him. I knew exactly what I was getting myself into. And I did it anyway, because he was too beautiful not to.

I tell myself to be reasonable. It isn't possible to fall in love that fast. It was hot sex and nothing more.

When I first saw those girls and left his room, Ruby and Rose took care of me. Ruby found me first. I wish Travis hadn't seen me in my hot mess of a state but there were too many emotions to hold back. Ruby had never seen me melt down like that and she was almost as upset as I was. I'm usually the steady one, the shoulder to cry on. This time I needed her. She and Travis said they'd handle Vaughn and I agreed to that.

Rose bundled me into my first class seat home and became the voice of reason. She knew first hand, after all, what it was like to play with fire and get burned. *It was always going to happen this way, Gi. You knew that going in. It hurts, believe me, I know how much. But you have to pick yourself up and dust yourself off and move on.*

When I showed her the texts Vaughn sent me, she said, "Jackson used to send me texts like that too. *While* he was in bed with other women."

My sisters got me through it. I cried it out and the next morning I got on with my life.

I can't bring myself to regret a single second of my time with Vaughn. I didn't delete his texts but I didn't reply to them either. I loved him, I lost my virginity to him, and now he's back with his harem and I'm back with my books.

It's been two days. I go through the motions. I pretend to be fine.

One day, maybe I will be.

Or maybe you won't.

I still love him. Too much. *With everything I have.* Am I ruined now for everyone else? How could anyone possibly compare to Vaughn Tucker?

Damn him.

I figure it's okay to love him with a small piece of my

heart forever. He was my first and it meant something. *It meant everything, just like he said.*

I just wish that piece of my heart didn't feel like the whole damn thing.

I'm in a meeting with Professor Tate about my field work next week. "Your essay about the psycho-dynamic model was excellent, Gigi. It's worth keeping that subject in mind when you start sitting in on sessions with patients on Monday morning. Remember that some people who take drugs do it as an unconscious response to a bad experience they might have had in the past. So they might not be addicted to the substance itself at all. They're using the drugs to cope and to mask the feelings they have that are related to the event, even if they don't realize that's what they're doing. Sometimes the fix can be as easy as addressing the event and getting good therapy. Now, do you have any questions about Monday?"

"What time do I need to be at Summerview?"

"Nine a.m. sharp. Dr. Clark will meet you at reception. She's the director of the facility and you'll be working alongside her. Remember to complete the case study notes and submit them to me by next Friday."

I assure Professor Tate I will, we end the meeting and I make my way out of her office and down the stairs. My phone rings and I take it out of my bag warily. Vaughn hasn't called me since the night I left. Which is a good thing, I remind myself. Who knows, maybe he's still with those supermodels.

It's Ruby. "Hi," I say. "What's up?"

"Gi, I wanted to let you know that Vaughn is … well, he's in the hospital."

"What? Why?"

"He took something. I'm not sure what. I was waiting to call you until I knew more."

No. "Is he okay?"

"He's going to be fine. They're still keeping him sedated, though. He woke up and tried to …"

"Tried to what?"

"Escape."

Oh my God.

"They caught him trying to climb out the window of his hospital room since there were guards at his door. So they had to sedate him. Roxie's worried. They're trying to figure out what to do next."

What if he was telling the truth in his messages and texts?

"I just thought you might want to know, Gi. I'll keep you posted, okay?"

"I want to come see him."

"No, Gi. You can't. He's not allowed visitors. And I don't think it would be a good idea anyway. It would just make it harder for you."

"Ruby?"

"Yeah?"

"When did it happen?"

"Just … a few hours after you left."

Oh God. All this time I've been waiting to be there for the person

I could help, like I couldn't help my father. What if it's true that Vaughn is The One, just like he said?

I realize my face is wet with tears. My blood feels like its iron is being pulled by Vaughn's magnet. I want to go to him so badly.

"We're still in Seattle but they're thinking about moving him. When I know more, I'll call you, I promise. Okay, Gi?"

"Okay."

"Are you okay?"

No. "I just hope *he's* okay." I need him to be okay.

"He's going to be fine. It wasn't life-threatening. They're more worried about his state of mind and his crazy behavior." I have this terrible feeling I know exactly *why* he was acting crazy. *To get back to me.* "Gi, I have to go but I'll call you later on."

"All right." We end the call and I go home. I walk across the field and let myself into Vaughn's cabin.

I don't care if he breaks my heart. He's already done that. By hurting himself.

I text him a message.

> Vaughn, I believe you. I didn't at first. I'm sorry about that. I hope you're okay. Please be okay.

I almost don't add it, but to hell with it. Nothing can hurt as badly as this. I just want to be honest with him.

> It was the best night of my life. I miss you
> so much.

I send the text.

Then, because if I sit around with nothing to do I'll go insane, I clean his cabin. It's dusty from years of being empty. I find some cleaning stuff under the sink and wipe down all the surfaces. I vacuum and clean the bathroom and change the sheets on the bed.

By the time I'm finished it's late.

I check my phone but there are no new messages.

So I crawl into Vaughn's bed.

I don't need him to be perfect. I just need him. Exactly as he is. He's already shown me what I was looking for. And it's enough. It's more than enough. It's everything.

Please be okay. Please come back to me.

Please.

THE WEEKEND IS a special kind of hell. I get updates from Ruby. Vaughn is completely fine, health-wise—in fact better than ever and strong as an ox, according to Travis —but he's still extremely "restless" when he wakes so they're keeping him medicated. He's still not allowed to have visitors aside from his family. They're moving him to a place where he can be monitored, she's not sure where, but they're all on their way back to Tennessee.

I almost demand that she give me Roxie or Travis or Kade's number. I almost call them and tell them that I *know* what he needs. I know why every time he wakes up he's agitated. *Because I'm not there.*

But they're his family. I've known him for only a few weeks. Maybe they know more than I do. The doctors will be careful with him. He's getting the kind of care he needs.

I can only hope.

On Monday morning, I get to Summerview right on time. I go inside the front door. A woman with dark hair in a white coat is there to greet me. "I'm Dr. Clark. You must be Gigi Hayes."

"Yes. Nice to meet you."

She shows me around the offices. "You'll be sitting in with me on a session with a patient that came in over the weekend. He's one of the most high-profile patients we've ever had, even though we get plenty of them. Which is why I need you to sign this non-disclosure agreement before I fill you in more on his background."

"Of course." As I sign the form, a sixth sense makes all the tiny hairs on my arms and the back of my neck rise. *It's him.*

"He's been a real handful. He's convinced he doesn't need to be here. He's tried to escape twice and we've had to use some unconventional techniques to restrain him."

"*Restrain* him?"

"Yes. It's the only way we can allow him to be awake. And the language that comes out of his mouth is somewhat eye-opening. Just to warn you. Although when we try to hold conversational sessions with him, he refuses to say a word."

"Can we see him now?"

"Yes, we'll be holding the session in his room. He still needs to be locked in. He almost escaped yesterday. We can't risk that happening again."

My poor Vaughn. They think he's crazy.

He's not crazy. *He just wants the kind of comfort only I can give him.*

I follow her into the elevator and we arrive in a patients' ward. The doors are made of metal and there are bars on the window at the end of the hallway. It's like a prison.

There are two guards standing outside one of the doors.

Let me guess.

Dr. Clark unlocks the door.

I follow her inside.

And there, strapped to a propped-up bed, is Vaughn.

His bloodshot eyes get wide when he sees me.

It's a strange thing. He's dressed in a hospital gown that clashes completely with his suntanned skin and his huge, corded muscles. His wrists and ankles have been restrained with steel cuffs and a there's a belt strapped across his chest. The shadows under his eyes are more pronounced, like bruises that add to the other ones he's collected over the past few weeks. His hair is unkempt and his eyes look wilder than ever. Even like this, he's the most beautiful thing I've ever seen.

And he's still wearing my rosary. Like karma has somehow chosen him.

He's mine.

His gaze is so intense. It makes my heart beat even faster. But there, behind his feverish rage, is a relief that's so profound I *know* he was telling me the truth. I can read his devotion in the sapphire blaze of his eyes.

"Vaughn, this is Gigi Hayes. She's a student and she'll be sitting in on our session today. I'm hoping we might make a little more progress than we did yesterday."

"I'll tell you anything you want to know," he says, still staring at me.

She gives him a surprised glance. Then she offers me an empty chair and pulls up another one.

"Let's pick up where we left off yesterday." Dr. Clark spears straight to the point. "The question I asked you is this one: what emotions are you attempting to hide from when you take drugs or drink excessively?"

Vaughn's eyes haven't left me since I walked into the room. I can sense that he wants to be honest with me. He wants to explain. "Regret. Sadness. A fanatical wish that I could rewind time and do things differently on one particular night."

The doctor blinks at him, clearly not expecting this kind of honesty. "What night?"

"The night I killed my parents."

The room gets very quiet. The doctor opens his file, checking something. "It says here your parents were killed when their car hit a tree. It says that your father's blood alcohol level was almost three times the legal limit." She pauses. "*You* didn't kill your parents, Vaughn."

"Not with my bare hands. But it was my fault they left that night."

She reads further. "Your father regularly drank excessively."

"Yes. He did."

"Tell us what happened that night."

Vaughn's fists are clenched and his muscles are taut. "I fought with him. I couldn't understand why he needed that crutch so badly, when there was so much about his life that was beautiful. It made me angry that he couldn't kick it. And that his sorrow ran so deep. I guess I was trying to jar him out of his state of mind. I wanted to help him, but I didn't know how. I wanted to do something—anything—that would make him see that he was hurting us. He was hurting *her* most of all. My mother. So I fought with him. But he was stronger. My mother cried and told him to stop. He stormed out. And she chose to go with him, even though I begged her not to. Ten minutes later, they were both dead." Here's the source of all his pain and his angst. Right here. "The difference between me and my father is that I don't get fucked up because I have to. I get fucked up because I want to. Because it helps quiet the memory."

"It wasn't your fault," I hear myself say.

His eyes are stormy. "But I was responsible. You can't know what that feels like unless you've walked through the fire."

"I can," I tell him. He's watching me, waiting for me to continue. "My father died of a drug overdose. A long, slow, agonizing one that cost him everything. He fought it for a long time. And I never knew what he was going through. No one did. I suspected something was going on with him but I didn't push hard enough to find out. I wish so much that I had. I wish I'd tried to comfort him and be there for him as someone he could have trusted. *I* could have talked him off that ledge like no one else could have. I don't know how I know that but I do. So I *do* know what the weight of it feels like. Because I carry that regret every single day. Just like you do."

I've never said any of that out loud before. And this is supposed to be Vaughn's therapy session, not mine.

The doctor is studying me gently. And noticing the intensity in Vaughn. "We can blame ourselves for our parents' mistakes but it's important to realize that, in any family dynamic, parents have the power. They're the ones that control almost every situation, especially as it relates to their own daily lives. They're also flawed human beings, like we all are. They make their own decisions based on reasons we can never entirely know."

Her words resonate deeply, I think for both of us. The thing is, she's right. It sounds so reasonable to hear it spoken like that.

"Vaughn, it wasn't your fault that your parents made the decisions they did that night. Just like Gigi's father's addiction wasn't her fault. It's easy to feel responsibility because you feel your loss so deeply. Grief is the price you pay for love. But it's very unlikely either one of you could have changed the outcome. Tragedies can't always be controlled, or prevented, as much as we wish they could. Both of you need to come to terms with that and forgive yourselves."

I think of the butterfly wing. All the things that have led to this point. All the variables in our lives that have brought us into this room, together, to somehow hear words we both really *needed* to hear. How our pain overlaps. We can see it mirrored in each other. We can share it. And we can help each other overcome it, instead of living our whole lives being consumed by our regrets.

"It wasn't your fault," the doctor says again.

Vaughn's gaze is locked on mine. Our connection feels visceral, almost physical, even through the air. A current of soul-touching energy.

The doctor's phone rings. She answers and has a brief conversation, then ends the call and stands up. "I'm afraid I'm going to have to cut this short. There's an emergency in C wing which could take a while." She turns to me. "Do you want to stay? I think it could be helpful to Vaughn to talk through this. It seems your presence is calming to him."

"Yes. I'd like to stay."

"Vaughn? Would you like to continue this conversation?"

"I sure would, doc."

She hands me a beeper. "His restraints are locked and there are two orderlies outside the door armed with sedatives. Push this button if you need help." She places it in my hand. "Vaughn, you did well today. It's not easy to talk about the things that hurt the most. I'll be back in a few hours."

With that, the doctor rushes out the door.

We're alone.

"Imagine running into you in a place like this," he says wryly.

"Imagine."

I'd almost forgotten the squally energy of him. It radiates off him like heat. "Do you believe me now?" he asks. "About the reason you left?"

"Yes."

"I'm sorry about that."

"It wasn't your fault." I was the one who propped his door open. I should have known that women would go to extreme measures to get close to Vaughn Tucker.

"I was trying to get back to you."

"I know that now, Vaughn.

His eyes, behind the ever-present blue smolder, are kind. "I'm sorry about your father."

It helps, partly because he *understands* in a way very few people could. "It feels good to share that. I've never told anyone. Not even my sisters know the real reason he died."

"I'm glad you told me."

"And I'm glad you told me, about your parents. I'm so sorry that happened to them. And to you."

"I guess it's time for me to forgive him. And myself."

"I guess that's true for both of us."

He's so gorgeous, sitting here in the most unromantic of places, lighting up the room like he always does. The cinnamon of his skin and his masculine virility look out of place inside these stark prison walls. His thick black hair is a glorious mess. I smooth a curl of it out of his eyes, feathering the backs of my fingers across the bruise on his cheekbone. "What happened to you?"

"I got tackled. Trying to get back to my girl." He smiles, and I'm falling, falling. *God, I'm so in love with him.* His slow grin is relieved, and easier. Already, I think we can both feel the difference. Sharing our secret burdens has begun to lighten the load.

I touch the metal cuff at his wrist. "Let me take these off you."

"They're locked. The doctor has the key." Despite the

setting and the situation, a devil-blue glint spangles behind his eyes. "I guess I'm at your mercy, baby girl."

Baby girl. The endearment reminds me of all the blazingly sensual, life-changing things he did to me. "I guess in that case ... I could do anything I wanted."

That slow, lazy grin. "I guess you could."

"I guess if I wanted to kiss you, you couldn't stop me."

His voice is quiet, his accent deepening. "I guess I'd have to just sit here and take it."

I sit next to him on the bed. I lean closer, brushing my lips softly against his.

Vaughn sighs, like the touch of my lips is almost too much for him to bear. "I mean, I've had women go to lengths to try to tie me up before, Gi, but this is really taking it to another level."

"Shh," I say softly, kissing him more deeply.

He takes my mouth hungrily, almost desperately. "*God*, Gi. I missed you so much. Please don't leave me again. You'll fucking kill me. I need you. Move in with me."

I kiss him so lovingly, licking little nips, welcoming his tongue as it slides deeper.

I let my hand rove down his chest, across the tight belt of his restraints. "I'm going to take such good care of you, Vaughn Tucker," I whisper. "I'm going to give you everything you want."

He groans.

"Quiet," I scold him, letting my palm slide over the now-giant swell under the thin layer of his hospital clothes. I gently squeeze his thick length. "You're filling out that gown like nobody's business."

"Oh, hell." His breathing is heavy. My touch, after all he's been through, seems almost painful to him. "Be reasonable, sweetheart."

"She said she wouldn't be back for a few hours. And we can't really leave you like *this*. It's *way* too big …" I pull the fabric up so I can take his hot bulk in my hand. " … and *much* too hard. We need to do something about this."

"*Gi. Fuck.*"

"Look," I murmur, feathering my fingers over the creamy moisture seeping from the broad head of his cock. "You're already starting to come a little. I bet it wouldn't take much to make you come a whole lot."

"*Ah, God.*"

"Do you want me to stop?"

"*No.*"

"Good. Because I wouldn't anyway. I want to taste you too much. I want to suck on your big cock and make you come."

"Goddamn, darlin', you're a bad, bad girl."

"You like when I'm bad." I move lower, taking his slick, rock-hard length in both my hands. His fists are gripping the sheet, his big muscles tensed, like he's strung out on a torture wrack. I lick the moisture, sipping and licking, running my tongue along the vein on the underside of his heavy, perfect cock. "Is my halo dirty yet?"

"Almost," he groans.

I take him deeper, fitting him between my tongue and the roof of my mouth, sucking strongly as I use my hands to squeeze and rub and work his pleasure. It doesn't take long. His body shakes, straining against his shackles. All his violent energy is channeled in one forward direction. His cock jerks and his thick jets of cum fill my mouth in milky bursts. I swallow as much as I can. I want him inside me. I want his life force to mingle with my own and become part of me. I lick him until I've taken all of him.

Then I wipe my mouth with my arm. *Damn.* Talk about a wild side. I don't even want to *think* about what would have happened if Dr. Clark had come back early. Luckily for my future job prospects, she didn't.

I rearrange Vaughn's coverings. I sit next to him, fingering my rosary that's hanging around his neck. I want him to keep it on. I want it close to him.

His color is high but he's calmer now. "I love you," he says, his voice rasped.

I stare at him, not quite expecting it, even though I've already admitted to myself a dozen times that I feel the same way. Deeply. Irrevocably.

He breezes past my shock. "You're a dirty little angel and you're all mine."

"All yours," I agree softly, blushing. Which is kind of ridiculous at this point.

"Gi?"

"Yeah?"

He's quiet for a few seconds. In the connective silence, as he stares into my eyes, our bond, even though it's so new, feels profound. "You've ruined me for anyone else and that's the truth. You need to know that. The minute you walked into my life, that was it. That very first morning, I knew it then. When I followed you and sat on that tree branch by your fence, I knew. I'd never seen anyone so damn beautiful. I knew you were the one. All those things you've read about me, they were true. Before. But not anymore. I don't care about anything else anymore. I just want you."

I don't know why but my eyes are suddenly filled with tears. "You have me, Vaughn."

"No more nerds in comfortable shoes." He's joking, but just the mention of it makes his irises flare.

"There was never anyone else, Vaughn. You know that. I've already told you that." *It was always supposed to be you.*

"Good." With that settled, he smiles. "Gi?"

"Yeah?"

"Can you do me a favor?"

"Anything."

"Can you get me out of here? Today? Please. I don't want to spend another minute apart from you. Go tell my family. Don't take no for an answer. Kade will listen to you. The other two can be thick-headed but I know you can talk them around. Can you do that for me?"

"Of course I can." I kiss his lips again, softly, slowly, with all the love I feel for him. "I'll tell them. I won't take no for an answer."

I get up to leave and he watches me do this, his expression sort of anguished. "How's the Porsche?"

"I … I drove the minivan."

"You don't like the Spyder?"

"Well, Rose spent a lot of time sitting in it so I told her she could take it for a drive. I haven't seen her since."

He gives me an exasperated look. "All right, then. She can keep that one. I'll get you a McLaren. Or maybe a Ferrari. What's your favorite color?"

"Bye, Vaughn. I'll see you soon."

"Don't let them talk you out of it, Gi. They can be stubborn."

I blow him a kiss and open the door, where the two security guards are still standing. "Luckily, so can I."

I PARK the minivan in the driveway and I head straight across the field. The tour is over and the band is home now, hanging out at Travis's country house next door. Ruby comes home occasionally but she's basically moved in with him.

It's early afternoon and the sky is overcast. It looks like it might rain later. The air is warm and humid.

I can hear music coming from Travis's barn so I walk toward it. The door is open a crack so I ease through and step inside.

They're all here. Travis and Kade have their guitars hooked up to their amps and they're playing a song. There's a huge Persian-style rug on the dirt floor and all their equipment is set up there, including Vaughn's drum kit. Ruby and Roxie are lounging on piles of hay in the old stalls, talking and listening to the brothers play. Sunlight streams in from several open windows and the gaps between weathered slabs of wood.

They all stop what they're doing when I walk in.

"Hi," I say.

"Hey, Gi," says Ruby. "How'd work go?"

"It was good. But I need to talk to ya'll about something important." I walk closer to Travis and Kade and they're kind of riveted and intense. Kade's the one I focus on. His hair is several shades lighter than Vaughn's, and longer. His vibe is quieter than Vaughn's, but no less forceful. His eyes are vividly blue, a shade lighter than Vaughn's. He's just as burly as Vaughn and Travis, and his plaid shirt strains against the flex of his muscles as he unplugs his bass guitar. He's wearing blue jeans and dusty cowboy boots.

"I need to you to sign Vaughn out of Summerview," I tell him. "Today."

They all stare at me. Ruby and Roxie get up out of the hay and come over.

"Gi," Ruby starts, "what are you talking about?"

"I saw him there. He doesn't need to be in rehab. We talked through a few things with the doctor and he shouldn't be in there."

Kade and Travis exchange a glance. Kade runs a hand through his hair. "Vaughn's been out of control for a while. He took it too far the other night. It's best if he takes some time out."

"I can help him. I can do more for him than they can. They're restraining him and it's not helping him to be imprisoned like that. I'll take care of him."

"They called and told us about that," Kade says. "They said they had to do it to keep him safe. To keep him from hurting himself."

"He only did what he did the other night because of me. I know he won't do it again. I'll make sure he doesn't."

Roxie puts her hand on my arm. "Gigi, you don't know what he's capable of." She's an inch or so shorter than me, gorgeous, with a sprinkling of freckles across her nose, long dark hair and those blue eyes that are so similar to Vaughn's.

"I *do* know," I tell her. "We've spent some … time together. I'm not fully trained yet but I know I can help him. He wants me to. I'll stay with him in his cabin and I'll make sure he's okay."

"That's a huge burden on you," says Travis. "Vaughn can be unpredictable. We don't want you getting hurt." I know what he's referring to. Vaughn's status as a player. His rule. My hot mess of a state the other morning.

"He won't hurt me. We've already worked through all that and I know I can help him like no one else can. Please trust me to try. I promise that if he has any problems or if I think he needs more help, I'll come to you and tell you that. I won't compromise his recovery."

They all glance at each other again, clearly uneasy about the decision.

Ruby links her arm through Travis's. "Well, if there's anyone who can fix Vaughn, it's my sister. She fixes everyone. All the time. It's what she does."

Her pronouncement makes my eyes sting. I kind of want to hug her.

Ruby smiles at me. "I think you should let her try," she says to the three of them.

Kade, as Vaughn predicted, is the first one to relent. "We could give it a shot. If you're absolutely sure, Gigi."

"I'm sure."

Travis is harder to win over. "You were really upset the other morning. I wouldn't want that to happen again."

"That was my fault. It was a misunderstanding. He didn't do anything wrong."

Travis contemplates me. I can see he's surprised by what I'm telling him, but also that he believes me. "If you're sure. For his sake, I'm sure the process would be a lot more enjoyable if you were the one to do it. For *your* sake, I hope it's as easy as you say it will be."

"It'll be fine," I assure him. "I know how to fix him."

Travis's mouth quirks in a half-smile. He glances down at Ruby. "If you're anything like this little one, I have no choice but to give you the benefit of the doubt. I only have one favor to ask."

"What favor?"

"Looks like we might need to borrow that minivan because there's no way in hell we're all going to fit in the Shelby."

THE FOUR OF us wait while Kade goes in and signs Vaughn out of the rehab. It takes a while. No doubt they tried to talk Kade out of it but, eventually, the two of them walk out the door, with Kade's arm slung around Vaughn's shoulders like he's happy to have his brother back. Vaughn sees me sitting in the back seat and climbs in, his swarthy beauty and outrageous star quality wildly clashing with the lack-luster interior of our old minivan. The look on his face is now seared into my memory for the rest of time. Relief. Happiness. And just a pure kind of love that's not the kind of thing you forget.

He pulls me onto his lap and holds my face in his

warm hands. Then he kisses me like his family *isn't* watching intently.

"Wow," says Roxie.

Vaughn and I move into his cabin.

His family seems to have accepted me. They can see the change in Vaughn and their relief is easy to read. They treat me like a miracle worker.

As for Momma, she didn't even blink when I told her I was moving in with Vaughn. Instead, she hugged me tight and told me she'd make picnic baskets full of food for us. "When you know, you know," she said.

Rose is in love with her new car. She's also been dating a techie computer whiz named Tyler who runs his own company. He's tall with dark brown hair, sort of lanky and handsome in a more clean-cut way than her usual. Definitely not a bad boy, but Rose said he's a rock star of a different kind. A bad boy of making money, she laughed. His car is even fancier than hers. Last weekend he took her to London on his private jet and I've never seen her so happy. "There's no roller coaster," she told me. "He calls me when he says he's going to. He makes time for me. He listens. It almost seems *too* easy."

"Maybe because he's your perfect match."

We'll see, but each day he becomes more and more besotted with her. It's good to see her finally experiencing the kind of relationship she deserves.

Five or six days of enforced rest and relaxation has turned Vaughn into a beast of raw, savage physical energy. He's playful but at the same time absolutely voracious. My classes are over and I was able to defer my field work until next semester. Both Professor Tate and Dr. Clark are half in love with Vaughn themselves so they're helping me do a lot of the work online.

Which is a good thing because Vaughn will barely let me out of his sight.

Or his bed.

All his cravings have now converged into one.

Me.

It's late afternoon and I'm laying on the couch reading a book. Vaughn's been sitting outside on the porch with one of his guitars and his practice drum kit. He's been working through rhythms and chords. I like listening to him.

The music stops.

I stand and go outside, leaning against the railing of the porch.

All he's wearing is a towel around his waist after our swim in the pond an hour or so ago, where we made love right there in the water, with me wrapped around him, his cock deep and hot in the coolness of the pond. Everything about him is a spiritual awakening.

He puts his guitar down. "Hey, gorgeous."

I go to him, and he pulls me onto his lap.

"Are you going to move more of your stuff in?" he asks me. "All you have is that one small suitcase."

I haven't really had a chance to go home and organize

my things. Vaughn keeps asking me to move in with him and I have, even though I haven't unpacked my small bag. I say it absent-mindedly as I look out at the view, without much thought. "I have to leave tomorrow—"

"What?" He grips my arm painfully. "You said you'd stay."

"I only mean—"

"You said you wouldn't leave me."

I can read there the ferocious tension in him, like a bubbling cauldron of emotions has suddenly overflowed. "Vaughn. You're hurting my arm."

He loosens his grip, but his expression is no less furious. "I won't let you go."

His emotions are still so new and so raw. "I only meant I was going to go over to help Momma bake some pies for a few hours."

He's still staring at me, deathly quiet.

"You can come with me if you want. My mother would love that."

His exhales in a rough breath.

"Vaughn." I place my palm on his chest, trying to soothe him. "I'm not *leaving* you. I'm right here."

If I didn't know better I'd almost say there's a shine to his sapphire eyes. He lifts me and I wrap myself around him. I can feel that he's very hard. Like this, he carries me inside and takes me to bed. "Don't say things like that to me, darlin'. I can't fucking handle it. And I need my fix. Right now. I'm jonesing for my candy-pink pussy."

"Already?" I tease him, trying to soothe him. "You just had a fix."

"I need another one."

"I'm yours. Anything you want."

He carries me inside, laying me onto the bed, pushing my light cotton sundress up to reveal my nakedness. He nuzzles against my full breasts, licking the underside of my nipple, latching on. "What I'm going to do is to take you deep and slow. I'm going to torture you, like you torture me. I'm going to make you wait for your orgasm this time."

I always come very easily. Just his touch gets me hot as hell, every time. I smile at his pronouncement because … well, it's unlikely.

Vaughn kisses a soft trail up my inner thigh, sending ripples of sensation across my skin.

His teeth bite me gently. He breathes in the scent of me, wrapping his arms around my thighs to keep me in place. "Oh, fuck it, you're too perfect to wait for anything." He eats hungrily into me, covering me with his mouth and tugging firmly as his fingers slide into me, stroking along with the rhythm of his mouth.

Just like that, I'm pulled into a sudden vortex of deep, ecstatic pleasure. Vaughn milks my pleasure with his mouth, then, just as the waves begin to slow, he lays himself over me and thrusts thickly into me, gripping my hips with his brutally strong hands. In and in. Deeper and deeper. His climax comes just as suddenly, overcoming him as he growls my name and spills himself deep inside me.

I hold him close for a long time. I play with his hair. His weight is heavy and warm.

Later, when his mood has calmed, he wraps a blanket around us and we sit on the porch and watch the sunset over the hills. "You want to hear the song I wrote today? It's for you."

"For me?"

"Yeah. For you."

He picks up his guitar and he starts to play. The orange and vermillion hues of the sky illuminate him as he strums like he's some kind of masterpiece the universe wants to show off. And then he starts to sing.

When you're young, everything's
a firefly night and a garden of
dreams. No one tells you the
fireflies are bombs and the dreams
turn to dust.

No one says the high fades to
black as you rise and you crash.
As you burn and you bleed. And
when hell rises up and you're
too tired to try, there she is.

My strawberry girl with the tiger-
striped eyes and the rock 'n roll
soul, there she is. Taking my hand.
Lighting my fire like she's made of
the sun. Fixing my scars like she
was always the one.

No one tells you the loss will first
kill you and then make you brave.
No one says it's the love most of
all that will drive you insane.
As you burn and you fly.
My sunshine girl with the wildfire
touch and the calm to my storm,
there she is.

HE STOPS STRUMMING, smiling almost self-consciously.

I take the guitar and set it aside. I climb onto his lap
and I kiss him. "I love you, Vaughn."

It's the first time I've said it.

His eyes get very blue.

His kiss is feverish, almost desperate. I straddle him
and he helps position me, so I'm sliding down onto his
surging cock, taking him all the way inside. We both say
the words, our souls mingling right along with our fierce,
wild, all-consuming love.

I WAKE IN THE NIGHT. I reach for him but his side of the bed is empty and cold. "Vaughn?"

There's no reply.

I get up and walk into the living room.

It's dark but the moon hangs full and low out the window, spilling its glow onto the wooden floor.

Vaughn is sitting on one of the leather couches. I can already sense a volatility in him. A quietness that isn't quiet at all.

I notice it then. On the coffee table in front of him is a whiskey bottle and a shot glass.

Not good, but I refuse to judge him, whether he's touched it or not. We knew this would be a part of his process. There were always going to be bumps in the road.

I walk over to him, my bare feet making no sound.

He looks up at me. His hair is low across his eyes, shading the blueness of them, which makes me feel uneasy. He's in a stormy, dangerous mood. "Do you want me to leave you alone?" I whisper.

"No." His voice is low. Aggressive.

Which makes me instantly, shamelessly wet, despite everything. I know too well what his aggression feels like.

I'm naked. Not scared, but careful.

I reach out to gently push the fall of his hair to the side, so I can see the ember-shine of his dark eyes. He's wearing a pair of jeans, low on his hips, and nothing else.

I can tell he's in a dominating mood. His inked muscles look huge and coiled with simmering power.

"Did you drink some of it?" I ask him softly. Just to gauge what I'm dealing with here.

"No."

All his demons are close to the surface, I can feel them, messing with his head. Those tragic memories have teeth but they're also just thoughts on a repeating reel. *I'm the here and now. I'm stronger than they are. I'm all about physical pleasure and I know I'll win. I'm going to make sure of it.*

I move closer, standing between his spread knees. He's in a dark mood but I know what he needs right now. I know how to ease his cravings. Lightly, I touch my finger to my nipple, circling it, teasing it until it becomes beaded and taut. I do the same to the other one as he watches me. I lean closer, offering my nipple to his mouth. "Suck on me," I whisper. "Use me. I'm so wet for you, Vaughn. There's nothing I wouldn't do for you."

He lets me feed my nipple into his mouth. Very gently, he bites me. Holding my sensitive flesh lightly between his teeth, his tongue touches the tip.

Fresh heat wets my pussy. I'm swollen and tingly.

Vaughn sucks my nipple deeply into his mouth and his eyes close, almost rolling back like he's experiencing a kind of ecstasy.

The brimming passion in him takes my arousal to a

different level. A greedy, primal one. I want to feast on him and take him inside. I want to feed on his beauty.

He takes my full breasts in his warm, rough hands, squeezing them almost painfully until both my nipples are close to his mouth. He sucks strongly in rhythmic pulls on one, then the other, until I can feel the building pleasure saturating me even more. He unzips his jeans, placing my hand on the broad, wet head of his cock. I kneel down, pushing his jeans lower until he's fully revealed to me. His fist is in my hair. I touch my nipples to the slit, rubbing against him and wetting my breasts with the beginnings of his pleasure, squeezing his thick length between them.

"Climb onto me," he commands. He pulls me onto his lap so I'm straddling him. His hot bulk slides against my wet pussy and I gasp, trying to take him inside. "Greedy girl."

I want my pleasure to squeeze him and milk him and make him mindless with pleasure, so there's no room for anything else.

He takes his huge cock in his fist and lifts me, touching the head against my clit, mingling our wetness, pushing himself just inside me. The tip slides in easily but he's so thick, my body resists him. He won't tolerate resistance. He grips my hips and thrusts, forcing the slide of his long, thick length all the way inside me, until I'm absolutely impaled on him. I moan and grip him, adjusting to the beautifully-brutal invasion. It's the most intimate thing in the world, this need. Our gazes lock. It's a spiritual experience, being so owned by him, stretched and fully possessed as we stare deep into each other's eyes.

There's so *much* of him it's almost uncomfortable. In a good way. In exactly the way I need him to be. He's a part of me and I want to keep him here, just like this, forever. "I meant what I said, Vaughn. I love you. Can you feel me?"

He stares at me and I can see then that he *can* feel me. I've won against the dark thoughts that plague him. He's fully here with me now and he's feeling what I just said to him, with his whole heart.

And his whole body.

"Gi," he whispers.

"I think I always knew, just like you did. From that very first moment."

Vaughn takes my mouth in a tender kiss. He holds me in place as he thrusts into me. I ride him, meeting each upward drive, working him, squeezing him with my inner muscles as I suck his tongue into my mouth.

He groans with low surprise as his cock jerks violently inside me, spilling his liquid warmth. The thick, bucking motion and the jetting gushes of his release set me off in an electric burst of pleasure that jolts through my core and my belly, sending currents all the way to my fingers and toes.

The orgasm lasts a long time, the ripples gently clenching around his deeply-insinuated barely-softening length.

I lean my head against his chest and he holds me like that for a long time. I can hear his heartbeat and it's perfectly in sync with my own.

"You're my cure and my love." His voice is gravel-edged with lust and emotion. "Please don't ever leave me again."

"I'm not going anywhere."

"Ever."

"Not ever."

We lay on our sides and he slides deeper inside me. My leg is wrapped around his waist and his warm hand is on my thigh. "In that case, I might even ask you to marry me and have my babies and grow old with me."

"I might even say yes." His answering smile, his kiss and his lovemaking are the answer to everything I ever wondered about.

"Mine was always the future you were supposed to change, Gi. I guess there's a reason things happen like they do. It was always supposed to be me."

Gigi

I NEVER DID END up leaving his cabin. We stayed there for a month and hardly left.

When his cravings rise up to haunt him, I give him everything I have. I suck on his cock until he forgets about those other urges. I swallow his lust and his fear. And in return, he gives me even more. He feasts on me with all the passion of the madman he is. He makes love to me like he can't get enough. Like he'll die if he doesn't get as close as it's possible to do. He's half insatiable beast and half fallen angel, too beautiful to deny. And I give and give and give, because it's the only thing I want to do. Anything he wants.

It's been getting easier.

Each day, he seems lighter. He still has staring contests with the whiskey bottle, which he keeps in the middle of the island in the kitchen as a test he's determined to pass.

But then, two days ago, he poured it down the drain and threw the bottle in the trash.

I stuck a photo Roxie gave me of his parents on the fridge with a magnet shaped like a heart. He went sort of still the first time he saw it, but he hasn't moved it and it's become something that's just there now, to look at against the backdrop of different moods and emotions.

At long last, we've both forgiven ourselves. We talk about it, late at night. Tragedies happen. There doesn't always have to be someone to blame. Life is a rocky road, with deep, craggy canyons and also mountaintops with the most beautiful views.

Yesterday, Vaughn told me to pack my bag. He said we were going to the Bahamas.

We took a private jet and arrived last night. A car drove us to the estate, which is outrageous. It's literally beyond my wildest dreams. The house is huge, Colonial style with modern detailing. It's surrounded by palm trees. There's a deck with an infinity pool that looks right out over a sugar-sand beach.

I didn't know a place like this even existed.

And, with Vaughn, I had my first swim in the clear, turquoise ocean.

When I asked him how long we could stay, he told me as long as I want. The house is mine, he said. He bought it for me. When I tried to protest, he silenced me with a lusty kiss and after that I got side-tracked from my protests.

We stayed up late and drank sparkling water under a full moon.

Now, it's early morning. Vaughn is wrapped around me, spooning me, our limbs tangled, his muscular arm snug around me. He likes to sleep this way, so I don't get away, he jokes. Even asleep, his cock is hot and hard against my backside. I arch against him, wriggling to get closer. I'm still full of his wetness from our lovemaking in the night.

Carefully, I maneuver until I can feel the head of his cock slide just inside me. Writhing gently, I take him deeper. I want him to wake up this way, hot and sweet with pleasure, so it's the first thing he thinks about. I rock back against him and he slides deeper. Then I sway forward. Then back. Each time, I take more of him, squeezing him silkily.

I hear a lecherous murmur against my ear, as his fingers pinch my stiff nipples. "You trying to fuck my big cock without me noticing, darlin'?"

"No," I tease him.

"Someone's a horny girl this mornin'". His accent is always thicker when he's inside me.

"I can't help it. You feel too good."

He rolls me onto my stomach, keeping himself inside me. He lifts my hips and positions me with my knees spread, making love to me slowly and so, so deeply. His fingers play my nipples while his other hand finds my clit and gently works the slippery nub. "You want me to pump your tight pussy full of my hot cum again, don't you, sweetheart? You're a greedy girl. You want my babies. You want me to get you all hot and sticky with it."

"Please, Vaughn."

I come hard around him. Feeling him drain himself deep inside me, I decide I don't want to wait too long.

He pulls me into a warm embrace, my head resting against his chest. With our bodies still rippling, I look up at him. "Vaughn?"

"Yeah?"

"You do want babies?"

He stares down at me, his expression stern, his handsome face so enchanting to me. "Of course I want babies. I want a whole bunch of them."

"I do too."

He smiles. "You just say the word and I'm all in."

"I don't want to wait too long."

"Well, then it's a good thing I've got a diamond in my pocket."

"What?"

He slides himself from my body. He sits up and holds his hand out to me. "Come on."

"Where are we going?"

"Put your best dress on."

I laugh. "Why?"

He goes to my closet and chooses a white silk sleeveless dress. "Come here."

I go along with it and he slips the dress over my head.

He pulls on a pair of board shorts. Then he takes my hand and leads me down to the beach, to my favorite palm tree that dips low over the sand.

Vaughn takes a small box out of his pocket. He gets down on one knee.

I gasp. *"Vaughn."*

He opens the box. It's literally the biggest diamond I've ever seen in my life.

"Gigi Hayes. My Gi. I'm not perfect. But I do love you more than I've ever loved anyone or anything. And I'll spend every hour of every day trying my hardest to deserve you. I'll support everything you want to do. I'll take care of you. I'll spend every day trying my hardest to make all your dreams come true. My family already thinks you walk on water and when I asked your mother the other day if she would give us her blessing, she asked me what took me so long. You're the one, Gi. You're my girl. My true love. The love of my life, from that very first day. I love you. I'm crazy for you. Will you marry me?"

My tears are making him blurry. "Yes, love," I laugh through my tears. "Yes."

He slides the ring onto my finger and picks me up, twirling me in a slow circle. He kisses me deeply. "Here's the part where we live happily ever after."

Taking care with each other and loving each other with our whole hearts, that's exactly what we do.

EPILOGUE #2

THREE MONTHS LATER, we got married on the beach, with all our families around us.

Travis gave me away. Ruby, Rose, Scarlett and Roxie were my bridesmaids. They all wore pale yellow silk dresses with flowers in their hair. Vaughn flew an up-and-coming New York designer—a friend of his—down to our house to make my wedding dress exactly the way I wanted it. Luca's design was to die for. A fitted bodice inlaid with tiny pearls and a silk skirt weaved through with white feathers. Vaughn wore a tux and looked so handsome in it I almost jumped him before we could even say our vows.

Momma sat in the front row and cried the whole time. She said she knew Daddy was watching from up there on his cloud, smiling down on us, so proud of his family.

I wore my rosary in his honor. Vaughn and I share it.

Whenever one of us feels like we need it, if the emotions are closer to the bone for one reason or another, it's like a talisman and a reminder. There's no one to blame for the past. We're strong and we're together and we're so in love it sometimes hurts. We lean on each other and we hold each other up. Vaughn is the most beautiful thing in my life. I could live a thousand lives and never get enough of him. He's my rock, my best friend, my lover, and now, my husband.

We both cried and laughed as we said our vows and kissed so much they had to remind us it was time for cake.

All our guests stayed for a week and we had the best time. Scarlett and Johnny have relaxed into parenthood and Clementine is a gorgeous little cherub with Johnny's blue eyes and bright red hair. Rose brought Tyler, and the day after the wedding he proposed to her in the same spot Vaughn proposed to me. She said yes.

Vaughn's three cousins came with their wives and by the end of the week, they all felt like close friends. The McCabe brothers are all gorgeous men who love their women as fiercely as the Tucker brothers do. Bo is a star quarterback with an athletic build and those trademark blue eyes that seem to run in the family. His wife Millie is sweet and has an almost ethereal beauty. Caleb is ridiculously buff, intense and quieter than his brothers and cousins. He and his wife Violet have a beautiful, caring relationship and sort of satellite off each other, like they're deeply aware of each other and very much in tune. Violet is studying psychology and she and I had a lot to talk about. And Gage is as cocky as they come, and so smitten with his stunning wife Luna it's entertaining to watch.

Kade had a nasty break-up with a girlfriend he was dating when I first met Vaughn, who didn't want to give him up. But there's been a new development on that front. Vaughn, Travis and Roxie have never seen him so besotted before. I guess he's like his brother and his cousins: once they fall, they fall *hard*. But I'll let the two of them tell that story themselves …

Vaughn and I spend as much time in the Bahamas as we can. It's our retreat and our getaway. Vaughn also bought us a house in Franklin, just outside of Nashville, right next door to Travis and Ruby's main house. It sits on ten acres and has ponds and gardens and a swimming pool off the grand patio. There are seven bedrooms, a chef's kitchen, a movie theater and a recording studio. Vaughn insisted on bringing in an interior designer—another celebrity friend of his—who redesigned the whole place, room by room, exactly as I wanted it, with inspired, expert advice along the way. My favorite room is the library, where I sit for hours with my books in the comfortable chair that sits in the sun, or the mahogany desk by the window with a view of the hills. I finished my degree and with Vaughn's encouragement, I've started working on my PhD.

Vaughn bought me a white Maserati MC20 and a red

Aston Martin DBX. I'd never heard of either of them before but I have to admit they're fun to drive. Not that I drive them all that much. I'm always with Vaughn and he usually drives us in his blue Ferrari F60. We also have drivers who take us everywhere we need to go. It's one of the things that took some getting used to, but as long as I can be with him, I just go with it.

We often spend time at our cabin in the country, where Vaughn and his brothers practice in the old barn, which they've converted into a much more modern and high-tech recording studio.

Vaughn also has an apartment in New York City, a loft in SoHo, which I absolutely love. Vaughn takes me there to spoil me, he says. He takes me on shopping sprees, to Broadway shows and even to Fashion Week, where we got to sit in the front row. He held my hand the entire time.

Our wedding got a lot of media attention. *The Alpha Playboy Superstar Drummer Has Finally Met His Match*, read one headline. *Hearts all over the world are breaking, but Vaughn Tucker only has eyes for his gorgeous new bride.* The article was accompanied by photos of us. In each one, Vaughn has his arm around me, or is gazing at me sort of adoringly, or holding my hand. It's become a detail the press seems to love talking about.

We've given a few interviews but Vaughn prefers to keep me to himself, he said. When we do go out in public, the paparazzi are rabid. I don't think I could ever get used to it. I'm more than happy to stay out of the limelight.

Our addiction to each other hasn't changed. Our bond has only deepened.

Vaughn went to some therapy sessions and insisted I go along with him, but he was so open and resolved about the things we'd already talked about, Dr. Clark agreed with him when he said he wasn't cured, but he *is* at least in control. For now. She checks in on him every week to see how he's doing. I told the doctor I'd call her if I thought he needed to see her but, so far, I've only needed to do that twice.

I'm careful with him. I'm aware of his moods and his vulnerabilities. He tells me when he's feeling the blues and it's those times that I give him even more.

It's not perfect every day. Vaughn has fallen off the wagon twice, for a day each time. I took care of him. I gave him all the love I have. I called the doctor and we went to see her. We talked it through and he met with the doctor more regularly for a while.

It hasn't happened again and Vaughn said the tears in my eyes were enough to make him realize that nothing is more important to him than making sure I never cry for that reason again. And I haven't. He said that knowing I've forgiven him before he even falls is the greatest gift anyone has ever given him.

We take it day by day.

He insists I go on tour with him, and I was surprised

by how much I love it. I get to be with Ruby, after all, and the shows are amazing to watch. The superstar lifestyle is another one of those things that took some getting used to, but I've found I adore traveling. It's something I always wanted to do but never imagined I would. We've been all over the United States and Canada, and even to London, Paris, Rome and Madrid. Next year the band is planning a tour of Australia and New Zealand and I can hardly wait.

Their recent tour ended just over a month ago and, this weekend, we're back in the cabin. I'm waiting for Vaughn to come back from the barn, where the band is starting to put their new album together. I visited Momma, who just got engaged to a man she's been seeing for a while who we all love. His name is Earl and he's fun, laughs all the time and, best of all, he makes Momma laugh. She's happier than I've seen her in seven years.

I told her my news but I haven't told Vaughn yet.

In the end, we decided I'd stay on the pill until after the band's most recent tour. Vaughn said he couldn't wait to get started but I wanted to enjoy some time with just him for a while, uninterrupted.

About six weeks ago, I stopped taking it. As soon as I did, Vaughn insisted we spend three whole days in bed. Let's just say he was very dedicated to his mission.

Vaughn's love for me infuses my life. He dedicates every waking hour to my happiness. I've found that the complex layers of his personality, once peeled away through patience and gentle affection, reveal amazing revelations. My husband is full of life. He's volatile at times. He can be aggressive and is so strong it sometimes shocks me. But underneath his strength and his hundred-proof masculinity, at the very heart of him, is the kindest, most loving person I've ever known. His love for me is unconditional and overwhelmingly heartfelt.

He's highly tactile, and when we're alone together, spends all of our time close to me, touching me, and caring for me, not only physically but emotionally too. He *gets* me, on a level even my sisters don't.

And now that we're trying for a baby, his protective instincts have become almost manic. I'll need to break the news to him gently.

I hear him come in. He comes through the door and takes off his shirt. "It's hot out there," he says, tossing it onto a chair. His thick hair is romantically mussed, his broad, inked chest suntanned and buff from his drumming. Soon after our wedding, he got my name tattooed on his chest, over his heart, close to his mother's name. But mine has a red heart around it and an arrow through it.

"How was practice?" I ask him.

"It was good." He sits next to me on the couch. "But I missed you. How's my strawberry girl?"

"I went to see Momma for a while. She baked you a pie. And she's already started knitting."

He smiles, not getting my meaning at first. "What for?"

I kiss his lips. "For our baby, Vaughn. Who's due in a little less than eight months."

"What?" Even though he's been more than a little enthusiastic about getting me pregnant, I've wondered about how he might react. He had a complicated and, in the end, tragic relationship with his own parents, especially his father. I wondered how that might make him feel. But there are no layers to the look on his face. It's pure awe and the kind of undiluted happiness that's become one of the unexpected blessings of our marriage. He takes my face in his hands. "*Gi.* Holy fuck. That's the best news I've ever heard in my life. Are you sure? Are you okay? Are you feeling sick?"

"I feel fine. I did a test this morning. I'll go see the doctor as soon as we get back to Nashville."

He kisses me deeply. Then he opens the robe I'm wearing and lays me back. "Let me look at you, darlin'. This is *amazing*, Gi. A *baby*. *Our* baby. I can't believe it. What do you think it'll be? What should we name him? What if it's a girl? Holy hell, sweetheart. Look how gorgeous you are." He slides his hands gently over my bare breasts. He kisses my stomach. "Hey, little baby. We love you so much. We're going to give you the best life."

I let my fingers weave through Vaughn's thick, silky hair as he gazes up at me with awe. *I love him so much.*

"Are you sure you're okay? Maybe we should go and see the doctor now."

"I'm fine, Vaughn. I feel perfect."

"That's because you are perfect. I just hope I can be one tenth as perfect as you are."

"What do you mean?"

"What if I don't do it right?"

"Do what right?"

"Being a father." There were always going to be a few doubts along those lines.

"I think if you're half as good a father as you are a husband you'll do it better than anyone ever has. Now come here." I weave my fingers through his hair and pull him up to me, kissing his lips. "You're going to be the best father in the world," I whisper in his ear.

He kisses my neck, moving to my breasts, worshipping me with his mouth like he's drinking from me. He kicks off his jeans and pushes his rock-hard cock gently, at first, inside me, getting me wet with his huge, hot bulk. Until we're as connected as two bodies and souls can be. He's as deep as I can take him. My arms and legs are wrapped around him. Our gaze is connective and real. Even our words are joined. We say them together.

I love you.

Thank you for reading **Nashville Nights**. If you

enjoyed Vaughn and Gigi's story, please consider leaving a quick review or rating on Amazon. Reviews help authors!

Below I've included the first chapter of **Nashville Days**, Travis and Ruby's story, a sexy standalone and the first book in the Music City Lovers series. It's my tribute to hot summer days and finding the kind of love that feels like the real thing from the very first day.

xoxo,
Julie

Please come join my Facebook reader group, Julie Capulet's Romantics, where I share cover reveals, insider info and we discuss all things romance!

Sign up for my newsletter to receive my free bonus content and get access to sneak peeks and exclusive giveaways!

Visit my website @ www.juliecapulet.com

Every song he wrote was about a girl he hadn't met yet. Then she walked into his life.

Travis Tucker is a country-rock superstar. With four number one albums, sold-out tours and millions of fans, he's living the dream. But somewhere along the way, the spotlight lost its shine. Travis can never find the one thing he's been writing all his songs about: *real* love. So he decides to buy himself a country getaway to work on his next record and clear his head.

Ruby Hayes is a small town girl with big dreams. Finally free of boarding school, she plans on spending the summer writing songs on the piano in the abandoned farmhouse next door. Then she's on her way to Nashville.

When Travis finds Ruby, singing like an angel at his piano, he falls *hard*. Now that he's finally found the girl he's been searching for, Ruby ignites in him a wild obsession that's hotter than the Tennessee sun. And she has no idea who he is.

For Ruby, things get complicated. With a voice that's somehow familiar, like he's already a part of her, Travis is a temptation she can't resist.

The summer becomes a feverish haze of hot nights, shared lyrics, and the kind of spark that blazes into wildfire.

But summer can't last forever. Can their love survive beyond it, with the demands of Travis's high-profile life, Ruby's ambition and a jealous best friend threatening to come between them?

Or is this a love story written in both the music and the stars?

Nashville Days is a steamy standalone small town rockstar romance starring a hot, hopelessly romantic lead singer and the sweet & sassy songbird who steals his heart. Perfect for fans of Elsie Silver.

Music City Lovers

Chapter One

TRAVIS

"I want to thank ya'll for coming out tonight, Austin. You know we love you." The crowd roars.

We play our last song, our newest number one hit. I can barely hear my own voice as a hundred thousand people sing along with me. It's a crazy feeling, having *this* many souls touched by your words and so fully invested, singing their goddamn hearts out. They know every note. They've lived their lives to these lyrics. They've loved, cried and laughed to these tunes. They're filling up the night with their emotion, swaying to the slow rhythm. The lights of their phones shine like a galaxy of stars.

And when we hit that final chord, the thundering cheer of the crowd is deafening. Vaughn climbs down from his drums and the three of us stand there together on stage for a few seconds, taking it all in. The applause of a hundred thousand people is something you don't ever really get used to. The adrenaline rush is just as pure as it was the very first time.

We take a final bow and exit the stage, where a swarm of security surrounds us and ushers us through a bullet-proof corridor toward our tour bus. I can still hear them chanting my name. But we've done our encores after playing for three and a half hours. We're getting close to the end of our 48-show, 38-city tour and I'm feeling it.

The highs and lows and the creeping exhaustion that sets in after giving it everything you've got for months on end. We have two final shows left, both at home in Nashville. It's been by far our biggest tour yet.

I feel lit by the crowd, the music, the whiskey and the wine, the satisfaction of pouring my heart and soul into something real. Something that touches people and connects them. Every single show has been sold out. Our record is number one. Four of our songs are in the top ten. And the momentum just keeps on building.

We get to the bus and it's crowded, with groupies and people from the band and hangers-on. Our opening act, Jackson Cole, and his entourage are here, like they always seem to be. The fame and the women are new to him. He's overdosing and finding his feet, maybe. Riding our wave, to a certain extent, but whatever.

Vaughn pours three shots. Roxie gives Kade a hug, then me. She's relieved. Turns out our little sister is a genius at managing us. This tour has been bigger than we ever imagined. Now we can play our last two home shows and finally take a much-needed break before we start another 12-show West Coast tour next month.

I collapse onto one of the plush chairs. I tip back the whiskey Vaughn hands me. One of the groupies puts her hand on my arm and leans close to me. "Travis, you were amazing tonight. You're *so* good."

Do I know her? I don't think so. She might be a new one. It all starts to blur at the edges after a while. They all start looking the same. I'm no saint but I also need to *feel* something before I'll act on the constant stream of attention and adoration I happen to get. Right now I'm not feeling much of anything.

Kade hands me a beer.

"Hell," he says, sitting in the chair next to mine and clinking his bottle against mine. "Texas always has insane crowds. I could hardly even hear us." As usual, Kade's new-ish girlfriend Carmen is hovering around him. Roxie's not a fan. Come to think of it, neither am I. I don't usually care much who my brothers hang out with, but this girl seems to have an effect on Kade that's messing with his head. He's more moody when she's around. Jackson joked that she's our Yoko, waiting in the wings, whispering in his ear all the time about running away together so he can work on his solo album. I don't think that's his plan. Not now, anyway. We're on too much of a roll. And I can't worry about it tonight.

Vaughn laughs and cranks up the music, chugging from the bottle of Jack he's holding. He's got a fat joint in his other hand. A groupie with a lot of piercings and a ridiculously short skirt puts a pink pill on his tongue. Another girl is unbuttoning his shirt. His black hair is unkempt and long. His eyes are bloodshot, which makes them look even more blue than usual.

Roxie pulls one of the girls away from him. "What did you give him?" She pries Vaughn's mouth open but he grins at her, sort of guiltily.

"Too late," he says.

"*Vaughn*," Roxie scolds him. "Booze and weed is one thing. You said no drugs."

"Come on, Rox, I'm celebrating. Give me one night."

"*One* night? You've had three whole *months* of nights."

"I'll go cold turkey after the tour," Vaughn tells her. "I'll take a break."

We've all heard that one before. My brother is out of control, is what it boils down to. And he's only getting worse.

Vaughn has always walked a fine line. Like our father did, until it killed him. Kade and I can easily keep up with our younger brother when it comes to the whiskey—and usually do—most of the time. The difference is, we have downtimes. We lay off when we're not touring. We clean up when we feel like it.

Cleaning up isn't something Vaughn's done in a while. I'm not sure he's even capable of it at this point. Kade and Roxie and I have talked about it. We decided to finish the tour, then we'll sit him down and talk it through with him. Get him some help or check him in somewhere if need be.

None of which is happening tonight.

We're driving all night tonight so we can get back to Nashville in the morning. There's no doubt this party will still be going when we get there.

This bus has been the hub of our non-stop bender all

the way through. We all got into a groove of it for the first month or two, but after a while you find yourself getting more and more strung out from the total lack of sleep and peace and quiet. Even before we left, we were hounded like this. We have a loft warehouse we've converted into apartments, a recording studio and an office headquarters in downtown Nashville. We tried to keep the location under wraps but our fans found out about it, like they always do.

"That show was mayhem," says Vaughn. Not that he minds. Mayhem might as well be Vaughn's middle name. As if to confirm this, he blows a couple of smoke rings at me.

Tonight I'm not in the mood to fight my way through crowds of people just so I can go to bed.

What I need is some real sleep. Uninterrupted by banging and knocking and people trying to get in.

I need a quiet place to hang out for a while, I decide. A secret getaway. An old house out in the country somewhere, far from the city and the rabid fans and the never-ending parade of groupies, where there's space and fresh air and days with nothing to do except write. I can't remember the last time I was *alone* for more than a few hours at a time.

I'll find myself someplace off the beaten track, where no one even knows I'm there. I'll sleep and daydream and clear my head. Maybe Vaughn can spend some time there too, and dry out. And Kade, without the girlfriend.

All three of us. We'll work on our next record. We'll write our masterpiece, uninterrupted.

I send a message to a real estate agent I sometimes use when I buy new properties. I have three houses: an apartment in Nashville that's part of our headquarters, my own house in Franklin outside Nashville that I need to get a lot more security for because people have set up fucking camps around the peripheral fences, and a condo in L.A. None of them will be either empty or quiet. I have a lot of friends and an open-door policy for the most part, which I'm now starting to severely regret. All my houses have become magnets for hangers-on and their non-stop parties.

I'm looking for another house, I text him. *A farm, maybe, at least a half hour outside Nashville. Something remote. Very private. Surrounded by a lot of land. Maybe with a barn or something I can soundproof and convert into a studio. ASAP.*

Three girls surround me. One of them touches the top button of my shirt. I'm not in the mood to party tonight, go figure. I'm strung out. *Burned* out. I'm twenty-five years old and I already feel like I'm hanging on to the end of a fraying rope. I've been burning the candle at both ends for as long as I can remember and I suddenly feel a new urge for some goddamn solitude.

One of the girls touches my hair. Another whispers in my ear. "You're *so* hot, Travis. I love you so much."

I don't even know her name.

One of the girls weaves her fingers through mine.

"We want to show you something in one of the bedrooms, Travis. *All* of us."

My phone pings with a message. It's from my real estate agent. Damn, he's fast. "Maybe later." I don't know, maybe I've become jaded. I don't want to fuck just for the hell of it, not that I ever really did. I'm not an out of control player like Vaughn and I'm not a soulful romantic like Kade. I fall somewhere in the middle. I have a good time without getting serious.

But sometimes—like right now—it occurs to me that I never quite *feel* as much as I wish I did. Never in a way that makes you want to hang on to it or get excited about it or make it last. Never in a way you'd write a goddamn song about. Which is too bad. Because I write a lot of songs. Songs about falling in love and chasing after that one and only true love because you think your heart will break if you can't spend every hour of every day with her until you die.

The truth is, I'm just guessing. Because I've never experienced anything close to that kind of intensity. Which, tonight, feels sort of … sad. All these desperate souls, looking for that one magical, elusive person they can fall in love with to the point that nothing and no one else matters.

Most of them will never find it. *I* might never find it.

Which is sort of tragic when you think about it.

Like now. Women are literally hanging off me. And I

feel exactly … nothing. No spark. No interest. Just … boredom. A craving for something *real*.

I stand up and move away, as much as I can in the smoky, noisy, jam-packed space. People are getting loose.

I check the message. *I've got a new listing you might want to see. It's been sitting empty for 4 years and needs some work but it's a premium property. Beaut house. 5 bedrooms. 40 mins east of Nville, remote. Sits on 100 fenced acres with its own pond, a large barn and 3 cabins. Listed at 3.5m. It's bank-owned and available immediately.*

I follow the link and scroll through the photos.

Wow. The place is mint, but he wasn't wrong. It looks dusty and unkempt. In a good way. In a no-one-will-ever-suspect-I'm-there kind of way. I'll leave it like that. I'll become a hermit for the next few weeks and completely tune out. There are pictures of the barn too. It's huge and rustic. And the old cabins, dotted around the property.

The offer is almost too fucking good to be true.

I text him back. *Let me know where to transfer the $. I'll pay cash tonight.*

I'll move in immediately. Hell, I'll drive out there as soon as we get back.

We exchange a few more messages. He confirms that the sale has gone through. He'll have the power turned on. He'll courier the keys so they're there by the time I get to Nashville.

A strange longing settles into me that feels almost like

hope. More than that. An eerie sense that something's about to happen.

"All I wished for was to experience that spark you read about, just once. What I wasn't expecting was the Fourth of July and heaven on earth all rolled into one." ~ Stella

Bass player Kade Tucker is known as the Magic Man, and not only for his riffs. After breaking off a disastrous relationship, he swears off women. Only problem is, five minutes later, he might have just met the love of his life.

Stella Bell has always done what's expected of her. Until a secret letter and an unwanted proposal on the same day prove to be her breaking point. For once in her life, she's going to do something for herself. As fate would have it, that means taking a spur of the moment trip to Nashville.

A hopeless romantic, Stella has been hiding her true self for far too long. And when a gorgeous, mysterious stranger rescues her from a torrential downpour, she decides to go with it. The hot, dreamy Kade Tucker proceeds to enlighten Stella in every possible way, until she begins to realize that some dreams really can come true.

303

But will Kade's twisted ex and Stella's family secrets – and a very accidental pregnancy – get in the way of their HEA? Or is this a match made in Music City heaven?

Nashville Dreams is a sexy standalone rock star romance starring a hot musician and a sweet & sassy dreamer who's the one he always knew was out there somewhere. Now that he's found her, he has no intention of letting any one of her dreams go unanswered.

Music City Lovers

Roxie

Nate Boone. My brother's best friend and the country boy I had a serious crush on all those years ago when we were both just kids. A lot has happened since then but a part of me never really moved on. Who am I kidding, *all* of me never moved on.

And now I'm heading back to Sugar Mountain to see my bestie—Nate's little sister—and to catch up with the extended Boone family, who have always felt like my own.

What I find is that Nate Boone is *alll* grown up, hotter than the Tennessee sun and not quite as forbidden as he used to be …

Nate

Roxie Tucker. No one knows about our history and our connection because I walked away and never looked back. I had to. She was a hundred percent off-limits.

I haven't seen her in years, until she shows up out of the blue, so beautiful it hurts. And I now know why I could never get real or even think about committing to anyone else. Because they're not her.

I shouldn't, of course. She's like family. And my life is complicated.

But she's too perfect and the pull is too strong. She's my dream and the one I could never let go of. I lost her once and I have no intention of losing her again. She's mine. She's heaven on earth and I'm a hundred percent addicted.

Now that I've had a taste of forever, this time, I'll risk whatever it takes to keep her...

Nashville Lights is a steamy standalone small town brother's best friend romance, starring a sweet & sassy band manager and the love of her life.

Music City Lovers

ALSO BY JULIE CAPULET

I Love You Series

The Obsession Begins (free)

XOXO I Love You

XOXX I Love You More

Love You the Most (free)

Sexy Standalones

Max

Cowboy

McCabe Brothers Series

Hopeless Romantic

My Hero

Arrogant Player

Music City Lovers Series

Nashville Days

Nashville Nights

Nashville Dreams

Nashville Lights

Hawthorne U Series

Lovestruck

Paradise Series

Devil's Angel

Wild Hearts

New York Billionaires Series

Billionaire Boss

Billionaire Grump

Billionaire Devil

Billionaire Romantic

Standalone Rom-com

Beautiful Savages

ABOUT THE AUTHOR

Julie Capulet is an Amazon top 20 bestselling author of contemporary romance. She writes steamy he-falls-first romance with heart, heat and fairy tale HEAs. Her stories are inspired by true love and she's married to her own real life hero. When she's not writing, she's reading, traveling, walking on the beach and watching rom-coms.

www.juliecapulet.com